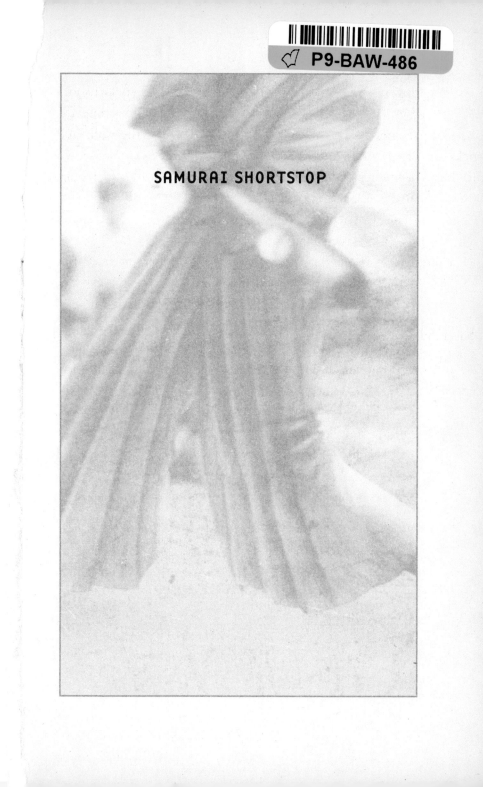

SAMURAI SHORTSTOP

SAMURAI
SHORTSTOP

Alan Gratz

DIAL BOOKS

DIAL BOOKS
A member of Penguin Group (USA) Inc. • Published by The Penguin Group
Penguin Group (USA) Inc., 375 Hudson Street, New York, NY 10014, U.S.A. • Penguin Group (Canada),
90 Eglinton Avenue East, Suite 700, Toronto, Ontario, Canada M4P 2Y3 (a division of Pearson Penguin Canada
Inc.) • Penguin Books Ltd, 80 Strand, London WC2R 0RL, England • Penguin Ireland, 25 St. Stephen's Green,
Dublin 2, Ireland (a division of Penguin Books Ltd) • Penguin Group (Australia), 250 Camberwell Road,
Camberwell, Victoria 3124, Australia (a division of Pearson Australia Group Pty Ltd) • Penguin Books India Pvt
Ltd, 11 Community Centre, Panchsheel Park, New Delhi - 110 017, India • Penguin Group (NZ), Cnr Airborne
and Rosedale Roads, Albany, Auckland 1310, New Zealand (a division of Pearson New Zealand Ltd) • Penguin
Books (South Africa) (Pty) Ltd, 24 Sturdee Avenue, Rosebank, Johannesburg 2196, South Africa • Penguin Books
Ltd, Registered Offices: 80 Strand, London WC2R 0RL, England

The publisher does not have any control over and does not assume any responsibility for author or third-party
websites or their content.
Designed by Teresa Kietlinski Dikun
Text set in Goudy

Printed in the U.S.A.

10 9 8 7 6 5 4 3 2 1

Library of Congress Cataloging-in-Publication Data
Gratz, Alan, date.
Samurai shortstop / Alan Gratz.
p. cm.
Summary: While obtaining a Western education at a prestigious
Japanese boarding school in 1890, sixteen-year-old Toyo also
receives traditional samurai training, which has profound effects on
both his baseball game and his relationship with his father.
ISBN 0-8037-3075-6
[1. Samurai—Fiction. 2. Fathers and sons—Fiction. 3. Baseball—Fiction.
4. Boarding schools—Fiction. 5. Schools—Fiction.
6. Japan—History—Meiji period, 1868–1912—Fiction.] I. Title.
PZ7.G77224Sam 2006
[Fic]—dc22   2005022081

FOR WENDI

Tama ukeru gokuhi wa kaze no yanagi kana

The secret to catching a ball
Lies with the willow
Swaying in the wind

—Haiku by Japanese baseball player
and poet Shiki Masaoka (1890)

Chapter One

TOYO WATCHED carefully as his uncle prepared to kill himself.

Before dawn, he had swept and cleaned his uncle's favorite shrine, down to polishing the small mirror that hung on a post at its center. When that was done, he carefully arranged new *tatami* mats on the dirt floor. Everything had to be perfect for Uncle Koji's *seppuku*.

Now Toyo sat in the damp grass outside the shrine as his uncle moved to the center of the mats. Uncle Koji's face was a mask of calm. He wore a ceremonial white kimono with brilliant red wings—the wings he usually wore only into battle. He was clean-shaven and recently bathed, and he wore his hair in a tight topknot like the samurai of old. Uncle Koji knelt on the tatami mats keeping his hands on his hips and his arms akimbo.

Toyo's father, Sotaro, crouched next to Koji. Though older than his brother, Toyo's father was slightly smaller, with a long, thin face and a sharp nose like a *katana* blade. They

1

used to joke that Koji's nose had been as straight as his older brother's, until it had been flattened one too many times in judo practice. But today was no day for jokes. In fact, Toyo couldn't remember either of them laughing for a long time.

Sotaro wore a simple gray kimono with the family swords tucked neatly into his sash. The sight was strange to Toyo. For as long as he could remember, the katana and *wakizashi* had been retired to a place of honor in their home. Carrying them outside like this was illegal, though his father would soon be using the swords to carry out an order signed by the emperor himself.

Uncle Koji bowed to Toyo, the ceremony's other witness. Returning the bow from his knees, Toyo touched his head to the ground to show his great respect for his uncle. His father nodded, and Toyo stood and picked up a small wooden stand supporting a short sword about as long as his forearm. The point and the edge of the blade were razor sharp. Toyo strained to keep his legs from shaking as he entered the shrine. Kneeling a little clumsily, he bowed low to the ground once more to present the short wakizashi to his uncle.

When he felt the weight of the sword lift from the stand, Toyo looked up at Koji. His uncle held the wakizashi cradled in his hands as though it were a newborn child. Uncle Koji closed his eyes, touched the flat part of the blade to his forehead, and set the wakizashi in front of him on the mat. He gave a quick smile then for Toyo, the same grin he always flashed right before getting them into trouble.

Instead of making him feel better, the grin deepened Toyo's sense of panic. He didn't want to lose his uncle.

Throughout all the preparations, he had fought to focus on something else—anything else. His first day of school at Ichiko tomorrow, his coming sixteenth birthday, even baseball. But when this ceremony was finished his uncle would be dead and gone. Forever. None of his strength, none of his compassion, none of his spirit would remain.

Toyo backed away, unable to meet Uncle Koji's eyes.

"For my part in the samurai uprising at Ueno Park," his uncle said officially, "I, Koji Shimada, have been sentenced to die. The emperor, in his divine graciousness, has granted me the honor of committing seppuku rather than die at the hands of his executioner. I beg those present here today to bear witness to my death."

Uncle Koji bowed low, and Sotaro and Toyo bowed in return.

He slowly untied the sash around his waist and loosened the kimono wrapped underneath. Pulling the stiff shirt down off his shoulders, Koji exposed his smooth round belly. He tucked the arms of the kimono under his legs, which made him lean forward. Toyo knew this was to help his uncle pitch forward if he should pass out during the ceremony. It would make his father's job much easier.

Uncle Koji closed his eyes and began the poem he had written for the occasion of his death:

> *"In the darkness after the earthquake,*
> *The Flowers of Edo burn bright and fast—*
> *Only to be replaced in the morning*
> *By the light of a new day."*

When he was finished, the samurai opened his eyes and put his hands on his stomach, almost as if he were saying good-bye to it. Then Koji took the short sword in his hands and turned the blade toward his gut.

"Brother," Koji said, "please wait until I have finished my task."

"*Hai*." Toyo's father nodded.

Koji looked past Toyo then, past the little path to the shrine, past the line of trees that circled the clearing. Whether he saw something in the distance or not, Toyo didn't know, but the faraway look stayed in his uncle's eyes as he plunged the wakizashi into his belly. Blood covered his hands and his jaw locked tight, but Koji held his grip on the sword, dragging it across his stomach from left to right. Toyo fought the urge to look away. To honor his promise to bear witness, he forced himself to watch as his uncle's insides spilled onto the floor of the Shinto shrine, the body deflating like a torn rice sack.

When Uncle Koji had sliced all the way across his stomach, he turned the wakizashi in the wound and pulled it diagonally up through his chest. Never flinching, his eyes remained steady and resolute. The knife reached his heart, and with the last of his strength Uncle Koji pulled the wakizashi out, laid it by his side, and fell forward on his hands and knees.

Toyo's father sprang to his feet, raising the long katana blade high over his head.

"Heeeeeeeeeeeeiaaaaaaaaaaaaa!" Sotaro cried. He brought the blade down with blinding speed and chopped Koji's head clean off his body.

4

The head rolled to a stop inches from Toyo, the eyes staring up at him. Toyo refused to let his father see his fear. As his father wiped the blood from the katana with a piece of paper, Toyo commanded his legs to stand.

"Did you watch carefully?" his father asked.

"Hai," Toyo said.

"You observed precisely how it was done?"

"Hai, Father."

"Good," Sotaro Shimada said to his son. "Soon you will do the same for me."

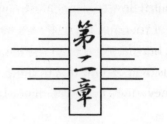

Chapter Two

A PHOTOGRAPH of Emperor Meiji was enshrined above the chalkboard in the ethics lecture hall. Toyo stared at the picture of the man who had sentenced his uncle to die. The emperor was a young man, younger than Uncle Koji. He sat awkwardly in a Western-style chair with his legs dangling down, rather than a more traditional pose on a mat with his legs tucked beneath him. He wore a modern military uniform, with medals on his jacket and a braided rope on his sleeve. His hair was cut short in the European fashion, and he had a moustache on his lip and a goatee on his chin. In his hand, the emperor held a sword pointed down to the ground like a cane.

Beneath the image of the emperor, the school's headmaster, Hiroji Kinoshita, stood at the lectern. He spoke at length about the school, and Toyo drifted in and out of his address.

"First Higher School—Ichiko, as we call her—is the most elite of schools," Kinoshita was saying. "For the next three years, we will be your family. Think of us, your educators, as your father, your fellow students as brothers. You will no longer have need of your mother, or of women at all. Ichiko is your mother now, her classrooms and dormitories your world. The life you had is over. A new one begins today."

"I hope this new one ends soon," Futoshi whispered. "I have to pee."

Toyo glanced at his friend. Like Toyo and the other nine hundred or so boys standing at attention in the room, Futoshi wore the black uniform of Ichiko. It was a strange sight after seeing Futoshi in the familiar middle school uniform they had worn for so long. Like they didn't yet belong here.

"Hai, me too," Toyo whispered back.

"Are you going to go out for the *besuboru* team this afternoon?" Futoshi asked.

"Hai," Toyo answered. "I just hope they don't already have a shortstop. Will you do judo?"

"Of course," Futoshi told him. "I'm the best."

Toyo smiled. Futoshi always thought he was the best at everything. He and Toyo were the only students from their middle school to pass the First Higher entrance exam. Two others had made it into Third Higher, and one was starting Fourth Higher next week. The rest would attend business or vocational schools.

"Your uniforms," Kinoshita said, drawing Toyo's attention, "mark you immediately as Japan's finest. Your black jacket and cap are symbols of excellence. You are to wear them with pride from the moment you rise in the morning until the moment your head touches your bedroll at night. You first-years will have noticed the brass badge on the front of your cap with an imprint of an oak and olive leaf. The oak leaf signifies *bu,* the ancient way of the warrior; the olive leaf symbolizes *bun,* the new way of scholarship and letters. Together, they represent the modern Japan—the place where the old and the new become one, where the powerful and the thoughtful combine to become even stronger."

The powerful and the thoughtful, Toyo echoed silently. The warrior and the scholar. If there was a better description of his father and his uncle, Toyo couldn't think of one. Uncle Koji had always been the fighter of the family—the first to stand up for what he believed with the steel of his blade and the courage in his heart. Sotaro was the scholar of the family. His weapons were his brush and his brain, and he wielded them to argue eloquently in papers, essays, and articles.

Toyo put a hand to the symbol on his cap. The oak and the olive leaves. Koji and Sotaro. He looked again at the portrait of the emperor above Kinoshita's head. Had Meiji written the death order himself, or had some bureaucrat done it for him? Perhaps Koji had been nothing more than a single sheaf in a pile of papers, stacked neatly on the emperor's new Western-style desk. "For refusing to give up his swords." Signed in pen and ink, but unread.

"What was it like?" Futoshi whispered.

Toyo blinked. For a moment, Toyo thought his friend had been reading his mind, but he knew Futoshi must have been wanting to ask him about it all day.

"It was . . . it was awful," Toyo said quietly. "Awful and . . . beautiful."

"Beautiful?" Futoshi asked.

"I don't know. Noble, somehow. Perfect. Until—"

Toyo fell silent. Koji was dead, and for what? Because the emperor had decided there should be no more samurai, and Koji could not give up being a samurai.

"Do you know what the Flowers of Edo are?" Toyo asked, remembering his uncle's death poem.

Futoshi frowned. He shook his head. "Edo is the old name for Tokyo. The *sakura*, maybe? Tokyo is famous for those."

Toyo doubted his uncle was talking about cherry blossoms. Koji's death poem remained one of the many things he didn't understand about his uncle's death.

"It is a great honor to attend First Higher School," the headmaster was saying. "You students of First Higher will someday stand in the upper crust of society. Whether in politics, the arts, or scholarly affairs, you are the future leaders of Japan. Good grades should not be your main focus. More important at Ichiko is the perfection of your character. Manliness. Honor. Public service. These are the lessons you will learn at First Higher."

"Good grades shouldn't be our focus?" Futoshi whispered. "I like it here already."

"In keeping with First Higher's goal to make you into leaders," Kinoshita said, "there will be changes to the way you live your lives here at Ichiko. Those of you who have been here for one or two years already will be familiar with faculty room inspections, hall monitoring, and curfews. Those practices end today."

There was a surprised murmur among the students. Toyo

and Futoshi got quiet with the rest of the crowd and listened attentively.

"As Ichiko graduates," Kinoshita said, "you will one day lead our country. Your dormitory will therefore be the training ground for state-craft. From this day forward, you will govern yourselves. You will be responsible for drafting your own constitution, writing your own rules, electing your own officers, and policing your own halls. In return for responsible self-governance, I pledge that I and the other faculty will not interfere without your permission."

Toyo and most of his fellow juniors didn't know how to react to this news, but the seniors across the aisle—the second- and third-years—were clearly buzzing. Quickly they came to order under Kinoshita's quiet gaze.

"Finally," Kinoshita continued, "before handing the program over to your student leaders for the swearing-in ceremony, I want to direct a few words to the first-years about the high wall that surrounds our campus. You may be tempted to think of it as something that keeps you from the outside world. But the great wall of Ichiko was not built to keep you in; it is to keep the vulgar world *out*. For you to lead a moral life while surrounded on all sides by extravagance and weakness is a formidable task. In this regard, the wall is your ally. Without it, you would be overwhelmed by bad influences and obscenity."

Toyo and Futoshi glanced at each other. They had grown up in Tokyo, and they had never considered it ill-mannered or obscene.

"You must view these grounds as hallowed," Kinoshita

told them. "The barrier that surrounds First Higher is sacred—a sacred Wall of the Soul. Inside it, you are safe. But understand, when you take just one step off the campus, everyone is an enemy. Think of Ichiko as a castle of rightness under siege."

Silence hung over the first-years as they considered Kinoshita's words. When Toyo thought about it, he found himself agreeing with the headmaster. In a way, Uncle Koji had been the victim of a dishonorable world. Toyo had never known a man of greater moral character than his uncle, and yet he had been sentenced to die because he refused to compromise his integrity. Perhaps they were already under siege from the outside world. All of them. All the time.

Kinoshita turned the program over to some of last year's senior leaders for the swearing-in ceremony, and the faculty filed out of the lecture hall.

"All right, first-years!" a senior said when the faculty were gone. "I hope none of you have to go to the bathroom, because we're going to be here a while. A *long* while. We'll begin by learning seven of our most important school songs."

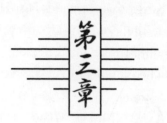

Chapter Three

TOYO HAD never had to pee so badly in all his life. Everything below his belt was on fire. Beside him, Futoshi had been silent for the last three hours. His knees were locked, and there was a look of intense concentration on his face. A boy ahead of them hadn't been so successful; his pants were soaked down his right leg and his head was bowed in shame.

Meanwhile, a seemingly unending stream of seniors had stepped up to the podium to yell and scream at them. First had come the songs. Long, exuberant songs about First Higher that they had to memorize. Then came the four tenets of dormitory life—self-respect, public spirit, humility, cleanliness—each given a lengthy explanation. Later had come more praise for the sacred Wall of the Soul, condemnation for being mama's boys, and harsh warnings that they should never think of, speak to, or act like girls.

At that moment, Toyo was willing to promise never to *look* at another girl if they would let him go to the bathroom. His eyes began to glaze over, and he felt himself wobbling.

Then everyone in the room was falling over—no, bowing. Bowing to the school flag. Toyo joined them, using the bow to hide his unsteadiness.

When he had bent over halfway, Toyo realized there was no way he could straighten back up without peeing in his pants.

Suddenly Futoshi was nudging him. "Stand up!" Futoshi croaked. "Run! What are you waiting for!?"

Clenching his muscles and looking up, Toyo realized the bow to the flag had been the end of the swearing-in ceremony. The first-years were practically trampling each other as they scrambled out of the lecture hall, and he allowed himself to be swept up in the mad dash for the door.

It took them all a desperate moment to realize none of them knew where the bathrooms were. Like birds released from a sack, they fled in different directions.

"Dormitory," Toyo grunted. "Have to be bathrooms near the dormitory."

He had never run so hard, not even when trying to steal home. Futoshi staggered behind him. Along the way, Toyo spotted the character for "Men" painted above a doorway.

"Here!" Toyo cried out for the benefit of his helpless classmates.

Futoshi was already a few steps ahead of him as Toyo bolted through the door to the bathrooms. He shoved his pants down as he crossed the room, almost tripping himself up as he hurtled headfirst toward a urinal and propped himself up weakly with both hands on the wall. Taking no care whatsoever to aim, Toyo gave in to the sweet release with a groan.

At the urinal next to him, Futoshi was talking to himself as he peed. "I am so sorry, my friend. I promise I'll never treat you badly again."

The door slammed open, and more first-years flooded inside. Throwing all sense of decorum to the wind, they crowded around Toyo and Futoshi and the other toilets to urinate together. Dozens more hopped and cried as they waited their turn.

"What are you doing in here!?" a voice demanded. Toyo was relieved enough to be able to turn around. A couple of seniors were working their way through the crowd, pushing first-years out of the way with little regard for their rather delicate situations. The largest of the seniors, a boy old enough to be growing a scraggly goatee, addressed the silent crowd.

"Didn't you see the sign above the door outside?" He turned to a trembling junior who was quite literally holding it. "What did that sign say?"

"M-men," the boy said.

"That's right. But I don't see any men here." The senior turned to one of his friends. "Do you see any men here, Moriyama?"

Moriyama laughed. "Just you and me, Junzo. Just you and me."

"You ladies should be in the women's guest bathroom, around the other side of the building," Junzo told them.

Half the first-years still in line ran to find the other toilets, women's or not.

Junzo laughed as the bathroom cleared out. "Just as I thought. A bunch of girls."

Toyo finished and stepped out of the way for the next person in line. As he moved toward the door, the big senior named Junzo stopped him.

"Who are you?" the senior demanded. "What's your name? Where do you come from? What are you doing here?"

Toyo didn't know where to start. "My, my name is Toyo Shima—"

"No," Junzo barked. *Whack!* He slapped Toyo across the face, bringing tears to Toyo's eyes. He quickly turned his face to the floor until he could control both his pain and his anger.

"Listen carefully, all of you," Junzo announced. "This is how you will always respond. When I ask 'Who are you?' you say 'I am a son of Ichiko.' When I say 'What is your name?' you will say 'My name is Ichiko.' I ask 'Where do you come from?' and you say 'My body and soul were formed in the womb of Ichiko.' And when I say 'Why are you here?' you say 'To honor Ichiko and defend Japan!'"

"Now," Junzo said, pointing at Toyo, "who are you?"

Toyo blinked away his tears. "I am a son of Ichiko," he said, gritting his teeth.

"What is your name?"

"My name is Ichiko."

"Where do you come from?"

"My body and soul are . . . my body and soul were formed in the womb of Ichiko."

"Why are you here?"

15

"To honor Ichiko and defend Japan," Toyo said.

"Louder!" Junzo demanded.

"To honor Ichiko and defend Japan!" Toyo yelled.

Junzo turned on another of the first-years and put him through the same routine. When the junior couldn't remember the answer to the third question, Junzo smacked him.

"You," Junzo's friend Moriyama said, stopping Futoshi as he tried to leave. "Who are you?"

"I am a son of Ichiko!" Futsohi screamed.

Moriyama smiled at Junzo. "I like this one. What is your name?"

"My name is Ichiko!" Futoshi cried even louder.

"Where do you come from?" Moriyama demanded.

"My body and soul were formed in the womb of Ichiko!"

"Why are you here?"

"To take a pee like everybody else!" Futoshi screamed.

Moriyama laughed once despite himself. Junzo reared a fist back to strike Futoshi, but Moriyama caught it.

"Wait, Junzo. I told you, I like this one. He deserves *special* attention."

Junzo lowered his fist. "You'll get yours during *the storm*," the burly senior told Futoshi with a grin. "Let's go, Moriyama. There are some girls in the other bathroom we need to talk to."

Before Moriyama could follow his friend, Toyo bowed to the senior for sparing Futoshi.

"Better not thank me yet," Moriyama told them. "Junzo never forgets. You first-years better not forget, either,"

Moriyama said to the entire room. "Nobody ever gets off easy twice!"

The juniors parted as Moriyama left the bathroom. "Oh," he said on the way out, "and we better not catch any of you peeing in here ever again."

"What's that supposed to mean?" Futoshi asked. "Where are we supposed to pee if not the bathroom?"

"We'll figure it out later," Toyo told him. "Let's just get to our athletic clubs and hope we don't run into the two of them any time soon."

• • •

Toyo carried his bat and glove down the path to the Ichiko baseball field. It was similar to the place he had played ball as a middle-schooler, a large, flat dirt patch near the back wall of the school. The foul lines were scratched in the ground with a shovel, and a net was strung between two poles behind home plate to help catch foul balls. The bases were canvas sacks the besuboru club had filled with sand.

The first person there, Toyo walked out to his familiar position at shortstop. In middle school, he had joined the baseball team for something to do after school, a way to avoid the long, tedious hours in the dormitory. But over time, baseball had become something more to him. He thrilled to the crack of the bat, the slap of leather on leather, the exhilaration of stealing a base. His fingers tensed inside his glove, anticipating a ground ball he could see only in his mind's eye.

Scratching at the dirt infield with his sandal, Toyo's nostalgia for those hot summer days was suddenly replaced by images of Koji's death. The dirt at the base of the Shinto shrine, dry and hard-packed like this, had swallowed Koji's blood before his very eyes.

A voice at the edge of the field startled Toyo from his reverie.

"Girls are not allowed on the field."

Toyo's heart sank. It was that Junzo, with a bat slung over his massive shoulder. Moriyama and a few other seniors stood behind him.

Toyo joined two other juniors who stood off the first-base line. Junzo and the other returning seniors collected on the infield.

"I saw some of you ladies in the bathroom," Junzo said, eyeing Toyo, "but if you don't know already, my name's Junzo Ueda. This is Tatsunori, our catcher. Kennichi, the third baseman. The best pitcher in Tokyo, Moriyama Tsunetaro. And our shortstop, Oda."

Toyo wilted. Of course the team already had a shortstop. Junzo introduced a few other seniors and went over the schedule, but Toyo was lost in his own misery.

"I don't care if we lose every other game this season as long as we beat American Meiji," Moriyama was saying.

"This is our year to win it all," Kennichi said, "it has to be!"

Junzo looked the first-years over and grunted. "We're not going to beat anybody with these ladies." Junzo pointed to the new recruits. "You, take third base. You, behind home plate. You," he said to Toyo, "first base."

"You want me to play first base?" Toyo asked.

"No." Junzo scowled. "I'm the first baseman. You take first base *foul territory*. Girls are *not allowed* on the field."

"I am a *son* of Ichiko," Toyo reminded him.

Junzo ignored him. "Everybody take your positions. Kennichi hits first."

Toyo dragged himself down the first-base line. Looking out over the field, he saw the Ichiko team had only two returning outfielders, and there was no one at second base. In his heart, Toyo was a shortstop—but he would play anywhere, just to be a part of the team.

On the mound, Moriyama took a few warm-up tosses that made Toyo forget everything else. The pitcher seemed to draw into himself as he went into his windup, only to unfurl like a banner in the wind, snapping the ball toward the plate. *Pop!* His fastball was so fast, Toyo couldn't imagine ever catching up to it.

"First pitch!" Moriyama called out.

Kennichi stepped in to bat. Kicking and firing, Moriyama sent the ball whistling toward home. *Thwink!* The third baseman knocked a grounder to short off the end of the bat.

Toyo instinctively took a step, then remembered his place. If he were at shortstop, he would've attacked the ball. Three quick steps to the right. Into the glove. Back to the hand. Across the diamond like an arrow striking a bull's-eye.

Instead Toyo watched as the senior shortstop backpedaled, tripped over his own sandals, and fell to the ground. The ball bounced into left field. *So they have an incredible pitcher and a rotten infield,* Toyo thought. *If only I could show them what I can do.*

Oda scrambled to the ball and hurled an off-balance throw. The baseball sailed over Junzo's head at first base and into foul territory, and Toyo easily snared it.

Without a word, Toyo walked the ball back to Junzo and dropped it directly from his glove into the first baseman's mitt.

"Girls are not allowed on the field," Junzo said.

Looking down, Toyo realized his left foot was across the line. He stared back at Junzo and made a great show of moving the few inches back into foul territory. Junzo smiled, and play resumed while Toyo watched from the sidelines.

It was going to be a long season.

• • •

Futoshi was smiling when they met up outside the dormitory before dinner.

"How was besuboru?"

"I don't want to talk about it," Toyo told him.

Futoshi quietly fell into step as they made their way to their assigned room on the second floor. Futoshi pointed to one of the doors as they passed.

"Look at the paper on that one," Futoshi whispered. "It's a mathematics exercise."

Toyo stopped for a look. The door was built in traditional Japanese style, with wooden slats like a window frame. Paper filled the squares, making them lightweight and luminous. But instead of the usual fine rice paper, this door had old pieces of homework pasted in the frames.

"Here's one from German class. And another from Chinese literature."

Every second door, including their own, was papered with old sheets of homework.

"Looks like we get one of the extra-special rooms," Futoshi joked.

Inside, a few of their new roommates were unpacking their things. Eight other boys were assigned to the room, for a total of ten, counting Toyo and Futoshi. The room was a broad, flat space with no furniture except a deep series of shelves built along one wall where the boys could store their bedrolls and personal items. A lone lightbulb with a metal shade hung from the high ceiling, but most of the light in the room came from the wall of paper windows that opened onto the Ichiko courtyard below.

The other boys in the room acknowledged Toyo and Futoshi with nods. No one was talking, and Toyo and Futoshi found themselves following suit. Without a word, they began to unpack their own sacks, delivered by porters to their rooms while they had been stuck in the swearing-in ceremony.

Most of the lower shelves had already been taken, and Toyo tried to climb up to the top ones with his gear in tow. When that failed, he tossed his bedroll at one of the high shelves, but it came tumbling back, knocking someone's brush case off with it. The bedroll flopped on Toyo's head, and he cringed, waiting for the sound of the brush case breaking on the floor.

It never came.

"Here, let me help," came a deep voice. Toyo peeked out from under his bedroll and saw the largest boy—or man—he had ever seen. He had a classic sumo wrestler's build—tall, heavy, and round—and he had caught the brush case in one of his massive hands.

Before Toyo could say anything, the large boy easily lifted the bedroll and the brush case onto the high shelf and stuffed them in.

"Thanks," Toyo managed finally. He bowed. "My name's Toyo. Toyo Shimada."

"Yoshihiko Fujimura." The other boy bowed back.

Futoshi joined them. "Wait, your name is Fuji and you're as big as a mountain?" he said.

"Hai," the big kid said. "And that's funny, because I've never heard anyone say that before."

"Seriously?" Futoshi asked. "I think it would be obvious, since you're Mt. Fuji–sized compared to the rest of us."

Toyo smacked Futoshi. "That's what he meant, *baka*."

"It's all right. Back home, everybody calls me Fuji," he told them.

"Where are you from?" Toyo asked.

Fuji shifted, as though he hadn't intended to bring the subject up. "The country," he said dismissively.

Toyo could tell he didn't want to say any more. "What about the rest of you?" he said to the room. "Where are you guys from?"

Slowly his roommates began to introduce themselves, and in no time they were sharing stories of hometowns, Ichiko oddities, and senior tortures. At dinner in the cafeteria, they sat together as a group, and later they stayed up long into the night discussing their early observations about Ichiko.

"Does anybody know why our door and windows are

covered with somebody's homework?" one of the boys asked as they lay awake on their bedrolls.

"We noticed that too!" Toyo told him.

"The first-years are assigned to the odd-numbered rooms, and the seniors get the even rooms," Fuji pointed out. "I don't know what it means, but only the odd rooms have the practice papers on the doors."

"And what's a 'storm'?" Futoshi asked. "That big baka Junzo said I'd get mine in a 'storm.'"

"Like a rainstorm?" one of the boys asked. "Do you think they'd make us sleep out in the rain?"

Toyo shrugged. "Who knows? We're not supposed to pee in the bathrooms."

"Aiiieeeee!" someone screamed, jolting everyone in the room. The cry was followed all at once by dozens more from somewhere in the bowels of the dormitory. The yelling escalated to a fever pitch, and the floors and walls started to shake with a sound like a hundred horses charging to their deaths.

"Earthquake!" one of Toyo's roommates shouted.

Toyo had been through enough earthquakes to know this wasn't one. He scrambled to the door and slid it open to peek outside. Up and down the corridor, he saw the heads of other first-years do the same. His friends joined him at the door as the stomping and shouting grew louder and closer. Doors rattled, pictures fell from walls, and floorboards jiggled loose.

"What is it?" Futoshi asked.

As the mob reached the top of the stairs, Futoshi got

his answer. Dozens of seniors, clad only in loincloths and headbands, surged into the hallway in a berserk stampede. Some banged on pots and pans, others beat the walls and doors with kendo sticks and canes. As they swarmed down the corridor like fire ants, the doors of curious first-years snapped shut.

"*This* is a storm," Toyo whispered in awe. And it sounded as if it was headed right for them.

"Shut the door," Futoshi hissed, scrambling away. "Shut the door!"

Toyo slapped the paper door shut. Behind him, his roommates hid in their bedrolls. Part of him wanted to run and hide with them, but another part of him was drawn to the storm. Quietly he poked his finger through one of the paper panels and peeked outside.

"Toyo!" Futoshi called. "Come on!"

In seconds the storm filled the hallway. Sticks beat mercilessly against the wall, the door, the floor. The sound was deafening.

But suddenly the swarm changed course, plunging into the first-year room across the hall. Toyo saw kendo sticks smash through the door, tearing its thin wood frame and school-paper windows to shreds. The boys inside cried out in fear, but soon the sound of the storm drowned them out. Still peeking through the hole, Toyo watched as dozens of seniors filled the room, smashing potted plants and pouring water into beds.

From his angle across the hall, Toyo could see one or two of his classmates cowering under their blankets. The seniors

24

fell on them, hitting, kicking, beating them with sticks—four or five seniors per boy. Soon the pain-filled cries of the first-years joined in the terrible chorus.

A crazed eye suddenly appeared in Toyo's peep hole, and if he hadn't fallen back in fright the baseball bat that immediately tore through the paper would have smacked him in the face.

The bat slid out of the hole and was replaced by the grinning face of Junzo Ueda. Toyo scurried to his bedroll, haunted by the soft laughter of the big senior as he stepped away.

From then on, Toyo could only hear the screams.

Chapter Four

THE MORNING after the first storm, Toyo saw two first-years with their arms in slings and another after the morning's cold baths gingerly wrapping a bandage around his swollen ribs. One boy was actually kept in the infirmary with a broken left leg. The room across the hall was in even worse shape—bedrolls soaked and shredded, door and windows totally destroyed.

And yet . . . no one spoke of it. The teachers asked no questions and the seniors went about their business as the juniors limped quietly to class. Storms were apparently an unquestioned Ichiko tradition. Every night, a different first-year room was stormed, and each morning there were new victims. In the rooms the storm had yet to hit, boys stayed awake all night long, whimpering under their blankets.

But despite their splints and bandages, the boys who survived the storms paraded around the school grounds like conquering champions. There was a swagger to their step and a self-assurance in their faces unmatched among those soon-to-be victims. Toyo envied their confidence, despite the obvious price.

After five nights, the seniors still had not attacked Toyo's room. Down the hall the storm came to a different room, and Toyo and his friends now knew better than to run to the door and watch. With relief they had once again been spared, they tried to sleep through the stomping and the screams.

Still feeling restless, Toyo sat up in a dark corner near the windows, the cloudy night outside obscuring the moon. Tomorrow was his sixteenth birthday. He wondered if his father would remember. Koji had, always bringing Toyo a small, hand-carved wooden sword. As a child, Toyo had worn them out or broken them each year, but as he had gotten older he had begun to treat them more kindly and to collect them. He regretted now the loss of those early swords, though he treasured the memory of using them. With nothing more than a sly grin from Koji, they would begin their battle, two samurai against the wooden posts that held the roof in place—ready stand-ins for a host of enemy ninja. Together they hacked and slashed at the beams until their wooden swords broke or Sotaro yelled at them from his study to be quiet.

A dark shadow inching across the room startled Toyo. The moon momentarily slipped out from behind a cloud, and Toyo saw the face of a boy tiptoeing toward the window.

"Futoshi, what are you doing?" Toyo whispered.

Futoshi shushed his friend. "Nothing. Just sneaking out."

"Are you crazy?" Toyo asked. Futoshi motioned for him to keep his voice down. "What if the storm comes and you're gone?" Toyo whispered more softly.

"The storm has already come and gone tonight. They never strike twice."

"You don't know that."

"Well," Futoshi conceded, "they haven't yet." One of the windows squeaked as he pushed it open. "Besides, it should be obvious by now they are saving us for last. They're trying to draw it out. Make us suffer."

Toyo knew he was right. The seniors were saving something very special for Futoshi, and it made sense to save the best for last.

"Where are you going, anyway?" he asked.

Futoshi already had a leg out the window. "Um . . ." He paused, clearly trying to think of a good lie. "To see the train?"

"Oh, sure," Toyo answered, "the train." The first trains to arrive in Tokyo had fascinated them when they were boys, but he doubted Futoshi would risk sneaking out to see one now.

"And how will you leave the campus? Sneak over the sacred Wall of the Soul?"

Futoshi thought about that. "If the wall is there to keep the bad things from getting in, it's all right to sneak out," he reasoned. "I just won't climb over it to get back in."

"I don't think that's—" Toyo started, but the sound of a window opening in the room next door silenced them. Futoshi pulled his leg back inside, and the two boys peeked outside. A senior from the room next door climbed up on the windowsill and leaned out over the edge.

"Do you think he's going to jump?" Toyo asked.

Soon they heard the sound of liquid showering the shrubs below.

"He's taking a piss," Futoshi realized. They sat back inside until the senior was finished.

"I think we know now how to avoid using the bathrooms," Toyo said. "At least at night."

The window next door slid shut, and Futoshi started to climb out his window again.

"Well, be careful," Toyo said. "And don't get caught."

"I don't intend to," Futoshi whispered, finding a foothold on the wall outside.

Toyo nodded toward the room next door. "And watch out for the dormitory rain."

• • •

Toyo met Futoshi in the courtyard after classes the next day. Toyo was taking the literature track, and Futoshi was in the science track. They shared only one class together—logic.

"You look tired," Toyo said, knowing Futoshi had been out all night.

"Not so loud," Futoshi warned him. "Do you want me to get in trouble?"

Toyo forced a smile. "Don't worry. You don't look any worse than all the other boys who waited up all night for a storm. Come on, let's go have a look at the new constitution the seniors posted."

They walked off together toward the tall clock tower that punctuated the courtyard. "I can't *wait*," Futoshi said. "Finally—no more cleaning rooms, no more taking baths, no more sneaking around. No more rules!"

Toyo shook his head. "You don't get it, do you? We can't live like monkeys."

"Why not?"

"We don't want to have to go running back to Kinoshita the first time something goes wrong. That would be the end of self-rule. If the seniors are smart, they'll make the rules more strict than the faculty did."

"*More strict?*" Futoshi cried. "You're crazy." A few juniors clustered around the posted constitution. From the way they were shaking their heads, Toyo knew Futoshi was going to be unhappy. As he read, he saw the seniors had christened the dormitory "Independence Hall." Toyo thought the name was fitting.

"Curfew at eight o'clock! That's worse than before!" Futoshi complained. "Look at this. No smoking, no spitting, no spending the night outside Independence Hall without permission."

"'Departures from campus for even the smallest errand must be reported to the gatekeeper,'" Toyo read aloud for Futoshi's benefit. "You think that includes sneaking out to see the train?"

"I think 'Slavery Hall' is a better name than Independence Hall. How do they expect to enforce all these rules, anyway?"

"There's an executive committee in charge of day-to-day operations," Toyo explained as he read ahead. "And there's a general assembly to advise them. They've already elected the executive committee."

"Nice of them to ask us," Futoshi said.

"First-years can't vote. Not for executive committee, anyway. And they've already assigned someone to oversee discipline in the dorm."

"Let me guess," Futoshi said. "Junzo."

Toyo didn't bother to tell his friend he was right.

A boy ran up to them. "Toyo Shimada," the first-year said. "Message for you."

The delivery boy handed over a slip of paper and went on his way.

"What's it say?"

"I'm to meet my father in the *dojo*."

"He's here? On campus?"

"Hai," Toyo said. "Amazingly, he remembered my birthday."

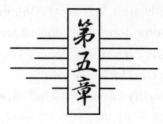

Chapter Five

TOYO STEPPED tentatively through the entrance of the quiet school dojo. The judo club training room was the customary place for receiving guests at First Higher School because it remained empty most of the day.

Sotaro sat on a tatami mat with his legs folded beneath him. Still as a statue, he looked customarily severe in his black kimono, his hair pulled back in a traditional samurai topknot. Toyo got down on his knees and bowed to his father, then sat on a mat across from him.

The silence between them grew thick as Toyo waited for his father to speak.

"Today is your sixteenth birthday," Sotaro said finally.

Toyo nodded. "Hai, Father."

A carved wooden box sat on the floor between them. Sotaro presented it to Toyo.

"This gift is of course inadequate," Sotaro said.

Toyo couldn't remember the last time Sotaro had honored him on his birthday. He accepted the box with a bow. It was engraved with an image of a cherry blossom, the Shimada family crest. Lifting the lid, he found two ink brushes inside—one long and one short—with handles made of elaborately carved whalebone. They were the most beautiful brushes Toyo had ever seen.

"I am not worthy of such a gift," Toyo said, bowing dutifully.

"It is nothing," Sotaro said. "Had the world not changed, on this day I would have given you your swords. Today you would have become a samurai."

Toyo's father paused momentarily, then dismissed the thought with a grunt.

"The great samurai Miyamoto Musashi once said the warrior's way is the twofold path of the brush and the sword," Sotaro told him. "Denied our swords, at least we can still have our brushes."

The twofold path. Toyo remembered the brass badge on his Ichiko cap—the olive leaf and the oak leaf. "The powerful and the thoughtful," Toyo said, both happy and surprised to connect with something his father said. "The two halves of the whole."

Sotaro brightened. "Hai. The samurai code. *Bushido*."

"Bushido," Toyo whispered. "Uncle Koji lived by bushi-do."

A cloud passed over Sotaro's face. "As do I. And when bushido demanded it, Koji was strong enough to give his life. But I—" Sotaro looked at the floor. "But I did not come here to speak of your uncle."

The subject of Koji was still a raw wound for them both, but Toyo had to know more.

"I thought Uncle Koji died because the emperor demanded it."

"*Koji died*—" Sotaro began forcefully, then calmed himself. "Koji died because he was *shishi*. One of the Men of High Purpose. They weren't fighting Emperor Meiji. Koji and the others helped restore Meiji to the throne."

"But he said—"

"The Men of High Purpose saw the soul of Japan dying," Sotaro told him, "and they fought to save it. They fought not a man, but a movement. They sought a return to the old ways, the ways of bushido. When arguments failed, they fought with their swords. But they did not succeed. Those samurai like your uncle who did not die in the uprising sought the only other honorable sacrifice—seppuku."

"But the emperor—" Toyo began.

"Koji was going to be punished—and he should have been. He rebelled against imperial decree. When he failed, he asked to commit seppuku rather than be subjected to a more common punishment like prison, and the emperor honored him by granting his request."

Toyo was astonished. "Uncle Koji—Uncle Koji *requested* it? He *asked* to die?"

"He was no longer able to win."

Toyo shook his head. "I don't understand anything about bushido."

"I know," Sotaro said sadly. "Unfortunately, there is no need for you to understand. Not anymore. Bushido is gone. Like a cherry blossom ripped too soon from its branch by the harsh winds of spring."

"Like Uncle Koji, I suppose," Toyo spat.

"Hai," his father agreed. "Like Uncle Koji."

"But he *wasn't* ripped from the branch too soon," Toyo argued. "You said yourself—the emperor only ordered him to die because he requested it! He made a choice. He *chose* to leave me all alone. Tell me how he could do that! What possible reason could he have for abandoning me?"

Sotaro said nothing, and Toyo realized his mistake immediately.

"Us," he corrected himself. "How could he leave *us* all alone?"

Whether his father was insulted or not, he was apparently in no mood to explain. But when had he ever been in the mood to explain anything? Knowing it was pointless to press him further, Toyo fell back on custom and bowed.

"I thank you again for honoring me with your gift."

"It is nothing," Sotaro said again ritually. He returned Toyo's bow.

Toyo stood to leave. Sotaro stood with him, and they bowed to each other once more. Without saying another word, Toyo walked away.

"Toyo," his father called.

Toyo stopped and turned, and he was suddenly struck by how old his father looked.

"There is . . . there is a Shinto festival this weekend. I wonder if you might like to join me in a visit."

Toyo felt his anger drain. First a gift on his birthday, and now a trip to a Shinto festival? What had gotten into Sotaro?

"Hai," Toyo said, bowing again. "It would be an honor. Father."

• • •

Practice was already under way, and Junzo glowered at Toyo from his position at first base.

"You're late."

Toyo bowed in apology—not that he understood what difference it made. But there were still two positions open, and he wanted one. He ran to his place down the first-base foul line.

"*Dabu pure* to third base!" the catcher cried, calling for a double play. *Dink!* He tapped the ball down the third-base line. The third baseman, Kennichi, charged hard. He reached low, plucked the ball with his bare hand, and fired the ball to second base as he fell.

One of the other first-years moved to the second-base bag. The ball popped into his glove. He pivoted, jumped, and threw on a line to first base to complete the double play.

One of the other first-years!? Toyo suddenly realized.

"I thought first-years weren't allowed on the field!" Toyo protested.

"I said *girls* weren't allowed on the field. Katsuya's no longer a girl," Junzo said.

"But what—how—?" Toyo stammered. The boy at second base had a bandaged shoulder from last night's storm, and he winced as he gave Toyo an apologetic shrug.

The only available place on the infield was now taken. Dejected, Toyo returned to his position in foul territory. Now he and the other first-year were competing for a place in the outfield. Ichiko was a good team—a great team, except for the obvious weakness at shortstop—and Toyo wanted desperately to be a part of it.

"Dabu pure to first base!" the catcher called. He blasted the ball down the line, but it skipped foul by inches. The ball shot past Junzo as he halfheartedly swiped at it.

Moving instinctively, Toyo stepped to his right and dove. The ball came up on a hop, and he squeezed it in his glove as his body hit the dirt with a *whomp*. Amid a flurry of dust and cotton and leather, Toyo popped up and launched the ball while still on his knees. The shortstop, Oda, was covering the second-base bag, and Toyo's throw was right on target.

The senior shortstop ducked like a rookie afraid of the ball, and Toyo's toss sailed past him into left field.

Moriyama whistled from the mound and nodded at Toyo. "Nice play."

Toyo looked up at the big first baseman, waiting for a similar acknowledgment. Instead, Junzo planted a sandal in the middle of Toyo's kimono and calmly kicked him back across the foul line.

"No girls on the field," Junzo said.

• • •

Toyo tossed his bat and glove on the shelf in his room and hurried to the dining hall. The cafeteria was a madhouse—at least on the seniors' side. They slurped their soup, laughed at bawdy jokes, and complained loudly about the quality of the food. The first-year side was a different story altogether. The juniors sat huddled around their meals, trying to remain as silent and inconspicuous as possible, lest they attract the unwanted attention of an upperclassman. Toyo went quickly and quietly to the table where the rest of his roommates sat. A servant brought him his meal.

"The food tonight stinks," Futoshi warned him from across the table. "It *always* stinks." The other boys at their table shot warning looks at Futoshi, but he ignored them. Having long since finished his food, he drummed his fingers restlessly on the table while he watched Toyo eat his rice.

"What did you get for your birthday?" Futoshi asked, but this time his roommates shushed him. Toyo wanted to answer, but didn't want to bring down the wrath of the upperclassmen on his roommates. He shook his head.

Across the room, a senior slammed his bowl on the table and called out to the kitchen. "This food is terrible! And you don't serve large enough portions! More rice! More rice!" he demanded. A servant rushed out with more rice and filled his bowl.

"That's so unfair," Futoshi whispered a little too loudly for his roommates' comfort. "How come they get seconds and we don't?"

Before anyone could stop him, Futoshi slammed his bowl on the table and yelled, "More rice here! I want more rice!"

The cafeteria went dead silent. Toyo's chopsticks froze midway to his mouth. All around them, first-years did everything they could to hide in their bowls. One of his roommates let out a small whimper.

Futoshi kept it up. "It tastes like rat," he yelled, "but I still want more stinking rice!"

All eyes in the room went to Junzo, the newly elected

master of dormitory discipline. His eyes narrowed as he considered Futoshi, then with the slightest tilt of his head, he nodded permission for the kitchen staff to bring another bowl to the first-year. A servant scurried to Toyo's table and nervously deposited a new bowl of rice in front of Futoshi.

It was the seniors' turn to whisper. Toyo couldn't hear what they were saying, but he knew every one of them was talking about Futoshi. If any of them hadn't known his name before, they all knew it now. His friend was a marked man.

Futoshi dug in to his new bowl of rice, seemingly oblivious to the attention he was receiving.

"Better enjoy it," whispered one of their roommates. "That's going to be your last meal."

"So they beat me up during the storm," Futoshi said with his mouth full. "They were going to do that anyway."

"Some things are worse than a storm," said a quiet kid from Osaka. Everyone looked his way without turning their heads. "Things like the clenched-fist punishment."

"The 'clenched-fist' punishment?" Toyo whispered.

"They say it's worse than a hundred storms," the boy told them.

Toyo watched as Futoshi choked on his rice.

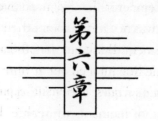

Chapter Six

"I PRAY there will not be a storm today."

It was the first thing Sotaro had said since they sat down to lunch almost half an hour ago.

"Hai," said Toyo. "That would be . . . most unfortunate," he added, thinking more of the Ichiko storm to come.

As usual, they ate in silence at the small table in the kitchen. This was the house Toyo had been raised in, but he felt no particular attachment to it. For most of his school life, he had lived in dormitories.

Toyo helped Sotaro clean the table and then wandered to the front room. There on a low cabinet the Shimada swords were on display—retired to a place of honor since the emperor had outlawed them. As he often did when he was a young boy, Toyo felt himself drawn to the long katana blade and short wakizashi. He ran his hand down the length of the katana's scabbard, remembering with a shiver when he'd seen it last.

A small scroll tucked underneath the sword stand caught Toyo's eye. It was addressed to his father, and it bore the official seal of the emperor. Toyo glanced over his shoulder to make sure Sotaro was not in the room, then quickly unrolled the piece of parchment. Buried in the official language of the Imperial court, one line jumped out at him:

"Sotaro Shimada's request to commit seppuku is denied."

It took Toyo a moment to realize he had stopped breathing, and he gasped as though he were coming up for air. He stifled the sound with a cough as the kitchen door slid closed, hastily stuffing the scroll back under the sword stand. Spinning, he found Sotaro watching him from the doorway. Had his father seen him?

"We should be going," Sotaro said. "Edo has become much more crowded since the emperor moved the capital here." His father still used the old name for Tokyo; hardly anyone else still did.

Toyo avoided his father's eyes as they changed into their sandals by the door. *Sotaro didn't take part in the uprisings like Koji did, so why should he want to kill himself?*

He rammed his indoor slippers into their slot. If Sotaro killed himself, Toyo really *would* be alone. But he was already, wasn't he? He had been alone since the day his mother died.

Why does he think he needs permission? He should just do it, if he wants to so badly, Toyo thought bitterly. *It's not like it will change anything.*

Sotaro frowned at Toyo, and for a moment he worried his father could read his thoughts. Following Sotaro's eyes, he realized he had put his sandals on backwards.

• • •

The walk to the Shinto festival was a long one. "We should take the streetcar," Toyo told his father. "Or at least a rickshaw."

"Once, the people of Edo were always ready to pack a sack and walk from town to town," Sotaro lectured him. "Now they ask, 'Does the train run there? How long will it take?'"

Toyo gritted his teeth and vowed to make no more suggestions.

Sotaro looked tall and officious today. People stared at him as he passed, the foot traffic on the street parting for him as it would for a streetcar. Almost every other man on the street had his hair cut short and wore a black, Western-style suit, a top hat, and leather shoes, but Sotaro still looked like a samurai. The sides of his head were shaved and the hair on top was pulled back and wound into a tight topknot. He wore a traditional kimono bearing the Shimada family crest, and he had thong sandals on his feet. Toyo burned with embarrassment.

He kept his eyes on the ground so he wouldn't have to watch the people stare. Soon they left the street, and his father was leading him down a strangely familiar wooded path. Looking up as they passed through the trees to a clearing where the Shinto festival was being held, memories returned to Toyo hot and fast. The festival was being held at the same temple where Uncle Koji had killed himself. But now the quiet little field surrounding it was filled with people dancing and singing. Jugglers and magicians moved about, and a puppet show drew laughter from the crowd. Toyo froze.

Sotaro noticed his son was no longer beside him and turned.

"What's going on here?" Toyo demanded. "How can they—how can they sing and dance here!? Don't they have any respect?"

"They have great respect," Sotaro told him. "When the honored die, Shinto holds that they become *kami*—spirits of our ancestors who continue to guide us through life."

"Shinto is just something to make people feel better about dying," Toyo said pointedly.

His father seemed to raise himself higher and look down on him.

"Koji is dead," Toyo persisted. "He's gone. Forever."

"He that is born must die," Sotaro said.

Toyo laughed humorlessly. "Thanks. That makes it all better."

As Sotaro simply turned and walked away, Toyo cursed to himself. *Why do I even bother?*

He found Sotaro watching a puppet show, of all things. Toyo crossed his arms and stared off into the distance.

"'The Tale of the Forty-seven *Ronin*,'" Sotaro said. "Do you know it?"

Toyo shrugged disinterestedly.

"Watch," Sotaro said. "A devious *daimyo* invited an enemy samurai lord into his castle. To kill a guest would break the code of bushido, so the visiting daimyo thought himself safe."

The wicked-looking daimyo stalked his enemy, his evil frown turning into a sly smile whenever the visiting daimyo turned around. Despite himself, Toyo was impressed by the trick.

"Likewise, it would have been dishonorable for the visiting daimyo to attack his host. But his enemy was very clever, and tricked the visiting daimyo into drawing his sword."

The visiting daimyo pulled out his sword on the tiny puppet stage, and the audience moaned in sympathy.

"The shogun, who maintained the law of the land, commanded the standard punishment for such an offense," Sotaro explained. "The visiting daimyo was ordered to commit seppuku."

"Just for drawing his sword?" Toyo frowned.

He stood transfixed as the wooden daimyo dragged his short sword across his belly and a red blossom of silk spread from his stomach. The puppet collapsed, and the audience sighed appreciatively.

"That's ridiculous. Why would he agree to die if he was tricked?"

"Because his shogun commanded it," Sotaro said. "The daimyo's samurai shared your anger, but there was little they could do. The shogun commanded no revenge be taken, for one death begs another, and another, and yet another, until there is no stopping it. Since they could not fight, those most dedicated to their lord performed seppuku."

Loyal samurai sat on folded knees and dragged their short swords across their bellies. More red silk ran, and the puppets collapsed to the applause of the audience. Toyo raised his hands in frustration.

"This is crazy."

Sotaro ignored his comment. "Those who chose to live became ronin."

"Ronin?" Toyo asked.

"Lordless samurai," Sotaro explained. "Drifters. Men with no past, no future, no allegiances, and no home in the present."

One of the ronin puppets sat at a little table, drinking sake. Suddenly he flipped the table aside, making the audience jump. Their surprise turned to awe as the little puppet drew his katana.

"One of the ronin was ashamed he had not committed seppuku like the others," Sotaro narrated. "He refused to accept the murder of his lord, and he convinced other ronin to join him. Forty-seven ronin in all."

"This makes more sense," Toyo said. He stepped closer to his father where he could see better. Though there were not forty-seven ronin puppets to be counted, their numbers filled the stage.

Toyo's eyes widened as the ronin ignored the shogun's order and stormed the castle of their enemy. *Click! Clack! Click!* Their tiny wooden swords hacked and slashed through the daimyo's guards. When the battle ended, a dozen ronin remained—but they were more than enough to take care of the evil warlord. The homeless samurai fell on him, and the puppet's head popped off into the audience to the laughter of the crowd. Toyo grinned as a young boy down front snatched up the puppet head and danced around with it.

The audience quieted down as the impressive figure of

the shogun marched onto the stage. The surviving ronin bowed before the nation's ruler.

"The ronin avenged the death of their daimyo, but they broke the shogun's law," Sotaro explained. "By his order, they committed seppuku."

The ronin drew their swords and dragged them across their bellies. As ribbons of silk filled the stage, the audience cheered. Toyo was dumbfounded.

"That makes no sense!" he protested. "Why are these people celebrating?"

"The ronin died honorably," Sotaro explained, "as heroes."

His father walked away, and Toyo followed on his heels. "That doesn't make any sense either. First the shogun orders the daimyo to kill himself even though he didn't deserve it, and he did. Then the shogun ordered the ronin not to take revenge, but they did it anyway. How does that make the daimyo honorable and the ronin into heroes?"

Sotaro stopped and looked Toyo in the eyes. "Sometimes a man must do what is in his heart," he said, "not what the law tells him."

Sotaro held Toyo's eyes for a moment longer, then moved away to watch a sumo match. Toyo shook his head and followed.

Standing to one side, Toyo tried to read his father's face. Would he follow the path of the forty-seven ronin? Would Sotaro disobey the emperor's order and obey his other master—bushido? His face betrayed nothing.

"The Record of Ancient Matters says that the gods Takemikazuchi and Takeminakata sumo wrestled each other for ownership of the Japanese islands," Sotaro said.

Toyo dragged his attention from his father to the ring. The two wrestlers, easily three hundred pounds each, were naked except for the black silks they wore wrapped between their legs.

"The sumo ring is the only place where the samurai tradition of *shobu*, one-on-one combat, still survives," Sotaro said.

Each sumo wrestler took a pinch of sand, tossed it over his shoulder, and then began the ritual planting of the feet and slapping of the legs that marked the beginning of a match. When they finished, the two huge men grunted and threw themselves at each other, trying to shove the other from the ring.

Shobu, ronin, bushido, thought Toyo. *Is Sotaro trying to share part of his life with me, or tell me good-bye?* Sure, they had never been close—but Sotaro was the only family Toyo had left.

He turned to his father. "If bushido is so important that Uncle Koji and forty-seven ronin would die for it, shouldn't I learn it?"

Sotaro's eyes fixed on him, and for the barest of moments Toyo thought he saw a glimmer there—then it was gone. "No," he said, looking away.

Toyo frowned. "Why not?"

Sotaro sighed. "The day you were born, the emperor ordered the samurai to put away their swords. We were the only class with a reason to oppose his move toward a more modern Japan, and our katana were the outward symbol of our power," Sotaro said. "On that day, I knew the old Japan, *my* Japan, was truly dead. But I swore to your mother before she died that I would raise you to survive in the new Japan, even though it is no longer my world. And so I have. You, Toyo, you will do more than survive. You will succeed."

"So you will not teach me the way of the warrior?" Toyo asked.

Sotaro stared vacantly at the sumo match. "Bushido is dead."

One of the wrestlers tossed the other sumo from the ring, and the delighted crowd cheered.

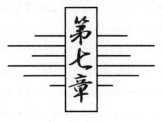

Chapter Seven

TOYO FETCHED his bat and glove for baseball practice Monday afternoon. Rushing out of his dorm room—*oof!*—he slammed into a human wall.

"Sorry, Fuji," said Toyo.

"It can't be helped." Fuji shrugged.

"Fuji, aren't you in an athletic club?"

The big first-year shook his head.

"Why don't you try out for the Ichiko sumo team?"

Fuji frowned. "No thanks."

"But it's easy," Toyo said. "All you have to do is push another guy out of a ring."

"There is far more to sumo than that," Fuji corrected him.

"Oh," Toyo said. "Sorry."

Fuji sighed. "I trained as a sumo wrestler at my middle school."

"Really? Where you any good?"

"I had to quit. It . . . it got in the way of my studies."

Toyo didn't quite believe him, but felt it was too impolite to say so.

"Okay then," Toyo said. "I guess I'll see you in the cafeteria after practice."

• • •

"First-year challenge," Junzo said. "Race to first base."

Toyo had just watched another fielding practice from the sidelines, and he immediately perked up at the opportunity to prove his worth. With nothing better to do, he had been studying the team, and he was convinced his team could be *great*. But first he had to *make* the team.

"Not you, Katsuya," Moriyama said as Toyo and two other boys lined up. "You're already on the team."

The new second baseman stepped away, leaving Toyo and the other boy, Michiyo. *Small and thin*, thought Toyo. *Probably a fast runner*.

"We're looking for a new center fielder. He must be quick," Junzo told them. "Do your best."

Michiyo lined up in the batter's box to the right of home plate. Toyo took a place next to him in fair territory.

"Ah-ah-ah—" Junzo started, but Toyo didn't need to hear the rest.

"I know, I know," Toyo said, moving around Michiyo into foul territory.

Toyo dug the edge of his sandal into the loose dirt around home plate and bent low.

"Go!" Junzo cried.

Toyo sprinted hard. Halfway there he was huffing, his sandals thunk-thunk-thunking along with his pounding heart. He could feel Michiyo drop back, and as they flew past first base, Toyo's foot was the first to cross the line.

Toyo pulled to a stop down the line, and Michiyo hobbled up alongside. They both rested their hands on their knees as they gasped.

"I'm usually much faster," Michiyo said between breaths. "Last night someone kicked me in the leg during the storm."

"That was—your room?" Toyo panted. He saw now that Michiyo was clearly favoring one of his legs.

Michiyo nodded. "You ran a good race, though. Congratulations."

"We have made our decision," Junzo said.

"Wait," Toyo told him. "It wasn't a fair race—"

"Michiyo will be the new center fielder," Junzo announced.

Toyo stopped. "But—but I won the race."

"Hai," Junzo said. "But Michiyo is a man."

"What!?" Toyo cried. "You mean there was no way I could win? What do I have to do?"

"I told you," Junzo said. "Be a man."

"What's the use when you won't let me prove it," said Toyo as he picked up his bat and glove and stalked off the field.

● ● ●

Toyo's roommates looked like he felt. Every face at his cafeteria table was haggard from staying up night after night, waiting for the storm. Michiyo's room had been hit three days ago, and Toyo's room was the only one left. The seniors were clearly playing with them. Trying to make them snap.

Toyo rubbed his eyes. He had been losing sleep too—but

51

not over the storm, and not over baseball. It was Sotaro. Every day now Toyo worried someone would bring him the news his father had committed seppuku without calling for him. It was a deep ache that grew in him as each day passed.

Toyo stayed lost in his own thoughts until he got a whiff of something putrid. "What *is* that?" he whispered.

"It smells like dead rat," said Futoshi.

The kitchen staff wheeled out large serving carts with piping hot pots of rice and stacks of serving bowls. As a cart passed them, Toyo saw Futoshi flip something into one of the steaming containers.

"What was—" Toyo started to ask, but Futoshi kicked him under the table. Toyo glared at his friend.

A different cart stopped beside their table, and the servant began dishing out bowls of rice. Toyo chanced a sniff. Not too bad.

A chair screeched across the room and everyone turned. Staggering back from his table, a senior pointed at his bowl with a disgusted look on his face.

"There's a dead mouse in my rice!" he cried.

The boy next to Toyo spit the rice out of his mouth, spraying Futoshi. Around the room, boys gagged, coughed, and spewed rice all over each other.

"I have a mouse in mine too!" Futoshi cried. Before Toyo could take a good look, his friend jumped on the table and hurled his dish at a wall. The bowl exploded, showering the area with rice.

In moments the air was filled with hundreds of flying rice bowls. The seniors attacked the juniors, and the first-years retaliated. The servants jumped out the windows.

All the anger and frustration from his baseball practices welled up in Toyo. In the swirling chaos, he spied Junzo's big ugly head across the room, took careful aim, and launched his throw.

Suddenly everything froze except Toyo's bowl, arcing gracefully through the air until it struck Junzo square on the back of the head. But Junzo didn't move. Headmaster Kinoshita stood in the doorway, tracing the flight of the bowl back to Toyo and locking eyes with him.

"What is going on here!?" demanded Kinoshita.

Everyone scrambled back into their seats.

"What is going on here!?" Kinoshita asked again. The answering silence was thick. "Is this the consequence of self-government? Is this what you choose to do with the freedom you have been given? Throw your food against the walls and destroy your cafeteria?"

The headmaster let his words sink in for a moment. Toyo looked to Futoshi, but his friend had his head bent low.

"Who are your elected officials?" Kinoshita asked. His fury had cooled to contempt.

Junzo and a few of the newly elected executive committee members slowly stood.

"We will discuss this incident in detail," Kinoshita said, "after I deliver the message I was bringing. Toyo Shimada! You are to proceed to the school dojo immediately. It is your father."

Toyo's dark imagination whirled during the longest walk of his life, crossing the cafeteria with every eye on him. His uncle's seppuku had been no secret. Did any of them suspect as Toyo did now that Sotaro would be next?

As Toyo neared the door, he saw Junzo smirk. The senior dragged his chopsticks across his stomach like a mock seppuku, and Toyo broke into a run.

• • •

Gasping as he reached the doorway, Toyo tried to force his heart to stop beating so fast before he entered the dojo. He bowed at the entrance as ceremony required, then stepped inside.

Sotaro was kneeling in the corner of the room. His eyes were closed and his back was straight and tall. Toyo felt a great weight leave him. He slipped off his shoes and walked softly to his father. Halfway across the room, he saw the family katana and wakizashi sitting beside Sotaro. His father's words the day of Koji's seppuku came back to him in a flash:

Soon you will do the same for me.

Toyo suddenly stumbled over his own feet. He shook as he sat in front of his father. He wasn't ready for this; he hadn't prepared. How could he stand beside his father as Sotaro had done for Koji, take the family katana in hand and—and—

Toyo bowed to his father, but he couldn't take his eyes off the swords.

"I am sorry for the interruption of your school activities," Sotaro said. It was a courtesy, nothing more.

"It is nothing," Toyo said. He burned inside. *I can't do this. I can't do this. I can't do this. I can't cut the head off my own father.* Would Sotaro allow him to refuse? Toyo glanced up and found Sotaro looking through him.

"My death—it scares you," Sotaro said.

Toyo returned his eyes to the floor. "No, Father. I mean—hai. I—"

"You are scared because you do not understand bushido," Sotaro sighed. "You were right. I *should* have taught you. Then you would understand the true sacrifices a samurai must make. That way you would understand what Koji did, and why I wish to follow him."

Toyo bowed to apologize for his fear.

"It is time you understood what it means to live and die by bushido," Sotaro said. "Koji was only the beginning of the lesson. I will finish it for you."

Not right here, Toyo thought. *Not now, with the eyes and ears of Ichiko on us.* It would be a more secluded spot, wouldn't it? Like the Shinto shrine? His mind swam, insanely considering all the details: *Who will help build the funeral pyre? Where will I find the sand to spread over the thickening blood? How will I move the body all by myself? How will I collect the head . . . ?* Toyo felt dizzy.

Sotaro interrupted his whirling thoughts. "Rather than attend your afternoon study sessions, you will join me in the dojo. Here we will begin your bushido lessons."

"Lessons?" Toyo repeated.

"The headmaster agrees that these private lessons would be beneficial for you. Nonetheless, I have assured him you will rise well before the first bell each morning and attend to all your assigned work."

"But you said there was no longer room for bushido."

Sotaro sighed. "True. Bushido will not help you enter the

5 5

Imperial University. Nor will it help you on your government service exams. But it *will* teach you character. It *will* allow you to assist in my seppuku correctly, without fear. And bushido *will* make you a samurai, even in this new Japan."

Sotaro stood. "We begin in two days' time."

Toyo rose, and he and Sotaro exchanged bows. On his way out of the dojo, all the anxiety Toyo had felt on the way returned tenfold. Learning bushido wouldn't keep his father from killing himself—it would hasten it. But what was he to do? Was there any way to learn the way of the warrior and still save his father's life?

Lost in his thoughts, Toyo almost didn't see Headmaster Kinoshita and Junzo until they were right in front of him. Junzo was dragging another student along behind him. With a rough tug from the upperclassman, Futoshi stumbled into view.

"Ah. Toyo Shimada," the headmaster said darkly. "Just the boy we were looking for. Your interview with your father is at an end, I take it?"

"Hai, but what—" Toyo started.

Junzo clamped a hand on Toyo's shoulder.

"Join us in my office, won't you?" Kinoshita said.

Chapter Eight

"YOUR ACTIONS in the cafeteria today were disgraceful," Kinoshita said from behind his desk. "You in particular, Shimada, after the special dispensation I gave your father to come to Ichiko and instruct you in the ways of bushido."

Junzo and Futoshi shot curious looks at Toyo, who was already protesting. "But I didn't—"

"Silence!" Kinoshita commanded. "I saw you on a table. All of you."

Toyo cursed inwardly. He had bigger concerns than Futoshi's childish pranks. How was he supposed to focus on keeping his father alive when he had to deal with nonsense like this?

"On the first day of school, I promised to stay out of student affairs," Kinoshita continued. "But a food riot is more than a student affair. It is an attack on Ichiko herself. Therefore I must intervene, to an extent. As promised, I will not mete out punishment. That is for your executive committee to do."

Toyo caught Junzo's sly sidelong glance. He definitely *did not* need this.

"What I *can* do is address the issue of cafeteria quality," the headmaster went on. "To protest without taking action is meaningless. But the dining hall is a branch of the school administration, not a student organization. It has been out of your control—until now."

Toyo looked to Junzo and found a mirror of his own confusion.

"I beg your pardon, Headmaster-san?" Junzo said.

"Since the students were unhappy with faculty supervision in the dormitory, I granted self-rule. Since you are clearly unhappy with your meals in the cafeteria, I now transfer that responsibility to you as well. If you wish the cafeteria to be better, you *students* must fix it."

"But Headmaster-san, none of us know the first thing about running a kitchen," Junzo argued. "How will we arrange it?"

Kinoshita held up a hand. "How you organize yourselves is not my concern. If you wish to eat, you must work."

Junzo looked forlorn, and Toyo felt an unwilling tug of sympathy. How in the world would they ever coordinate six hundred students in the preparation of their own meals?

"Perhaps once you cook your own food, you will be less inclined to throw it across the room," said Kinoshita. "Dismissed."

Outside the headmaster's office, Toyo and Futoshi jumped as the senior kicked a hole in the wall and turned on them.

"The executive council isn't going to be happy about this," Junzo warned them. "*I'm* not happy about this. How are we supposed to run a cafeteria?" He got in Futoshi's face, and then Toyo's. "Do *you* know? Do *you*? We're all going to starve now, and all because of *your* little stunt."

"My little stunt?" Futoshi said, playing innocent.

"I know you are behind this, Futoshi. You and Toyo."

"I had nothing to do with it!" Toyo protested. "I—"

"You two started this mess," Junzo interrupted, "and that's exactly what I'm going to tell the executive council—whether it's true or not."

Junzo stalked away.

"Gaaaaah!" Toyo cried in frustration. He stormed off toward the dormitory with his friend on his heels. "I do *not* need this right now, Futoshi. I have other things to worry about. Not to mention the fact that none of us will ever have a decent meal again."

"When have we ever had a decent meal?" Futoshi argued. "I can cook better than any of those baka."

Toyo spun on his friend. "Can you cook better than them for *six hundred boys?* Well?"

"You got up on that table too. I saw you," Futoshi said quietly.

Toyo closed his eyes. His friend was right. Futoshi was quiet for the rest of the walk back to the dorm, and Toyo said nothing more. Their roommates were having a hushed conversation as the two boys entered, and they immediately got quiet.

"Hey, guys," Futoshi said. Fuji was the only one who would look at him, but no one said hello.

"Oh, come on," Futoshi pleaded. "You guys aren't mad at me too, are you? It was a joke."

"It's not just the mouse," one of the boys said finally. "It's the talking back in the bathroom. Asking for seconds. Everything you've done to anger the seniors."

"So they're mad at me." Futoshi shrugged. "Why do you guys care?"

"Futoshi," the boy from Osaka said, "your storm is going to come down on all of us."

"It won't be that bad for all of you, will it?" Futoshi asked.

"Everybody's saying this is going to be the worst storm ever," said a boy named Hideki. "That they're going to kill us."

"I wrote a letter to my parents," said Yamamoto. "I've asked them to come and get me. To take me home."

Toyo heard a sniffle. *Was somebody actually crying?*

"I'm so tired of this!" Toyo yelled, startling all of them. "I'm tired of walking around this campus worried about what I say or who I say it to. And I'm tired of seniors stopping me in the hall to ask me trick questions. I'm tired of people telling me I'm a girl. And I'm tired of waiting for somebody to come in the middle of the night and beat me like an old tatami mat. I am tired of being *afraid*. Aren't you?"

He had everyone's attention now, and rather than fight down his anger and frustration, he let it all pour out.

"You know what? Futoshi was right. The food in the cafeteria was terrible. If we think so, why can't we say so? And why can't we ask for more if we want to? Or talk? Or laugh? Or have a good time? Why do we have to put up with this?" Toyo pointed at his friend. "Futoshi is the only one of us who's shown any courage at all—and instead of respecting him, everybody blames him. Well, I don't. From now on, I'm going to stand up to the seniors too."

"You can't!" Hideki said. "You'll make things worse!"

"*How?*" Toyo demanded. "Here, what were the seniors going on and on about the first day of school? Manliness. Honor. Integrity. How 'manly' is it to hide under our blankets every night whining about the storm? Where's the 'honor' in that? They're the ones who told us to be like Alexander the Great, not act like girls. I say we do what they told us."

"What would you have us do?" Fuji asked. "Start food riots? Get thrown out of school?"

"No," Toyo said, frustrated. "Just . . . stop being afraid. Stand up for ourselves."

One of the smaller boys named Satake quailed. "Stand up for ourselves?"

Up to that moment, Toyo hadn't been sure where he was going, but suddenly it all came together. He looked around at his roommates' disbelieving faces. "Why not? I mean it. Today Kinoshita told me and Futoshi that protest without action is worthless. If we want things to be better, it's up to us to fix them."

"Impossible," one of the boys said.

"*Not* impossible," said Futoshi. "We just have to earn their respect."

"Should we have our own storm?" someone offered.

"No," Toyo said. "But maybe we don't just lie down for theirs. When our turn comes . . . when it happens . . . we fight back." He let that thought linger for a moment, and he could see them looking at each other, searching for solidarity.

Fuji was the first to speak. "I am tired of being afraid."

"Me too," someone else said. Another boy nodded.

"So am I," Yamamoto said. "But there aren't enough of us."

"Then we use our brains," Toyo said. "We turn their numbers against them. We know they're making us wait, trying to make us sweat it out. Let's use that time to . . . to come up with a plan."

"I say we do it," Fuji told the room. Others nodded and agreed, some more reluctantly than others.

Toyo clapped his hands. For the first time since arriving at Ichiko, he felt truly alive. He studied their room, looking for any advantage they could gain on their attackers. A plan suddenly came to him, and it was so simple, he laughed out loud.

"When they come for us, we're going to be ready," Toyo told them. "And here's how we're going to do it . . ."

Chapter Nine

TWO NIGHTS had passed, two nights with no storm. Toyo and his roommates had established a night watch schedule, which at least let most of them get a good night's sleep. Even so, Toyo was having trouble focusing on what his *sensei* was saying at the front of the classroom. Today was the first day of bushido lessons with his father, and it was all he could think about.

As the final bell of the afternoon sounded, Toyo quickly stuffed his books and brushes in his desk. He worked his way upstream against the flow of students headed for the dorm, picturing himself all the while with the family katana in his hands, training to become a master swordsman like Uncle Koji. Was it possible?

As he neared the entrance to the dojo, Toyo slowed. He knew better than to enter loudly and out of breath. Calming himself as best he could, he took three deep breaths, bowed to honor the dojo, and stepped inside. Sotaro was already there, sitting serenely in the center of the room. A mat was laid out across from him, and Toyo slipped off his shoes and went to it. He bowed deeply to his father, crossed his legs underneath him, and waited.

And waited.

And waited.

Staring at the floor, Toyo tried to show respect. Had he done something to anger his father? Worse, had Sotaro decided teaching Toyo bushido was a waste of time after all? Toyo shifted uncomfortably.

His eyes fell on the sword at Sotaro's side. The family katana. He imagined the weight of it in his hands, the power it contained flowing from the blade to the hilt and up through his arms. Then suddenly the joy of cutting through the air with it was replaced with the thought of using the sword on his father. Toyo looked up to find Sotaro watching him and quickly returned his eyes to the floor.

"Tell me something you learned in school today," Sotaro said.

"We, um, we learned . . . the lights in the night sky are stars like our own sun," Toyo stammered.

Sotaro frowned, and Toyo took that as an invitation to explain.

"They're, um, they look so small because they are millions and millions of miles away. It takes the light so long to reach the Earth that some of them may be dead and gone before we ever see their light."

"Why would you learn such a thing?" Sotaro demanded.

"What?"

"What purpose does such knowledge serve? Will you be going to the stars soon?"

"No, of course not—"

"How will this information help you get a good job? Will your knowledge of deceased stars help you repair the Unequal Treaties the West forced us to sign? Will it help you build cities? Manage the economy? Lead Japan?"

"No, but if we're to join the community of enlightened nations, shouldn't we—"

"The stars in the night sky could be sunlight pouring through holes in a dark blanket that hangs over the earth, for all it matters," Sotaro said.

"But that's ridiculous," Toyo argued, speaking quickly so Sotaro couldn't cut him off again. "If it's true, shouldn't we understand it? Why be ignorant when we can know the truth?"

Sotaro dismissed Toyo's argument with a wave. "Your knowledge is useless. I shall have to speak to Headmaster Kinoshita-san about this. It is most disappointing."

Toyo huffed, but he knew it was pointless to protest. His father never wanted to understand.

"All the more reason for our first lesson," Sotaro said. "I want you to put away everything you learned at school today. Let it settle into the back of your mind, along with all your concerns, your hopes, your regrets, your desires. Even your wish to take this sword in hand and feel its power."

Toyo startled at the ease with which his father could read his thoughts.

"Clear your mind. Let it become empty," Sotaro counseled him, "so it is not filled with the past or the future, but with the present. The now."

Toyo tried. Putting away everything he had learned at school was easy. Ignoring his desire to learn bushido was harder. He also caught himself thinking about Futoshi and the food riot, the storm, their plan, his roommates, Fuji and his mysterious reasons for not going out for sumo, the Shinto festival . . . Toyo was astonished. One thing led to another . . . and everything led him back to Koji.

"It will be difficult at first," Sotaro said. "The very act of trying to forget will cause you to remember. To help focus your thoughts, listen for the sound of the wind in the sakura." Sotaro paused. "Do you hear it?"

"How can I hear the wind in the cherry trees when they are outside and we are inside?"

"Try," Sotaro commanded.

Toyo listened, but he heard nothing.

"To become a samurai," Sotaro said quietly, "you must learn Zen. The way of the sword is the way of Zen. Zen teaches us to listen for the sound of the wind in the sakura when there is none."

Toyo listened very hard, but all he heard was the thumping of his own heart.

"Zen will teach you to find harmony with everything around you, and when that happens, you will understand the way of things," Sotaro explained. "Zen allows the samurai to see, to feel, to anticipate. When you are one with the world, the world is one with you. Do you understand?"

"No, Father," Toyo confessed.

"In the dojo, you are to call me sensei," Sotaro said. "For I am your bushido teacher."

"Hai, sensei," Toyo said. *But how is listening to wind that isn't there going to teach me how to be a samurai?*

• • •

Late that night, Toyo sat in a corner of his room trying to hear the wind in the sakura. Try as he might, he couldn't bring the sound to his mind.

"You're not going to sleep, are you?" Fuji whispered.

Toyo opened his eyes. Fuji was the only other boy awake at this hour. He was huddled over the flickering flame of a covered lantern, still doing homework.

"No," Toyo whispered, trying not to wake their slumbering roommates. "I'm meditating. Or at least I'm trying to. My homework assignment, from my first bushido lesson. You don't have to stay up, you know. It's my watch shift."

"I would be up anyway," Fuji told him. He returned to his work, but there was something more he wanted to ask. Toyo could see it in his face.

"Did you practice much with the sword?" Fuji asked without looking up.

"No," Toyo said. "I never got to touch it. We just argued, like usual, and then we sat around trying to hear the stupid wind in the stupid sakura."

"'The wind in the sakura'?" Fuji repeated.

"I'm supposed to be able to hear it any time I want. But I don't even know what that's supposed to *sound* like. I mean, how is wind blowing through sakura trees supposed to be different from wind blowing through any other tree?"

"You're not just supposed to hear it," Fuji said. "You're

supposed to see it too. In your mind. It's a way to focus your thoughts."

"That's what Sotaro said! How did you know that?"

"We were taught to meditate before our sumo matches," Fuji said quietly. "They told us to imagine we were the ceaseless river pushing an immovable stone. I didn't really understand what they meant until I went down to the river and really thought about it. After that, I could picture it any time I wanted to."

Toyo bowed his thanks and Fuji returned to his work.

"Hey, Fuji," Toyo whispered. "What really made you quit sumo?"

Fuji stiffened up. "I told you that it interfered with my studies," he whispered.

"That can't be the only reason," Toyo pressed. "In middle school I played besuboru, and it always got in the way of my homework. But I did it anyway."

"Besuboru is not a samurai game," Fuji said.

"What does that have to do with anything?" asked Toyo.

"Sumo is a samurai sport, and where I come from, everyone else who wrestled sumo was of samurai descent. But I am not."

"But everybody is the same now," Toyo told him.

"You say that because you are samurai. But it is not true."

Toyo didn't know what to say. Wasn't everyone in Japan now a *heimin*, a commoner? Wasn't that why the samurai had been stripped of their swords and positions—to make everyone equal? He was about to ask Fuji that very question, when Toyo heard a noise in the hall outside. It was only the softest creak of floorboard, so soft that had Fuji not looked up in alarm at the same time, Toyo might have thought nothing of it. But no one left their rooms at night for anything—not even to go to the bathroom. That's what dormitory rains were for.

A creak in the hall could mean only one thing.

"Wake the others," Toyo whispered. "Get into position!"

Fuji doused his light and roused his roommates. Toyo hid his beautiful brush set under a loose floorboard and climbed under his blanket. The dormitory was deathly quiet.

"Are you sure it's the storm?" Futoshi whispered groggily.

The stomping started slowly. Carefully. *Boom . . . Boom . . . Boom . . .* Pots and pans joined in the clamor, beating time with the trudging feet. *Boom . . . Boom . . . Boom . . .* The dormitory shook, the stomping like thunder exploding over and over again outside their room.

"I'm sure," Toyo said.

And then, when it didn't seem possible, the storm grew louder. Faster. BOOM-BOOM-BOOM. BOOM-BOOM-BOOM. Like a mad, giant bull, tamping its feet before a charge.

"It sounds like every senior in school is down there!" one of the boys shouted over the din.

"Six hundred boys can't fit in this room!" Toyo shouted. "Stay focused!"

The storm began to move slowly up the stairs. *Achingly* slowly. BOOM-CH-CH-BOOM. BOOM-CH-CH-BOOM.

It advanced down the hall, rattling the walls and sending their possessions crashing down from the tall shelves. BOOM-CH-CH-BOOM.

Toyo squeezed the handle of his baseball bat. "Hang on!" he cried. "It will all be over soon!"

One of the boys sobbed once.

BOOM-CH-CH-BOOM. BOOM-CH-CH-BOOM.

The storm surged to their door, the walls threatening to come apart at the seams.

BOOM-CH-CH-BOOM. BOOM-CH-CH-

And then silence.

"Girls of room thirteen!" Junzo's voice boomed from outside. "Send Futoshi Ogawa out alone, and the rest of you will be spared!"

A tense silence filled Toyo's room, and he knew they were waiting for *him* to answer. Could he hand over his best friend?

"No," came Fuji's deep, strong voice. "Futoshi stays."

"*Bonsaaaaaaaaaaai!*" Junzo cried, smashing the wooden door frame with his bat. *Crick-crash!* Two dozen seniors streamed in, filling the room. They banged pots and pans and stomped their feet—BOOM-CH-CH-BOOM, BOOM-CH-CH-BOOM. An earsplitting cry of rage went up— "*Aaaaaaaiiiiiiiii!*" and soon every senior joined in: "*AAAAA-IIIIIIIIIIIIIIIIIIIIIII!*"

The upperclassmen showed no mercy. They fell on the motionless forms hidden in the bedrolls with abandon, jabbing and punching. Junzo kicked one futon so hard, it flew across the room, scattering the clothes that were stuffed inside. Junzo bent to pick up a kimono, and realization dawned on him.

"They're stuffed with clothes!" he cried. "They're not in their beds!"

One by one the seniors shook the bedrolls, revealing mounds of dirty clothes.

"*Bonsaaaaaaaaaaaai!*" Toyo screamed, matching Junzo's cry. The ten men of room thirteen stripped away their blankets and leaped down from the shelves where they had slept the last two nights. They took the seniors by surprise, landing solid blows with their fists and stolen kendo sticks. *Smack! Thwack! Crack!*

"*Haaawooooo!*" Junzo cried, throwing back his head and howling. The smile in the senior's eyes frightened Toyo—and then a pan was coming his way and he lost Junzo to defend himself.

In flashes, Toyo saw his friends in action. Fuji waded into the crowd and tossed seniors over his head. Futoshi took one boy down with a sweeping leg kick learned in the dojo. Ducking a boat paddle, Hideki kicked a senior in the gut.

"Stay together!" Toyo yelled, smashing an upperclassman's kendo stick in half with a level swing of his bat. "Don't get separated!" He whirled left to deliver a blow to a senior's backside, but his bat crashed into Junzo's. The big brute was grinning like a Komodo dragon.

Shifting positions, Toyo and Junzo faced each other like samurai. As they thrust and parried, their baseball bats rang with the *thwack* of hardwood against hardwood. Toyo fought off a heavy swing from Junzo, then caught another by spreading his hands out like he was bunting. Pressing down, Junzo forced Toyo to his knees and then raked the barrel of his bat sideways, scraping Toyo's knuckles. Toyo lost his grip, and Junzo sent the bat clattering across the floor.

A sharp blow to the back sent Toyo sprawling, and through half-lidded eyes he saw most of his roommates on the floor with him. Even mighty Mt. Fuji was ridden to the ground. *Smack! Thwack! Crack!* They were beaten worse than if they had hidden in their bedrolls like girls, but at least they had shown their fighting spirit. At least they had proven to the seniors they were *men*.

"This is a nice bat," Toyo heard Junzo say from somewhere above him. Rolling onto his back, he saw Junzo was straddling him, testing the weight of Toyo's bat in his hands. "Light, but a nice bat."

Toyo closed his eyes, expecting another blow, but the sound of wood striking wood surprised him. He opened his eyes to find Junzo had used his bat to block a Moriyama kendo stick attack on Toyo's side.

"Don't break his arm, Moriyama," Junzo said. "He's our new shortstop."

Moriyama laughed and seared Toyo's backside instead.

"Leave these men alone," Junzo announced, dropping Toyo's bat on him. "The storm has ended."

The seniors filed out behind Junzo, each giving Futoshi one last kick on the way. BOOM-CH-CH-BOOM, the storm echoed. BOOM-CH-CH-BOOM.

Toyo felt as if his brain were going to shut down. He twisted his head to see if his friends were in worse shape, but his vision was too blurred, his words nothing more than a wheeze.

He could vaguely make out the shape of a first-year, peeking into the room from across the hall. The boy's sharp gasp was all Toyo needed to know what they must all look like.

The boy cursed. "Are you all right?"

"Oh . . . hai," came Futoshi's strangled voice. "Just . . . fine. Thanks."

The hacking laughter of his roommates was the last thing Toyo heard before he slipped into unconsciousness.

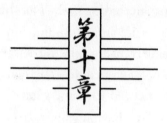

Chapter Ten

AS IF the agonizing pain wasn't enough, Toyo had what felt like a few miles of bandages wrapped around his chest. Toyo's roommates had similar injuries, but nothing so serious they couldn't at least hobble or drag themselves to class. They had gone to the infirmary as a group, some of them still laughing, but the doctor had asked no questions, and they had offered no answers. It was a quiet conspiracy.

Now they were "men." And Toyo had something manly to do.

He stepped across the foul line of the baseball field and dared Junzo to yell at him.

"Well?" Junzo said.

Toyo bowed and ran to his familiar position at short. He turned to Kennichi at third.

"Where's the old shortstop, Oda?"

"Off the team," Kennichi said. "Don't worry about it. We looked for a way to get rid of him all last year. He was only playing besuboru because he couldn't make the archery team."

Toyo made an X in the dirt in the place where he liked to stand. The dirt was still hard, reminding him again of Koji. If only what the Shinto priests said was true. If only Koji could become a kami, a helpful spirit. If only Toyo might still know him, even as a ghost.

"Let's get to it. We have a game soon against Waseda," Junzo said. "Who has the ball?"

The catcher, Tatsunori, hit ground balls to the infielders and fly balls to the outfielders. He smacked the ball between second and short, testing the new Ichiko infielder.

Toyo darted to his right and reached his glove across his body for the ball, but his hurt ribs flared, sending bolts of lightning up his body. Doubling over, he watched the ball take a bad bounce and skip into short left field.

"I hope you can make that play in a game," Moriyama said.

"I can," Toyo said, hugging his sides. But the truth was, he had always had problems going to his right.

"Next time, I want to see you dive for that ball, Shimada," Junzo called. "I thought samurai were supposed to sacrifice themselves for noble causes."

"What?" Toyo said.

"Headmaster Kinoshita said your father was giving you bushido lessons. From what your father wrote about samurai in today's paper, I expect you to slice open your belly if you make an error!" Junzo laughed at his little joke, then turned serious. "Your father says men like *my* father should have sliced open their bellies instead of putting away their swords. What about *him*? If your father thinks seppuku is so

75

honorable, why doesn't he do it himself? Ask him *that* the next time you see him."

Toyo's heart sank. Sotaro had set aside his swords to become a newspaper columnist, writing editorials for the *Asahi Shimbun*. Often he wrote about things like the Unequal Treaties forced on Japan by America and the West, but sometimes he attacked prominent Japanese too.

"Enough about samurai," Moriyama said. "It's time to practice hitting. Junzo, you're up."

Junzo tossed his glove away and grabbed his bat.

Moriyama took the mound and worked the ball over in his mitt. He glanced over his shoulder at Toyo. "You okay back there?" he asked. Toyo nodded absently.

Moriyama looked in for the catcher's sign, reared back, and whipped his long arm toward home. The fastball hummed up and in at Junzo, brushing him back off the plate.

"Sorry," Moriyama said, windmilling his pitching arm as though trying to get it loose. "Didn't do any warm-up pitches first."

On his way back up the mound, Moriyama winked to Toyo at short. Toyo smiled his thanks.

As batting practice officially got under way, Junzo kept the outfielders busy trying to hit a home run over the Wall of the Soul that formed the outfield fence. It was very different from Toyo's experiences in middle school, where most of the boys knew they couldn't hit that far. There had been an elegance to their games, an art to fielding grounders and getting the ball to where it needed to go. In Toyo's opinion, home runs disturbed the easy flow of the game. If he could change the rules, he would make any ball hit over the fence an out.

"Come on, Moriyama! You pitch like a first-year," Junzo joked.

"You want the hard stuff?" Moriyama asked. "Here it comes."

Moriyama delivered a screaming fastball out over the fat part of the plate.

"*Rrrrrrrrrrrrrrraaaaaaaaaaa!*" Junzo growled, blasting Moriyama's pitch to deep center. Michiyo sped back, but he ran out of room at Ichiko's sacred Wall of the Soul. The ball sailed over the wall and into the street beyond.

Moriyama slammed his glove to the ground in disgust.

"*Homu ran!*" Junzo cried, lifting his bat in the air triumphantly.

"Great, Junzo," Kennichi said, sitting on third base. "That was our only ball."

"Who's going to go get it?" Tatsunori asked.

"Maybe you should go get it, since you're the one who hit it," Moriyama told Junzo.

"Maybe *you* should get it, since you threw it!" Junzo told him.

"I'll get it," Toyo volunteered, surprising everyone. They stopped arguing and watched quietly as Toyo walked away.

Chapter Eleven

"HOMU RAN," Toyo explained as he passed the old guard at Ichiko's gate.

"Ah." Nishimoto nodded. "Junzo?"

"Hai," Toyo said.

The gatekeeper threw the bolt and pushed open one of the enormous wooden doors decorated with the oak and olive leaves of Ichiko. Toyo turned left outside the gates and walked along the crowded street in front of the school. Looking around, he just couldn't feel that everyone outside Ichiko's sacred Wall of the Soul was his enemy, but it certainly was a different world. Factory chimneys poured black plumes into the air and telephone lines crisscrossed the tangled rooftops. Gray ooze slid down a canal at the side of the street, carrying waste from homes and businesses, and advertisements for work in the city's textile mills were plastered on every available surface.

With a *ding-ding! ding-ding!* a streetcar rattled around the corner. People walking up and down the street parted, and Toyo stopped to watch. The streetcar was packed with

salarymen in black suits and top hats hanging off the sides. Sparks flew from the elaborate series of power lines above the car, and its bell clanged constantly, a warning to the citizens of Tokyo to make way or be crushed beneath the wheels of progress.

Toyo noted that some of the women he passed still wore traditional kimonos, but many wore Western-style dresses and had their hair cut short and shaped to hang down around their faces. None of them looked anything like the picture Toyo had of his mother, with her blackened teeth, plucked eyebrows, and white face powder. *Things have changed so much in the fourteen years since she died.*

Toyo turned down the street behind the baseball field to search for the ball among the shops and street vendors. A newsstand was hawking copies of the *Asahi Shimbun*, the paper his father wrote for, and Toyo bought a copy to find out why Junzo was so riled.

The smells from a hot *cha* stand drew Toyo farther down the street. Fingering the few coins left in his pocket, he looked over the pastries the little old shopkeeper sold with his tea. Toyo's mouth watered at the sight of the fresh buns filled with bean jam.

"Looking for a treat before you return to Ichiko?" the old man said.

"How did you—" Toyo started, then realized he was wearing the Ichiko uniform. He counted out enough money to buy two bean buns to sell to Futoshi—which would pay him back for the four he was going to buy for himself.

"You will want to try some of my cha as well," the old

man said, gesturing at the large pot of tea. "It has a special ingredient."

"What special ingredient?" Toyo asked.

"A strange fruit that fell from the sky," the shopkeeper said, lifting the top off the cha pot.

The Ichiko baseball floated in the tea.

"This fruit has a tough skin," the old man said, seeing Toyo's eyes widen, "so today I am using it only to flavor the cha. Tonight, I will cut it open and eat it myself."

"That's not a fruit!" Toyo said. "It's a besuboru!"

"A besu-boru?" the old man said.

"It's ours!" Toyo told him. "It belongs to the Ichiko besuboru club!"

The old man quickly covered the pot. "It is mine. It fell from the sky. Everyone knows good luck charms that fall from the sky belong to whoever finds them."

"That's ridiculous!" Toyo said. "How can—oh, forget it. You won't let me have it back then?"

"No," the old man said. He thought for a moment. "But you may buy a bowl of cha. If the besu-boru fruit ends up in your bowl, it will be yours."

Toyo sighed. "How much is a bowl?" he asked.

"Twenty sen," the old man said.

"Twenty sen!" Toyo cried.

"This is a special cha," the old man explained. "Besu-boru cha."

After buying the *Asahi Shimbun*, Toyo had enough to buy three bowls of cha. He looked at the bean buns sadly.

"I will take one bowl of cha," Toyo said.

The cha seller was happy to make a sale. He moved quickly, smiling as he took a bowl from a stack and lifted the lid to the pot. The old man scooped the bowl into the steaming tea, but it missed the baseball.

Toyo sighed. Only two more chances—but there was no sense letting a hot bowl of cha go to waste. He squatted nearby and unfolded the *Asahi Shimbun* on the ground in front of him. He found his father's column inside and read the headline: "Who Are We?"

"Many people are shocked that in this day and age a man like my brother, Koji Shimada, would still commit seppuku," Toyo read. "But what kind of a day and age is it when we can so readily forget bushido, the way of the warrior? For centuries, this was the code by which all samurai lived. And now? Men who once called themselves samurai carry black umbrellas instead of swords. Where once wheeled carriages were reserved only for the emperor, any fool with five yen can take the train. Dresses and suits have replaced kimonos. Ballroom dancing and bicycles have replaced judo and horsemanship. Business and opportunity have replaced honor and loyalty."

Another customer came by and ordered a bowl of cha. Toyo breathed a sigh of relief as the baseball swirled out of the way, and he started drinking his cha so he could order another soon.

"This cha tastes funny," the other customer said.

"Hai, hai!" The old tea seller smiled. "It is besu-boru cha!"

From the look on his face, the man beside Toyo wasn't

sure he liked besuboru cha, but he drank it anyway. Toyo went back to skimming the editorial as he finished his own bowl.

"When the pocket watches and the streetcars and the steam engines came to attack our noble way of life," his father wrote, "we should have taken up our swords and fought like samurai. Instead, we packed away our katana and embraced America and the other countries of the West, lapping up anything 'modern' like starving men who will eat rotting meat. Under bushido, a warrior knew when to sacrifice himself for a noble cause. And what more noble cause has there ever been than the death of bushido itself? My brother was right to fight against the changes of Emperor Meiji, and he was right to commit seppuku when he could not win—for if bushido is dead, what reason is there to live?"

Only Toyo knew why Sotaro hadn't followed his brother's example—yet.

Toyo downed the last of the cha and paid for another bowl. The old man dipped a new bowl into the tea, missing the baseball completely.

"Hey!" Toyo complained. "You stayed as far away from the besuboru as you could!"

"No I didn't," the old man said.

"You did!" Toyo cried.

The tea seller stepped in front of the cha pot, as though Toyo might steal the whole thing away. "Here is your cha," he said, setting the bowl on the countertop.

Toyo was furious. He stood and quickly tipped the tea back, burning his throat.

"Another bowl," Toyo rasped, slamming the bowl on the counter in imitation of the seniors in the cafeteria. "And this time, close your eyes when you fill the bowl."

"No!" the old man cried. "Take your money elsewhere. No more cha for you today."

"That besuboru belongs to Ichiko!" Toyo told the cha seller. "I demand you give it back!"

The man's wife came out from behind a curtain. "What's all this noise?" she asked.

"Nothing," the old man said, covering the cha pot. "This boy will not go away."

"He hasn't been honest with me!" Toyo cried. "He said I could have our besuboru if it floated into my bowl, but he's deliberately scooping away from it!" The old woman took one look at Toyo's uniform and smacked her husband in the head.

"What are you thinking, cheating an Ichiko boy?" she scolded the old man.

"But I didn't—" he started. *Thwack!* She silenced him with another whack to the head.

"This boy might be the emperor's advisor one day," the old lady warned him. "Maybe prime minister! And then where will we be, eh? Out on the streets, all because of your foolishness."

It felt strange to Toyo to have someone talk about him like that to his face, but he was close to getting the baseball back. He puffed himself up like one of the upperclassmen.

"I'm warning you," Toyo sneered, "I know many influential people."

The old woman lifted the lid to the pot and snatched the baseball from the hot cha.

"My besu-boru fruit!" the cha seller wailed.

"*His* besu-boru fruit," his wife said. She handed it to Toyo. "Why should we want it, anyway? It smells foul."

"Actually, it was fair," Toyo said with a grin, slapping his last twenty sen on the counter. "Now, I will take two—no, three bean buns." Three bean buns for twenty sen was less than the old man's original asking price, but Toyo wanted to see how far he could push his new status.

"Here, here—take four," the man said, bowing low. "And please forgive me."

Toyo smiled at his good fortune, and with ball, newspaper, and bean buns in hand, he marched off down the street. Before he reached the Ichiko gate, Toyo stopped to read the last part of his father's article and hurriedly eat his food.

"It is said the mirrors in Shinto temples are windows into our souls," his father wrote. "If Japan were to look into one of these mirrors, what would we see? What do we believe? Where are we going? Bushido once offered answers to these questions, but now we toss about on the rapids of change like paper boats, soon to be drowned. The last of the true samurai die the only honorable way they now can—by the sword—and the way of the warrior dies with them. If we do not join them, what honor can we find in this new life? In short, if we are not samurai, who are we?"

Toyo looked around at the salarymen in suits and the women in their dresses, at the streetcars and the bicycles and the pocket watches. Was this new, modern Japan so terrible?

Why could his uncle not exist here? Why did Sotaro want so badly to die?

"Better hurry or you'll be late for dinner," the old guard Nishimoto said as Toyo approached the Ichiko gate.

"That's okay," Toyo said. "I feel sick to my stomach."

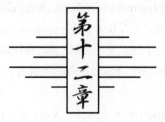

Chapter Twelve

TOYO SNEAKED a peek at Sotaro during meditation practice at the beginning of the bushido lesson the next day. Was this really a man who would kill himself for an outmoded warrior code? Toyo desperately wanted to understand what was so intriguing about bushido, but so far it had all been useless meditation and philosophical discussion.

Sotaro stirred, and Toyo quickly closed his eyes to pretend he had been meditating.

"Is your mind clear of thoughts?" Sotaro asked.

Toyo opened his eyes. "Hai, sensei."

Sotaro grunted as though he wasn't so sure, but he didn't challenge Toyo. Instead he rose and went to a small cabinet in the corner of the dojo. Toyo's heart leaped. Would Sotaro bring out the swords?

"Today," Sotaro said, "you will learn the samurai art of flower arrangement."

"What!?" Toyo blurted.

Sotaro returned with a bundle of flowers and a vase.

"What is the purpose of Zen meditation?" Sotaro asked.

"To—to find harmony with all things," Toyo answered.

Sotaro nodded. "Flower arrangement has the same purpose. Finding harmony with the whole. Samurai have long practiced the art of arranging flowers to help them find *wa*. Harmony."

"I don't remember Uncle Koji ever arranging any flowers," Toyo said.

Sotaro darkened. "Do you think you knew my brother better than I did?"

Toyo lowered his eyes. "No, sensei."

"Then if you have no further insights, let us begin today's lesson."

Toyo bowed slightly in apology.

"Now. See if you can find the *wa* in these lilies," Sotaro commanded.

Toyo studied the flowers. There were nine in all, with white, trumpetlike petals and long, thick green stems. They were freshly cut and dripped water. Toyo put them in the vase one by one. He tried to space them out evenly, but there were far too many for the small opening. There certainly seemed to be no *wa* in too many flowers forced into a tiny vase.

One by one, Toyo took the lilies out, trying to make the arrangement feel harmonious. Nothing seemed right, and Sotaro's face offered no hint of approval. Toyo put one or two lilies back in the vase, then frowned and took out all but one of the flowers. He angled the last one so it leaned over the edge of the vase, as though pouring out the contents of its white petaled cup. He crossed his arms unhappily and made it clear he was finished.

"An interesting arrangement," Sotaro said.

Toyo waited for his father to take him to task for giving up so easily.

"It is difficult to find harmony between many things, isn't it?" Sotaro asked. He studied the solitary flower for a moment longer. "You have created a most pleasing arrangement."

At first Toyo thought his father might be joking, and then remembered Sotaro never joked about *anything*. He bowed his thanks.

"You are skeptical," Sotaro noted. "Do you not see the wa in your arrangement?"

Toyo shook his head. "How can there be more beauty in one flower than there is in nine?"

Sotaro sighed. "Because the one embodies the beauty of the many," he explained. "It contains the harmony of the whole."

Toyo studied the arrangement again, trying to find the wa in the one. He frowned.

"Perhaps you will understand the simplicity of wa in the samurai tea ceremony," Sotaro said, and he got up to collect a small tray of cups.

Toyo bent low and thunked his head on the floor.

• • •

Trudging back to the dorm, Toyo felt tired. He had done nothing but arrange flowers and practice pouring tea all afternoon, but he was as weary as if he had taken a hundred swings with his bat. He didn't know how he would survive the two-hour baseball practice before dinner.

On his way he saw Futoshi leaving Independence Hall.

His arm was in a sling, and Toyo had to jog to catch up to him. "Hey—Futoshi! What's the hurry?"

"Oh. Have to be going, Toyo!" Futoshi said. He stopped for a moment. "I swear, I didn't have anything to do with it."

"Anything to do with what?"

Futoshi's eyes darted toward the dormitory, then back to Toyo.

"You mean you haven't seen it?"

"Seen *what?*"

"Never mind then!" Futoshi said, rushing away. "See you after athletic club!"

Toyo grabbed Futoshi by the sleeve of his Ichiko uniform. "Show me," he demanded.

Reluctantly, Futoshi led Toyo back into the dormitory. There, next to the stairs, was posted a special election notice for the executive council.

"You've been nominated for the executive council," Futoshi said. "To, um, to run the cafeteria."

"*What!?*" Toyo cried. He skimmed the notice. "This is impossible! First-years can't be on the executive council!"

"Actually, there isn't really a specific *rule* that says first-years can't be on the executive council," Futoshi corrected him. Toyo glared angrily. "Hey, I'm just telling you what I know." Futoshi shrugged.

"But first-years can't *vote* for executive council!" Toyo argued.

Junzo walked up behind them carrying his baseball bat and glove. "You're not voting, Shimada. You're just being elected."

"I don't know how to run a cafeteria!" Toyo said.

"Too bad. Because you and the other first-years are going to have to. Better run and get your bat and glove. Time for besuboru practice." Junzo slapped Futoshi's sling. "How's that arm doing?"

Futoshi winced. Junzo laughed and strolled off for the baseball field.

Toyo closed his eyes. "It should be your name up there, Futoshi, not mine."

"They must not think I'm 'Executive Council Material,'" Futoshi joked lamely. "Hey, look on the bright side—maybe you won't win."

"Of course I'll win." Toyo sighed. "I'm the only one on the ballot."

Chapter Thirteen

TOYO TRIED to think of it as a sign of respect, being the only freshman elected to the executive council, but he knew he was being punished, pure and simple.

Focusing his anger on his *former* best friend Futoshi, he slid open the door and entered the dining hall. It was still study period, and Toyo had another hour before he needed to be at the baseball field for the first game of the season. By Kinoshita's order, the cafeteria would become the full responsibility of the students by week's end. Toyo needed to assess things in order to be ready.

He saw half a dozen men working in the kitchen. Some chopped vegetables, others cooked rice, some stirred broth in huge kettles. Another servant piled bowls and cups on a tray. The kitchen staff moved in an orchestrated dance, wasting no time and no energy. It reminded Toyo of a baseball field with the ball in play.

One of the men spied Toyo. "Go away." He scowled. "Dinner is served at seven."

"I—I'm not here for a snack," Toyo said, stepping inside

the kitchen. "My name is Toyo Shimada."

"I thought every boy here was named 'Ichiko,'" one of the men laughed.

"Who are you?" one of them barked.

"I am the bastard son of Ichiko," another answered.

"What is your name?"

"I don't know," the man joked, "my mother abandoned me on the doorstep."

"Where do you come from?"

"My father's loins!" the man said. Everyone erupted in laughter.

"I—I am here to learn the ways of the kitchen," Toyo announced. "I have been elected to replace you at the end of the week."

The laughter went out like a candle and loathing lingered like smoke.

"So. You are the one who puts rats in our food," one of them said.

"No," Toyo began. "I am simply the one elected—"

"He thinks he can cook better than us," a servant sneered.

"It wasn't my decision—" Toyo tried to tell them.

"I give it one week," said the man cooking the rice. "They'll be begging us to come back."

"Tell you what," said another, "why don't you boys figure out for yourselves how much work it is to feed your stupid yammering mouths every day." He spat in the broth and stirred it in. "You'll find out soon enough, Ichiko. Now get out of here."

Toyo's face burned red as he left the kitchen with his tail between his legs. Stopping just inside the dining hall, he fumed silently. *How could they show such disrespect to Ichiko? Why didn't I stand up to them?*

Toyo took a deep breath and strode back into the kitchen. Puffing out his chest, he tried to recapture the attitude that had made the old cha dealer and his wife cringe a few days ago.

"That broth is spoiled," Toyo announced. "Throw it out, and I will observe how you prepare a new kettle."

The cooks ignored him.

"I—I said throw it out."

One of the cooks snickered, and Toyo shook in anger.

"*Rrraaaaaaaaaaaa!*" Toyo roared, kicking the container of broth with his best judo imitation. Hot water sloshed over the sides and the huge kettle rocked on its cradle, but it was far too heavy to turn over. Panting, Toyo watched as it settled back into position over the fire.

The kitchen crew stared at him like he was an idiot.

"You baka!" one of the men accosted him. "What do you think you're doing?"

Toyo's heart raced. Part of him wanted to run away and never come back, but instead he found himself thinking, *Koji would never back down, never run away.* As though his uncle's spirit guided him, Toyo picked up a long piece of wood stacked beside the fire pit.

"This broth," he said, cocking the log behind his head like a bat, "is *spoiled*."

With a home run cut, Toyo knocked one of the kettle's

supports across the room. The giant iron kettle clanged to the floor, spilling its contents. The scalding broth chased the barefoot servants up onto the tables.

"You're crazy," one of them began. "Do you realize—"

"Silence!" Toyo ordered, and this time they obeyed. "If we students were not already taking over for you at the end of the week, the disrespect you have shown Ichiko today would be enough to see you never work in Tokyo again. Do you understand!? We are the men who will lead this nation. We are the guardians of our country's future! When we rule this land, do you think we will not remember the men who insulted us and spit in our food?"

Not knowing what to say next, Toyo pretended to pause for effect. More prepared food sat on tables nearby, and he smacked the bowls, sending them clattering to the ground.

"The food you prepare in this kitchen is terrible," Toyo told them. "Worse than I would feed a dog. You will begin again. You will prepare a meal fit for Emperor Meiji and you will show me how it is done."

The servants nodded hastily, but none of them made a move down from the table.

"Well?" Toyo said. "We haven't much time. Get to work."

"W-we can't, Ichiko-san. You have broken the kettle and smashed all our bowls."

For the first time, Toyo saw what a wreck he had made of the kitchen. The outburst scared him a little, and he dropped the log onto the smoldering embers of the fire.

"Right," Toyo said. "Well, come down from there and let's see if we can fix it."

• • •

The cherry blossoms were blooming along the row of sakura trees that bordered the baseball field. The visiting Waseda team had already arrived and were taking infield practice.

Somebody else was there too.

"Futoshi," Toyo grumbled.

"Was that a fastball?" Futoshi called to the Waseda pitcher. "It was so slow I could count the stitches."

"Futoshi, what are you doing here?"

"You're going to have an easy time of it today, Toyo," Futoshi said. "Waseda is no good."

The catcher sniffed the Ichiko baseball. "Why does your ball smell like cha?"

Toyo led Futoshi away. "Don't you have judo practice right now?" he asked.

"Sure. But I can't practice with my arm in this sling," he said. "Besides, you need me here. I'm your *oendan*."

Toyo looked around. Futoshi was the only fan for either side at the game. "Some cheering section," Toyo said. "You know, I just spent an hour in the cafeteria because—"

"Time to focus on the game, Toyo," Futoshi interrupted. The pitcher bounced a curveball two feet in front of the plate, and Futoshi jeered him. "Good throw! That's the way!"

The catcher turned and gave Futoshi a tired look as his team left the field.

"I'll hold him down while you hit him," Toyo offered.

"Come on, Toyo," Futoshi said. "You're not going to stay mad at me forever, are you?"

95

"Pu-re boru!" the umpire called, imitating the American players. Play ball!

Toyo jogged to his place at shortstop, and Ichiko's pitcher, Moriyama, went to work, striking out the first batter on three straight pitches.

"Banzai!" Futoshi screamed. The catcher was so surprised, he threw the ball over Moriyama's head and Katsuya had to run it down at second.

"That's the way, Moriyama!" Futoshi sang, dancing behind the net. "Go, Ichiko! Go, go, Ichiko!"

Moriyama looked good the rest of the inning, until the umpire called ball four on a pitch that should have been strike three.

"That was a strike," Futoshi cried. "Are you blind!?"

The umpire glared at Futoshi.

Moriyama slammed the ball into his glove and paced around the mound muttering to himself. After that he threw nothing but fastballs, and Waseda did nothing but hit them. Three hits, another walk, and an inside-the-park home run later, Waseda was out to a 5–0 lead.

Toyo's team lost all focus. The catcher kept dropping balls he should have been catching, and the third baseman overthrew Junzo on an easy toss to first. To his shame, Toyo even made an error going to his right on a ball hit in between third and short. And Futoshi's antics on the sidelines were making *both* teams irritable and distracted.

In the top of the eighth inning, the score was still 5–0. Waseda had runners on first and second again, but Ichiko had already given up. Moriyama worked slowly to the next batter, starting him off with a couple of balls nowhere near the strike zone. Toyo's attention wandered.

Alongside the baseball field, the cherry trees bent in the breeze. His conversation with Fuji the night of the storm came back to him now, and Toyo tuned all of his senses to the sakura. Soon he was mesmerized by their swaying motion, carried away by the gentle *shirrr-shirrr* of the branches as the fragile cherry blossoms tore loose in the wind. Toyo felt at peace for the first time that day—maybe ever.

Remotely, Toyo heard the crack of the bat. His senses snapped to attention as the ball leaped off the bat, shooting straight for the narrow gap between third and short. Toyo came to life, moving quickly to his right. The third baseman crossed in front of him, but Toyo knew Kennichi had no chance. The ball ducked beneath the third baseman's glove, took another bounce, and Toyo was there. Reaching across his body, he swallowed the ball with his glove, pivoted, jumped, and launched the ball to Katsuya. He watched as the second baseman swept the bag with his foot, hurdled the sliding runner, and threw down to first.

"*You'rrre*—out!" the umpire cried.

A double play. The end of the inning. But rather than run off the field, the Ichiko nine stood motionless for a moment, marveling at the perfect execution of their play. Toyo looked down at the mitt on his hand, wondering how he'd been able to do it.

"Woo-*hoo!*" Futoshi cried, bursting the stillness of the moment. "That's the way to do it, Ichiko! Great play, Toyo!"

Futoshi's cheering woke everyone up, and they jogged in from the field to bat.

"Wow! What a play," Futoshi said, meeting Toyo as he came off the field. "You never made plays like that in middle school."

"I know," Toyo said. He stared at his mitt as though it were charmed. "I don't know what got into me."

"You looked really focused out there," Futoshi said.

"No, that's just it. For the first time, I *wasn't* going over the whole thing in my head. I just—I just did it. I don't know how, but I did."

"Maybe the ghost of your dead uncle put the ball in your glove," Junzo told him.

Toyo shook his head, but for the second time that day, he was convinced his uncle was with him—somehow.

The two teams lined up at home plate to bow to each other when the game was over, and after the visitors left, the Ichiko nine and their one-man oendan gathered around home plate.

"Moriyama, what happened out there?" Kennichi asked.

"I struck that third batter out!" Moriyama said, still arguing about the call from the first inning. "The umpire was blind."

"That baka couldn't umpire an archery tournament," Futoshi agreed.

"That didn't matter," Junzo said. "Things wouldn't have gotten out of hand if Tatsunori hadn't dropped the ball in the first inning."

"You try and catch a ball while a runner's sliding into you!" the catcher protested.

"And what about all those other balls you let go by to the screen?" Junzo challenged.

"Maybe his mitt has a bad kami in it," Futoshi said helpfully. He picked up Tatsunori's mitt and smacked at it. "Hey! Hey, you in there! Why are you playing tricks on us? Hm?" Futoshi handed the catcher's mitt to Tatsunori. "You should take this to a Shinto priest and have him scare off the bad kami."

"It wasn't bad kami, it was bad *play*," Junzo said.

"If it was so bad, *you* be catcher," Tatsunori said, shoving his mitt at Junzo. "I *quit*."

Tatsunori stormed off the field.

"Thanks a lot, Junzo," Moriyama said.

"He couldn't play, anyway." Junzo shrugged. "We're better off without him *and* Oda."

"Well, we're going to need a new catcher," Moriyama told the team. "Preferably before our next game. Any ideas?"

Chapter Fourteen

"FUJI, CATCH—"

Toyo tossed a bean bun across the room and his big roommate plucked it out of the air with ease, making Toyo smile.

"Thanks." Fuji nodded. He sat at a tiny table near the window, writing with a brush. The room was empty except for the two of them.

"What are you working on?"

Fuji took a bite of the bean bun, then answered. "English," he said. "It is . . . difficult."

"I know." Toyo sat on the floor across from him. "Have you ever met a *gaijin?*" *Gaijin* meant "outsider," but everyone used the word for Americans and Europeans in particular.

"Never," Fuji said. He put the brush to the paper while it was still wet and wrote the words *unequal treaty* in English.

"Not one?" Toyo asked.

Fuji shook his head. "I come from . . . a remote prefecture."

"I've met some," Toyo said. "They are incredibly ugly."

Fuji grunted. Toyo thought it might be a laugh.

"Why do you sit up here and study all the time?" Toyo asked. "Everybody else is in a club."

"I don't have time to join a club," Fuji said. "I need to study."

"But Fuji, *nobody* studies. I don't think Futoshi has opened a book since he's been here."

"It is an honor for me to attend Ichiko," Fuji told him. "I must take every advantage."

"But you already have. Every one of us is practically guaranteed to get into Tokyo University. You heard the headmaster on opening day. The development of our character is more important than grades. You need to loosen up and come out for an athletic club. Like . . . besuboru."

Fuji paused. "Besuboru?"

"We need a catcher," Toyo told him. "You'd be perfect."

Fuji grunted again, and Toyo was pretty sure it *wasn't* a laugh. "I don't have time," Fuji said. He finished writing a sentence in English and moved to a new line.

"Sure you do," Toyo said. "Seriously, Fuji, you don't have to study this hard."

"You and Futoshi might get by without working, but I must continue to do my best."

"What's that supposed to mean?"

Fuji sighed and put down his brush. "I mean no disrespect. Both you and Futoshi are good friends and deserve to be at Ichiko. But you do not understand where I come from. How I got here. Do you know the Akita prefecture?"

"That's far north, isn't it?" Toyo said. "On the Sea of Japan?"

Fuji nodded. "I am the only boy from my village to pass the test to attend Ichiko, and only the second from my entire prefecture."

"Only two boys from all of Akita?" Toyo wondered aloud.

"The other boy was samurai-born, but I am not. My family does not have much money, so . . . the village pays my tuition."

"Your village?" Toyo laughed. "You can't be serious."

Fuji bowed his head in shame. "Ten yen a year is a great deal of money for my family."

"I'm sorry," Toyo told him. "I didn't mean—"

Fuji put up a hand. "It is hard for many people to understand. My village has placed great faith in me. To think a peasant son of a rice farmer may attend the highest school in Japan and become a government official is a source of great hope to them. When I boarded the train for Tokyo, everyone in the village was there to encourage me to do my best. Along the way, at every station down the line, the people of Akita prefecture were waiting at the stations to cheer me on."

Toyo was stunned. There had been no celebrations, no cheering crowds waiting for him as he boarded the streetcar and crossed Tokyo. Toyo had taken the entrance exam, of course, but Sotaro had merely come home one day a month later and told Toyo he had been accepted.

"I had no idea it was such a great thing to get into Ichiko," Toyo said.

"Because you are samurai," Fuji told him.

"But there are no samurai," Toyo said. "Not anymore."

"There may not be samurai in name," Fuji told him, "but everyone knows whose family was once samurai and whose was not. Where I come from, such distinctions still mean a great deal."

"Tokyo is different," Toyo insisted. "Everyone is heimin now, commoners."

"You think so?" Fuji asked. "How many boys in the sumo club are not the sons of former samurai? How many on the judo club? The besuboru club?"

Toyo hadn't thought about it before, but all the boys on the baseball team were the sons of former samurai. He couldn't think of boys from peasant families on the other clubs either.

"Is that why you quit sumo? Because you were the only one who wasn't samurai?"

Fuji bowed his head. "It is enough that a commoner is allowed to attend Ichiko. I need not overextend myself."

"So you will sit up here and hide from the *former* samurai," Toyo scolded him. "And what will happen when you graduate from Ichiko, and then Tokyo University, and take a top position in the government? How will you hide from them then?"

When Fuji had no answer, Toyo continued.

"I count you among my closest friends at Ichiko, Fuji. And not because of where you come from or who your parents were. Because you were the first roommate to say hello to me. The first to agree we should fight back against the storm. The first to speak up for Futoshi when it would have been easier to throw him to the wolves."

As if on cue, Futoshi entered the room, talking with two of their other roommates.

"Hey, Fuji. Hey, Toyo," Futoshi said, dragging his futon down off the shelf.

Fuji stared at his homework.

"Think about it, will you?" Toyo asked.

"I will consider it," Fuji said. Toyo knew that was what people said when they wanted to say no but didn't want to offend someone.

Toyo bowed slightly for the kindness, regarded Fuji for a moment longer, then collected his notes on the cafeteria and left the room. In the hallway he sighed. If his friend wanted to sit in his room and hide for three years at Ichiko, there wasn't much Toyo could do to change his mind.

The sakura trees beside the baseball field beckoned, and now that the game was over and the sun was setting, the diamond was as meditative a place as anywhere else. Toyo settled in beneath one of the cherry trees and took a moment to calm himself. His senses came alive with the sound of the wind in the sakura, and he was sure now it was an experience he would be able to reproduce later. He let his concerns over Fuji and the lingering questions about samurai and commoners slip away as he focused on the task at hand.

With nearly two hundred first-year boys available, Toyo had to devise a schedule for all of them to work in the kitchen. Three meals a day, seven days a week—he needed cooks, servers, and clean-up crew. Toyo shook his head. Every way he tried it, he and his classmates were going to practically *live* in the kitchen. It wasn't fair.

But why did the first-years have to run the cafeteria by themselves? That's what the rest of the executive committee expected. Junzo had said as much. But they had elected *Toyo* to run the cafeteria. It was his decision now. He grinned to himself. He would simply schedule *everyone* to work in the cafeteria—first-years and seniors alike.

And if they didn't like it, they could elect someone else.

● ● ●

The next morning, Toyo nudged Futoshi awake with his foot.

"Futoshi, get up," he said quietly, trying not to wake the others.

"Why?" Futoshi moaned.

"Because we have to make breakfast."

"What?"

"Didn't you read the schedule? We have breakfast duty this morning."

Futoshi rolled away. "Why did you schedule me for breakfast duty on a Saturday?"

Toyo crouched low and spoke into Futoshi's ear. *"Perhaps you remember the small matter of a mouse . . ."*

Futoshi pulled himself up with great effort. He squinted in the darkness and muttered a profanity. "What time is it?"

"You don't want to know," Toyo told him. "Let's get this done, and we can spend our free day in the city."

Futoshi staggered toward the window. "So is it just you and me this morning?"

"Junzo's on the schedule too."

Futoshi unleashed a torrent of dormitory rain. "So," he said. "It's just you and me."

The early-morning walk to the cafeteria was crisp and cool. The lights were off in the dining hall when they arrived, and the naked bulbs hummed when Toyo flipped the switch.

"You realize this is going to be the only meal ever prepared by Ichiko students," Futoshi said.

"At least they can't say I didn't try," Toyo told him. "Come on. Let's get started."

Toyo stacked logs under the rebuilt kettle stand and lit the fire.

"What's on the menu this morning, Chef Shimada?"

"Same as every morning," Toyo said. "Rice and miso soup."

"Ah, miso soup," Futoshi said. "If memory serves—"

The kitchen door opened, and in walked Junzo Ueda.

"Junzo?" Toyo said. "You're here? I thought you—"

"My name was on the schedule, wasn't it?" Junzo grumbled.

"Hai." Toyo bowed. "Thank you for coming."

Junzo moved into the kitchen. "Don't thank me yet," he said. "Rice and miso soup?"

"Hai," Toyo said. "If you want to chop up the onions—"

"I don't chop," Junzo said. "Or peel."

"All right," Toyo said. "No problem. No problem. I'll chop the onions and peel the carrots. Futoshi, if you'll get some water, and Junzo, if you'll cook the rice?"

Junzo started to puff himself up, but he conceded and Toyo breathed a sigh of relief as everyone set to work. Futoshi filled the huge soup kettle, Junzo dished rice into the cooker, and Toyo chopped up mass quantities of vegetables. True, it was too early in the morning, and yes, Toyo had a million things he'd rather be doing, but he found a simple satisfaction in concocting a meal for six hundred students.

Junzo watched over Toyo's shoulder as he minced onions. The senior surveyed the ingredients and even tasted one or two.

"You know what this really needs," Junzo said after a moment. "Shiitake mushrooms. That's what my grandmother puts in miso soup. Makes it taste terrific."

"I think we have some in that cabinet." Toyo pointed. "I'll cut them up and add them."

"No, let me," Junzo said. "There's a certain way you have to do it."

• • •

Soon students began wandering in for breakfast. Peeking out the kitchen door, Toyo could tell many of them were surprised to smell something familiar cooking. More and more poured in, filling the dining hall. But of course everyone would be here, Toyo realized. No one wanted to miss the grand debut—and failure—of Head Chef Toyo Shimada.

Junzo came up behind Toyo. "Where are the servers?"

Toyo shrugged. "Waiting for food with everyone else, I guess."

Junzo cursed and pushed past Toyo into the dining hall. The light murmur of conversation quickly hushed to silence.

Junzo strode to a table where one of the assigned servers was sitting. "You," Junzo said. "Who are you?"

"W-what?" the first-year stammered.

"Who are you?"

The boy jumped to his feet, instantly realizing his mistake.

"I am a son of Ichiko!"

"What is your name?"

"My name is Ichiko!" the boy yelled to the silent cafeteria.

"Where do you come from?"

"My body and soul were formed in the womb of Ichiko!"

"Why are you here?"

"To honor Ichiko and defend Japan!" the boy cried.

"And to serve breakfast," Junzo told him. "Now get in the kitchen!"

The boy bolted for the kitchen door.

"Who else was scheduled to serve breakfast this morning?" Junzo called out to the room. A second-year boy in the back corner stood quickly and ran toward the kitchen.

"Good," Junzo said. "Ladies and gentlemen, breakfast will be out shortly."

Toyo and Futoshi helped the servers hustle two huge pots out of the kitchen, and under Junzo's watchful eye they filled bowls with rice and miso soup and set them in front of their classmates. When all the other students had been served, Toyo and Futoshi stood beside Junzo at the front of the room.

"Well, what are you waiting for?" Junzo asked the room.

"*Allez cuisine!*" he cried, mangling the French expression.

As one, the students jabbed a bite of rice with their chopsticks and slurped their soup.

"Who made this miso?" One of the seniors frowned.

"I did," Toyo said.

"Why did you add mushrooms?"

"*I* added the mushrooms," Junzo said. "When it's *your* turn, you can make it however you want."

"I love the mushrooms," the upperclassman said quickly.

The rest of the students reserved comment. Junzo, Toyo, and Futoshi took their seats, and the servers rushed over to feed them. Toyo looked around and smiled. For at least one glorious morning, the Ichiko students had managed to make their own breakfast without major incident.

Across the table, Futoshi slurped the last of his soup and slammed the bowl on the table.

"More soup here!" Futoshi cried. "More of this wretched miso soup!"

Dozens of bowls came flying at Futoshi. The first of them was Toyo's.

Chapter Fifteen

TOYO AND Futoshi nodded to old Nishimoto the gatekeeper as they left Ichiko for a stroll around Tokyo. The first morning of the student-run cafeteria had gone exceptionally well—even if the scheduled clean-up crew had a little more work to do today than usual.

"Are you going to stop asking for seconds now?" Toyo asked.

Futoshi found a piece of shiitake mushroom in his hair and popped it into his mouth.

"No." He grinned. "I'll just wait until a day when we have something easier to catch."

The Tokyo street outside Ichiko was still busy for a weekend, but the boys were able to settle into a comfortable swagger as they walked down the sidewalk in their black Ichiko uniforms.

"Where to?" Toyo asked.

"Oh, I don't know," Futoshi said. "Let's go down to Hashimoto Street."

"Isn't American Meiji on Hashimoto Street?"

"Among other things," Futoshi said.

Futoshi was up to something, but Toyo was happy enough to walk the streets of his hometown. A chance to spy on American Meiji wasn't bad either. Western learning and language were emphasized at Meiji, as well as Western sports like baseball. The most progressive families sent their children to be educated there. Sotaro, of course, had never considered it.

A low row of *yamabuki* bushes lined the grounds outside American Meiji, and Futoshi pulled Toyo into them when they got close to the school.

"What are you doing?" Toyo whispered.

"Look, there she is." Futoshi pointed.

Across the street from Meiji was a new school for girls, and half a dozen of them lounged on the front steps in their school uniforms. One kept looking their way, and it was clear she had seen them duck into the bushes. She sat up straighter and became more animated.

"Isn't she beautiful?" Futoshi asked.

"*Is that*—" Toyo started more loudly than he had intended. "Is that who you've been sneaking out to see every other night?"

The starry look in Futoshi's eyes was answer enough. "Her name is Mariko."

"Futoshi. Futoshi!" Toyo said, spinning his friend around. "Weren't you listening to the headmaster and the seniors opening day? We're not supposed to have anything to do with girls."

"They wouldn't say that if they met my girlfriend," Futoshi said.

"Your *girlfriend*! Do you know what will happen to you if anyone hears you talk like that?"

"I'm careful," Futoshi told him. "You didn't know until today, did you? And who knows me better than you do? Except maybe Mariko."

Futoshi's girlfriend leaned in to whisper something to a friend, and together they glanced at the bushes where the boys were hiding, and giggled. *The girl Mariko is talking to is very cute*, Toyo thought. *Maybe I could sneak out one night with Futoshi . . .*

He shook his head and turned away. The last thing he needed to do was fall in love with some girl and end up sneaking out to see her all the time. To demonstrate such weakness when he had been extolled to be like Alexander the Great? He couldn't believe Futoshi was taking the chance. The reaction at school would be swift and severe.

Behind him, Toyo heard the crack of a bat. The Meiji baseball club was practicing in the yard! *I'll do some advance scouting*, he thought. *Think besuboru, not girls. Besuboru. Besuboru. Besuboru.*

Toyo knew the Meiji team was easily the best high school team in Tokyo—maybe all of Japan. Now he knew why.

"They've got a red-hair for a coach!" Toyo said. The man actually had brown hair, but gaijin hair came in such strange colors, many Japanese called them all "red-hairs."

"What are you talking about?" Futoshi asked. "I don't see any of their sensei."

"Not the girls, you baka, the Meiji besuboru club! He's teaching them how to hit!"

"I bring you all this way and all you can think to look at is besuboru?"

Toyo started to lecture Futoshi on the dangers of femininity, when a shadow fell over them.

"See something interesting?" a voice asked.

Toyo and Futoshi stepped out of the bushes to find themselves face-to-face with four boys wearing the judo club uniforms of American Meiji.

"Shigeo," Futoshi said coldly.

"Futoshi," the boy named Shigeo said.

"You know this guy?" Toyo asked.

"I beat him once or twice in judo, back in our middle school days."

"You've taken too many blows to the head," Shigeo said. "*I'm* the one who beat *you*."

"I guess we'll see when Ichiko meets Meiji in the dojo," Futoshi said.

"Oh, I don't think you'll be with Ichiko much longer." Shigeo grinned. "Not when I tell them you've been spying on the girls across the street."

"We weren't looking at any *girls*," Futoshi lied.

"Oh no?" Shigeo said, stepping closer. "It sure looked like you were making eyes at my girlfriend. *Mariko*."

"*Your* girlfriend?" Futoshi said, gritting his teeth. "Why you dirty *eta*—"

Futoshi fell into a judo stance, and the four Meiji boys followed suit. Trying to avert a lopsided fight, Toyo stepped in front of Futoshi.

"We weren't spying on any girls," Toyo assured them.

"Then who *were* you spying on?" Shigeo asked.

"The Meiji besuboru team. I'm the new shortstop on the Ichiko team."

"Well." Shigeo smiled. "I guess I don't get to turn you in for spying on girls. But I do get to beat you up for spying on the Meiji nine." He dropped into his judo position again.

"Wait," Futoshi said. He stepped forward to guard Toyo. "What if we promise to show you one of Ichiko's new besuboru plays? It's guaranteed to make Meiji look stupid."

"What?" Toyo cried. "Futoshi, you can't—"

"What can Ichiko know that our gaijin doesn't?" Shigeo interrupted.

"Ever heard of an *endo ran?*" Futoshi asked.

Shigeo shook his head. Toyo frowned. These Meiji judo club guys didn't know the first thing about baseball, or they would know exactly what an endo ran was. "Endo ran" was the Japanese way of saying the English words *hit and run.*

"Maybe you teach me this 'endo ran' and we let you crawl out of here with only two broken legs." Shigeo grinned. "And you get to decide which two."

"You heard him," Futoshi told Toyo. "He wants to see an endo ran."

Toyo didn't understand. How could they demonstrate a play here, without a bat or ball or—

"An endo . . . ran," Futoshi repeated, stressing the words.

"Ohhhh," Toyo said, finally understanding. "Endo ran." Toyo nodded and crouched in a low base-stealing position. The three other Meiji boys stepped back to give him room.

"First, you have to imagine my friend Toyo here is on first base," Futoshi explained, "because he got a beautiful line-drive single off your terrible Meiji pitcher."

"Get on with it," Shigeo demanded.

"Next, pretend I am Junzo Ueda standing at the plate, ready to drive the ball over Ichiko's sacred Wall of the Soul." Futoshi took up a batting position.

"This better be good," Shigeo warned Futoshi.

"Oh, it will be." Futoshi grinned. "Ready? Watch Toyo first."

Shigeo's eyes shifted to Toyo.

"Endo!" Futoshi yelled, kicking Shigeo hard in the groin.

"Ran!" Toyo cried, and he and Futoshi were off to the races. Shigeo dropped to his knees as Toyo and Futoshi leaped the yamabuki shrubs and flew down the sidewalk. Futoshi threw a little wave to his girlfriend, and he and Toyo ducked into the maze of Tokyo's tiny back alleys. They ran all the way to Asakusa Park, laughing hysterically.

Futoshi grabbed a lamp pole and swung around it. Toyo laughed so hard, he got a cramp, and he collapsed to the ground.

"Endo ran," he gasped.

"Yeah," Futoshi said. "I guess it was more of a *kick* and run, but he got the idea."

"Seriously," Toyo said. "What if that boy *does* say something about you spying on those girls? You could be in for a lot of trouble."

"He was just giving me a hard time," Futoshi said. "Shigeo won't tell on me. We're friends."

"*Friends?*" Toyo said. "You kicked him in the nuts."

"Serves him right. He kneed me in the balls last year at a judo tournament and the ref never caught it. He pinned me in no time flat."

"I'm glad I'm not the kind of friend you kick in the nuts," Toyo laughed.

"No, you're the kind I get elected to run the cafeteria." Futoshi clapped Toyo on the back. "Come on, let's go climb Mt. Fuji."

The real Mt. Fuji—Japan's tallest mountain—was many hours' travel to the west, but a miniature Mt. Fuji had been constructed in Asakusa Park to allow the citizens of Tokyo to make pilgrimages to its mystical summit without leaving the comfort of their own city. Toyo and Futoshi paid the admission price and climbed up the trail that circled the huge landscaped hill. At the top, they stood on a little observation deck and looked out over Asakusa Park.

"I think I can see my house from here," Futoshi said.

Toyo couldn't see his house, but he could see the big Shinto shrine deeper into the park. It had a huge bell that could be rung to wake the spirits.

"Futoshi, do you think my uncle Koji is a kami now?"

If the question surprised Futoshi, he didn't show it. "Of course," he said.

"Seriously?"

"You can't die like that and not join the spirit world," Futoshi said as though it were a fact. "What did you *think* happened to him?"

"I didn't think anything happened to him. He's just dead."

"I think your uncle was too strong to just die," Futoshi said.

Toyo wanted to believe that, but before he could say so, Futoshi ran down the ramp.

"Where are you going?" Toyo called.

"Someone's on the rope bridge! Come on!"

"Oh, come on, Futoshi, not the rope bridge," Toyo said.

A small rope bridge with wooden planks had been built over one of the ponds in Asakusa Park, and it was the favorite spot for young couples to moon over each other. But the rope bridge was shaky, and rocking back and forth on it could tip any unwary occupants into the lily-filled water below.

It was one of Futoshi's favorite pastimes.

A man and a woman in Western clothes were at the middle of the bridge when Futoshi climbed up behind them and grabbed the rope railing with both hands. Toyo thought there was something strange about the couple, and as he drew closer he realized what it was.

"Futoshi, don't!" Toyo cried. "They're gaijin!"

The man and the woman turned at his cry, and Toyo saw he was right. The woman was pale-skinned and the man had a bushy moustache and beard.

Futoshi froze as he met the gaijin's eyes, and for a moment Toyo thought his friend would come to his senses and not go through with it.

He was wrong.

"*Banzai!*" Futoshi yelled, startling the two gaijin. He

pulled madly at the railings, rocking the rope bridge back and forth. The gaijin couple cried out, but they clung to each other rather than the rope railings. Together they toppled over into the shallow pond with a splash.

Futoshi jumped off the rope bridge and sprinted away. The water was only a couple of feet deep, and the gaijin man stood up in the pond while the woman thrashed about in her long, heavy skirts. Water poured from the sleeves of his gray suit as he pointed angrily at Futoshi, yelling something in English before finally helping his lady friend up out of the water.

Toyo spun around as Futoshi blew past, and for the second time that day, he found himself chased like a fox from a henhouse.

Chapter Sixteen

"CAN WE not go anywhere without you getting us chased off?"

Toyo and Futoshi worked their way through the crowded Tokyo streets they had run as children. Their destination was the Ginza District, the modern shopping area that was the jewel of the new capital.

"A bit of fun, for old time's sake," Futoshi said with a smile.

"And what if that gaijin comes knocking at the Ichiko gates asking questions?"

"How would he know where we go to school?" Futoshi asked.

Toyo pulled the cap off Futoshi's head and handed it to him.

"Oh, right," Futoshi said, looking himself over.

Together Toyo and Futoshi strode into the electric Ginza shopping district. The streets were packed with Saturday shoppers and sightseers, but the crowd was parting for them just like the day his father had carved a swath through the streets of Tokyo on the way to the Shinto festival. One glance at them made people step off the sidewalk to make way for them.

Just because we are Ichiko boys, Toyo marveled.

Walking through Ginza was always a treat, and soon Toyo was gawking like a country farmer. Glowing arc lights hummed over the entrance to the Mitsubishi Corporation, and the giant clock high atop the Seiko Watch Company ticked away the minutes. New Western-style brick row houses, completed after yet another earthquake had flattened the shopping district, guarded the gaslight-lined sidewalks.

"Hello, ladies," Futoshi said, bowing low to a passing group of girls about their age. The girls squeaked almost as loudly as their patent-leather shoes did as they scampered away.

"*More* of your girlfriends?" Toyo asked.

"I'm an Ichiko man," Futoshi boasted. "I don't need female companionship, remember?"

"Right," Toyo said skeptically.

"But I do need food," Futoshi said, changing direction. "Let's get something to eat."

There was a bean bun stand near Shimbashi Station, and Toyo and Futoshi bought as many as they could carry.

"We have to go see the trains," Futoshi said through a mouthful. Toyo nodded. A visit to the trains was as much a tradition as dunking people on the rope bridge.

Inside the station, the next train for Yokohama was already boarding. It hissed and bubbled as the engineers vented steam. The engine was three times as tall as Toyo, and as long as the distance from home plate to first base. Two men in the driver's compartment shoveled fuel into a great furnace in the train's belly, and Toyo could feel the heat all the way down on the ground.

"Incredible," Toyo said. "How can the new Japan not be better than the old?"

"Who's arguing with you?" Futoshi said, marveling at the engine.

A train whistle blew, and the incoming train from Yokohama slid up to the opposite platform. Toyo and Futoshi wandered over to listen to it moan and complain before it came to a stop. The stationmaster gave the all clear, and the passengers began to disembark. Toyo caught sight of a kimono and topknot among black suits and bowler hats, and he pulled Futoshi aside.

"My father just got off the train," Toyo told him.

"Really? You'll have to ask him what it was like."

"I have to get back to Ichiko right away. He'll be there soon for my bushido lesson."

"On a Saturday?"

"Sotaro's in something of a rush," Toyo said. He put a hand out to feel the burning heat radiating from the engine. "He may be gone soon. For a long time."

"You mean to someplace like Osaka?"

"No . . . someplace even farther away."

Futoshi waited for him to explain, but Toyo walked on outside the station. There, he saw a crowd gathered to watch a group of gaijin practicing baseball and he hurried over.

"What is it?" Futoshi asked as he caught up.

"The Shimbashi nine," Toyo said reverently. The team was made up entirely of American businessmen, sailors, and soldiers. Together, they were the closest thing to real baseball players in all of Tokyo, and they hit hard and threw fast.

"I thought you said you had to get back," his friend reminded him.

"Sotaro can wait," Toyo said, mesmerized.

One of the players arrived late to practice, and the others greeted him in English as he took his place at shortstop. Toyo cursed.

"What?" Futoshi asked.

"That gaijin! He's the one who works at Meiji."

"Is he? They all look alike to me," Futoshi admitted.

"It's him," Toyo moaned. "Meiji's getting help from a gaijin on the Shimbashi nine."

• • •

Back at Ichiko, Toyo sat across from his father in the school dojo and bowed deeply. Sotaro was tense, and Toyo was pretty sure he knew why.

"Is everything all right, sensei?" he asked, to be polite.

"Hai," Sotaro said. "Of course."

Toyo bowed slightly, accepting the lie as a politeness. That seemed to make Sotaro more frustrated.

"I don't know why I let the *Asahi Shimbun* make me ride the damn thing."

"What thing, sensei?"

"The *locomotive*, of course," Sotaro said. "An infernal contraption."

Toyo felt hurt. "I think the train is wonderful."

"Wonderful? What is so wonderful about that ugly, belching monster?"

"All the pipes and pistons. The giant wheels and the steam rushing out," Toyo gushed. "The smell of the coal and grease. The way it sounds when the engine slows and the cars lean into each other, groaning and squeaking."

Sotaro's sour expression told Toyo he was getting nowhere with his argument. How could he explain why he loved trains? Didn't Sotaro notice the way Toyo had been infatuated with them as a boy? Koji had noticed. His uncle was even less of a steam engine fan than Sotaro, but still it had been Koji who had taken Toyo on his first amazing train ride.

"They're a marvel of engineering," Toyo said, trying a more practical defense. "And useful, too. Trains save time."

"Save time?" Sotaro sneered. "That beast doesn't save time, it hurries it. Since it is quicker to go to Yokohama by train, we must go more often. And is this 'saved time' used to rest? To appreciate the beauty of Yokohama's shrines? To linger in the company of friends? No. We must now use 'free time' to get more work done. The time 'saved' is just as quickly spent."

"No, you don't—" Toyo breathed deeply. Arguing with Sotaro was like playing toss against a brick wall. No matter how hard you threw, the bricks never loosened.

"I just like them," Toyo said by way of ending his argument.

Sotaro grunted. "This serves no purpose. Let us practice our Zen meditation."

Toyo decided to forget the conversation ever happened. He emptied his mind, picturing the sakura that bordered the baseball field. Slowly Toyo's muscles relaxed as he felt the cherry trees sway and heard them rustling as though he were sitting beneath them.

"You've been practicing," Sotaro observed.

"Hai, sensei," Toyo said quietly.

They meditated silently for some time before Sotaro spoke again.

"Today would be a good day to begin your sword training . . . unless you feel you are not ready."

"No, no. I mean, hai," Toyo said eagerly. He calmed himself. "I am ready, sensei."

Sotaro nodded and took the two family blades from his side, placing them on the mat between them.

"The long blade is called a katana," he explained. "The shorter is called a wakizashi. Both are used in battle, as well as in ceremony like seppuku. Before Meiji, a samurai was never without his swords. He wore them everywhere he went. Even slept with them. To lose one's blade was the same as losing one's life, for the soul of the samurai is in his sword."

Sotaro drew the long katana and held it so Toyo could see it. He did not offer the sword to his son, nor did Toyo reach for it. Then Sotaro sheathed the blade and laid the katana back down. From beneath a cloth behind him, Toyo's father drew a long piece of wood cut to look like a sword.

"This wooden sword is a *bokkoto*," Sotaro told him. "It is to be your practice sword."

Toyo's shoulders sagged. "Uncle Koji gave me one of

these every year on my birthday when I was a child."

Sotaro's face became sharper. "You think you have mastered the bokkoto fighting imaginary enemies in our courtyard? Show me your skills."

Toyo flinched as his father tossed the bokkoto in his lap. Sotaro took another wooden sword in hand and stepped back, waiting for his son to stand.

"You said the soul of a samurai was in his sword," Toyo argued as he rose. "Can my soul really be found in this cheap piece of wood?"

"You have heard me quote Miyamoto Musashi many times," Sotaro said. "Do you know who he was?"

"A samurai?" Toyo ventured.

Suddenly, Sotaro attacked. High, low, high again. Toyo was never able to completely block any of the blows, and occasionally one slipped through to his face. Mucous and blood filled his nose, and an ugly black bruise welled up on his elbow. Sotaro stepped back, and Toyo lunged angrily with a wild swing at his head.

Sotaro easily stepped out of the way and rammed the end of his bokkoto into Toyo's bandaged ribs.

"Aaagh!" Toyo cried, falling to his knees. He held his burning chest with one arm and held himself off the floor with the other.

"Miyamoto Musashi was the greatest of samurai," Sotaro continued calmly. "He excelled at both the brush and the sword. He became such a great swordsman, in fact, that no one in his province could defeat him. And no one would dare practice with him, because he always won."

Toyo pushed himself off the floor with his wooden sword and stood ready again, one arm still clutched to his ribs. *Sotaro must not win.*

"Seeking to better himself in the samurai arts"—*Smack!*—"Musashi sold all his belongings"—*Whump!*—"except his blades and his practice swords." *Thwack!*

Toyo staggered away, his breath coming in hard, raking gasps, while Sotaro spoke as evenly as if he were still sitting in meditation. "Musashi then went on the very first warrior's pilgrimage, walking from province to province and taking on all challengers in shobu—the art of one-on-one combat."

Toyo tried to catch Sotaro in mid-sentence, but his swing was slow and clumsy. Sotaro slapped the broad side of his bokkoto on the base of Toyo's skull, then took his son's legs out with a cruel hack to the back of the knees. Toyo fell headlong to the floor and huddled there, his eyes screwed tight against the pain.

"Samurai young and old sought Musashi to test their skill, but no one in all Japan could defeat him," Sotaro continued somewhere above him. "Eventually, the great Miyamoto Musashi stopped using his blades. He fought katana with bokkoto. He fought steel with wood, and won every time."

So smug, Toyo thought. *So right. Always so right.*

Toyo stood and held his practice sword tight with both hands, willing himself to ignore the hundred places on his body that sang in agony. He forced himself to think of the wind in the sakura, and as he did, happier memories blew warm and muggy. Those hot summer days in the courtyard playing wooden swords with his uncle . . . what had Koji taught him then? Keep his sword up, his feet planted, his eyes on his opponent's sword—

Thwack! Sotaro's bokkoto found his ribs again, and Toyo dropped to the ground for the last time. His wooden sword skittered across the floor.

"What does this story tell us about the soul of Miyamoto Musashi?"

Toyo spat blood. Sotaro waited, but Toyo would commit seppuku before he answered him.

"It teaches us that very few saw the real soul of Miyamoto Musashi, for it was so great, almost none could understand it," Sotaro answered for him. "Your soul, like Musashi's, lies not in your bokkoto, but elsewhere. You simply have yet to find it.

"Now," Sotaro said, kicking Toyo's bokkoto back to him. "Again."

Chapter Seventeen

THE BEATING by Sotaro had been bad enough, but when it was over, his father made Toyo repeat the correct way to hold and swing a sword—five hundred times.

All the while, Sotaro preached "economy of movement." The litany of commands was unceasing. "Keep your elbows in tight," "do not step so far," "keep your head down," "square your shoulders." There were a hundred things to do correctly, and each got harder and harder to remember as Toyo's bruised and battered body failed to respond. He did them all, though. Five hundred excruciating swings, refusing to let Sotaro see his pain.

Now it hurt just to put on his glove for baseball practice.

"What happened to you?" Katsuya asked him.

"You look like you've been through a clenched fist," Moriyama joked. The mention of the mysterious punishment made a number of the seniors look away uncomfortably.

"Let's get started," Toyo said wearily.

"How are we supposed to have besuboru practice if we don't have a catcher?" Junzo asked.

"You should have thought of that before you ran Tatsunori off," Kennichi told him.

"His glove ran him off," Junzo argued.

"Did anybody talk to Tatsunori? Ask him to come back?" Moriyama asked.

Kennichi shook his head. "I saw him with the science club. He didn't seem to be sorry about leaving besuboru at all."

"Who's going to hit ground balls for fielding practice?" Sachio asked.

Toyo wanted to offer, but he could barely lift his bat.

"Kennichi. He can hit to all fields. He should do it," Junzo said.

"But when am I supposed to do my fielding practice?" the third baseman asked.

"Suguru, then. He never gets any balls hit to left field during games, anyway."

"I do so," Suguru protested. "Just because I get fewer chances doesn't mean I need less practice."

Toyo spied someone coming down the path to the field, and he squinted to make sure his swollen, bruised eyes weren't playing tricks on him.

"I think we should let *him* hit," Toyo said.

The team turned, and there at the edge of the field stood Fujimura.

Toyo went to his friend. "Fuji, you . . . you're here."

Fuji frowned at Toyo's injuries. "What happened to you?" he asked. "Who did this?"

"My father," Toyo said quietly. "Have you come to be our catcher?"

Fuji nodded. "I will—I will see if it is worth the time."

"It will be, I promise," Toyo said. He introduced Fuji to the rest of the team.

"I recognize you." Moriyama bowed. "I think you tossed me across the room during the storm."

"I did." Fuji bowed.

"Anybody ever call you Mt. Fuji?" Kennichi asked.

"You are the first," said Fuji. Kennichi laughed.

"So this is going to be our new catcher?" Junzo asked.

"Can you imagine someone trying to score when Fuji is blocking the plate?" said Toyo.

"Where did you play in middle school?" one of the boys asked.

"I have never played besuboru," Fuji told them.

Toyo saw the team's enthusiasm cool. He found a catcher's mitt and handed it to Fuji. "Here, take this and get behind homu plate. Moriyama will throw to you."

"What is a homu plate?" Fuji asked.

"Here, do what I do." Toyo's joints protested as he squatted behind home plate, but he was too excited to stop.

The big first-year grunted and took his position.

"Moriyama is going to throw the ball to you. Every pitch he throws is a strike, so you'll barely have to move your glove at all."

"What's a strike?" Fuji asked.

Toyo leaned in close. "How about I explain everything tonight back in the dorm, okay? For now, just follow my lead."

Fuji nodded, and Toyo stepped back. "Okay, Moriyama, toss one in here."

Moriyama looked unsure. He glanced at Junzo, but the muscular senior didn't respond. Moriyama shrugged and went into a weak windup. He lobbed the ball at the plate, clearly trying not to throw too hard to someone who had never caught a ball before. The ball bounced three feet in front of home plate and went flying off to the right.

Fujimura reached out and plucked it from the air.

"Wow," said Katsuya.

"Hey," said Moriyama.

"Hmph," Junzo grunted.

"That was great," Toyo told him.

"I thought you said I wouldn't have to move the glove," Fuji said.

"Well, every now and then maybe," Toyo confessed. "Throw for real, Moriyama."

Fuji tossed the ball back to his pitcher and settled in for another throw. This time Moriyama really wound up and fired. Fuji caught it like someone had tossed him a bean bun in the cafeteria. And he caught the next one, and the next one, and another one in the dirt.

"All right," Junzo said. "So Mt. Fuji can catch. How is he with a bat?"

"What's a bat?" Fuji asked.

Toyo grimaced and waved off the question for later. "He's a quick learner," Toyo explained. "He'll be fine."

"He better be," Moriyama said. "We've got three games coming up soon, including Meiji."

Toyo wondered if it was the best moment to mention it, but decided there was probably no better time. "About

Meiji," he told the team. "Today when I went by there I saw a gaijin who plays for the Shimbashi nine. He was teaching them to hit."

Someone whistled softly, and Michiyo tossed his glove in the air.

"All the more reason for us to get practicing," said Junzo.

The Ichiko fielders took their positions, and Toyo handed Fuji a bat and ball. Fuji tested the weight of the bat in his massive hands, then sniffed at the baseball.

"Why does the besuboru smell like cha?"

"Never mind," Toyo said. "What we need you to do is to stand here and hit the ball to the fielders so they can practice. You toss the ball in the air and hit it. Got it?"

Toyo demonstrated, then went to his position at short. "Okay, Fuji. Just hit the ball on the ground like I showed you."

Fuji tossed the ball in the air and took a swing, missing the ball by a foot.

"It's okay," Toyo said, getting ready again. "You'll get the hang of it."

Fuji took another bad swing. And another. He wasn't anywhere close to the ball. Toyo could sense the frustration in his teammates, but oddly no one was complaining. Not even Junzo.

The big first-year finally made contact on his next swing, knocking the ball a whole yard and a half in front of him, where it died meekly in the grass.

"All right," Junzo said. "Experiment over."

Fuji set the bat down on the ground and bowed. "Thank you for the opportunity," he said.

"Wait, wait, wait," Toyo said, running in from short. "All right, so hitting is a little harder than catching. You need a few pointers is all."

"Great," Junzo sneered. "Now Mt. Fuji is going to get batting lessons from a girl who can't hit the ball out of the infield."

"Don't worry about Junzo," Toyo told Fuji. "He's like that to everybody. Now here, watch. You're wasting too much swing. It's all about economy of movement."

Toyo took the bat from the catcher and mimicked Fuji's swing.

"You're also not using your hips. You must swing with your arms *and* your body. Like this."

After five hundred swings of the bokkoto, Toyo was able to imitate the stance from his bushido practice without even thinking about it. He stepped forward into a downward swing, slicing the air while his hips and arms moved together. Though his arms ached, he felt a power he had never experienced before.

"Moriyama, throw me a ball."

"Come on, this isn't batting practice," Junzo complained.

"He needs to see how to hit," Kennichi argued.

Moriyama went into his windup and delivered a fastball down the heart of the plate. Toyo marshaled what remained of his strength for one good swing. In his mind, the bat became a bokkoto and the ball was his father.

Thwack! Toyo drove the ball well into right field.

"Wow, when did you learn to hit?" Moriyama asked.

Toyo stared at his bat.

"Let's see him do it twice before we give him a medal," said Junzo.

Moriyama got the ball back and Toyo got set again. "Elbows in, step forward, swing with the body," Toyo muttered to himself, trying to remember everything Sotaro had taught him. "Keep your arms tight, stay focused, and . . ."

The ball zipped over the plate.

"Swing *through*," Toyo said, whacking the ball back up the middle. Katsuya dove, but the ball rocketed through into center field.

Wearily giddy, Toyo laughed. He suddenly understood what had drawn him to baseball in the first place—why he and the others loved the game so much. At its heart, baseball was Japanese. How else to explain the samurai nature of this gaijin game? It was at the same time both modern and ancient, mental and physical.

"Hey, Junzo," Moriyama joked from the pitcher's mound. "Maybe you should let Toyo teach *you* how to hit."

Junzo marched to home plate. "Nobody needs to show me how to hit." He took the bat from Toyo and stepped into the batter's box. "Pitch."

Moriyama delivered the ball, and Junzo cut the air with a mighty swing. He missed, and the ball snapped into Fuji's glove with a pop.

"You're sacrificing control for strength," Toyo told him. "If you shorten your swing—"

"Again," Junzo commanded.

Moriyama threw. Junzo swung and missed. *Pop!* Someone on the infield snickered.

"Again!" Junzo roared.

Moriyama tossed another pitch. *Whack!* Junzo drilled the ball deep to center, where it short-hopped the sacred Wall of the Soul.

Junzo flipped the bat away. "There. *That* is how to hit."

• • •

After practice, Junzo pulled Toyo aside to speak to him privately.

"Secret executive committee meeting tonight," Junzo whispered. "Before the tea assembly. Ten o'clock. Room ten."

Before Toyo could ask why, Junzo was walking away.

"What was that all about?" Fuji asked.

"I'm not sure. Did you know there was a tea ceremony in the dorm tonight?"

"A tea ceremony? I thought that was something only samurai did."

"It's not the same thing," Moriyama said, dropping in on their conversation. "A tea assembly is more like a party. Everybody sings school songs and performs skits and does sword dances."

"Sword dances?" Toyo asked.

"Well, not really sword dances. I mean, nobody in Independence Hall really knows how to use a sword. Somebody always breaks out his great-grandfather's katana and recites poetry while he swishes it around."

Toyo wasn't very impressed.

"Yeah, it's stupid," Moriyama confessed. "But some people really get into it. Me, I think I'll turn in early tonight. Get some, ah, studying done."

Fuji nodded. "As will I."

Moriyama raised an eyebrow, but said nothing more.

Chapter Eighteen

INDEPENDENCE HALL was still alive with activity when the Ichiko clock tower struck ten o'clock. It was easy for Toyo to slip out of his room and make his way to the secret executive committee meeting in room ten. There he saw a group of seniors huddled around a candle in the corner, and Junzo waved him over.

"Now that we're all here, we can get to business," Junzo said as Toyo sat down. Candlelight flickered over the senior's face as he bent forward to speak softly to the group. "It has come to the attention of a few of us that there are some who live in Independence Hall who do not uphold the . . . *spirit* . . . of Ichiko law."

"What are you talking about?" one of the boys asked. "The spirit of the law and the letter of the law are one and the same."

"No," argued another senior. "Though we have many rules, we cannot anticipate every crime. For some things, there must be an *unwritten* law—a standard to which all Ichiko boys aspire."

"Things like what?" asked another boy.

"Like wearing a fancy shirt under your uniform. Or putting your collar up," Junzo said.

"Like hiding things away and not sharing your possessions with your friends," an ally said.

Toyo immediately thought of the whalebone brush set tucked away under a floorboard in his room.

"Making up joke words to Ichiko songs," someone else threw in. "Writing anonymous essays in the school paper criticizing athletes and student government."

"Relations with the opposite sex," Junzo added, looking right at Toyo.

Toyo's heart skipped a beat. *Does Junzo know Futoshi has been sneaking out to see a girl?*

"There are already rules about consorting with girls," someone said.

"But no rules for *thinking* about girls," Junzo said. "For what goes on in a man's *heart*."

There were scoffs all around the circle.

"And how do you propose to determine what is in someone's heart?"

Junzo shifted so he sat a little taller. "There should be a group, an agency, dedicated to investigating and collecting evidence against anyone who does not live up to the Ichiko ideal."

The executive council sat quietly while they considered this. Junzo pressed his case.

"For Ichiko to achieve true greatness, we must think alike. Act alike. There is no room for individuality. Who are we? We are sons of Ichiko. What is our name? Our name is Ichiko. This goes beyond punishing criminals. We must think of this as . . . helping our friends become part of the mainstream."

"You want us to elect more members to the executive council?"

"No," Junzo said. "The executive council exists to enforce the written word of the constitution. This 'Mainstream Society' should remain separate."

"And once you discovered a 'friend in need,' what would you do then?"

"A quiet word with one or two members of the Mainstream Society should do the trick."

"And if a 'quiet word' is not enough?"

Junzo darkened. "There is always the clenched fist."

The invocation of the punishment's name unsettled one or two other boys in the circle. They shifted uncomfortably.

"Junzo is right," someone said finally. "There are too many boys who take being an Ichiko boy lightly. They prance around like girls or sneak out to visit the brothels, thumbing their noses at the rest of us and giving Ichiko a bad name."

"There should be no secrets between brothers," added another.

One of them nodded. "It is becoming a crisis."

"Then I suggest we take a vote," said the head of the council. "All those in favor of starting a 'Mainstream Society,' say hai."

One by one, the boys around the circle gave their answer until it was Toyo's turn to vote.

"Hai," Toyo said, making it unanimous.

After all, wasn't there harmony in the one?

• • •

In other rooms in Independence Hall, the "tea ceremony" started without them. In the room Toyo chose, three or four dozen boys wearing nothing but white loincloths and headbands were packed into a room where ten usually slept. It felt like a hundred degrees in the room, and the boys sweated profusely as they belted out one of the more popular Ichiko songs:

> "Behold, the flaming red of our school flag.
> It is dyed o'er the fumes
> Of our seething blood
> As we are moved
> By the spirit of life."

Toyo stood through a short skit, then made his way to the window to rain on the bushes below.

With a deep breath of the cool night air, Toyo gazed out over the main quad. He saw a shadow dart across the courtyard, and for a moment the person came into view under a lamppost. It was Futoshi, no doubt sneaking out to see his girlfriend again. Toyo felt a hint of panic. With the Mainstream Society investigating everyone, his friend's late-night visits might soon come to an end with a clenched fist.

"Nice night, isn't it?"

Toyo started and almost lost his balance as Junzo climbed up into the window beside him. The senior could easily see Futoshi if he knew where to look.

"Hai. Hai, I suppose," Toyo said.

Junzo looked away. "So, did you vote for a Mainstream Society because you agreed, or because that's how everyone else voted?"

Toyo thought for a moment. "Aren't they both the same reason?"

Junzo laughed. "Maybe so."

Futoshi finally moved out of the light in the courtyard below and slid into the cover of a hedge of yamabuki. Toyo breathed a sigh of relief and refastened his trousers.

"Do you know why the Ichiko yamabuki grow so tall?" Junzo asked.

It was too much of a coincidence. Junzo had to have seen Futoshi in the shrubs.

"No," Toyo said quietly.

"Because of the dormitory rain," Junzo said, starting his own stream. "Sometimes you have to piss on something to make it stronger. You'll see."

Chapter Nineteen

RAIN CLATTERED outside the dojo as Toyo finished another round of five hundred practice swings with his wooden sword. In the first few days he thought his arms might fall off, but now the bokkoto was becoming lighter and lighter, the five hundred swings easier and easier. With each swing he practiced staying within himself, focusing on the moment so as to execute it as perfectly as possible. At first he imagined himself swinging at Sotaro. Backing him into the corner. Striking him down. But it became hard to maintain the anger, and Toyo instead imagined himself with a bat in hand, not a bokkoto—lining a single up the middle.

Sotaro counted the five hundredth swing of the afternoon, and Toyo rested as his father moved a short pedestal to the center of the dojo.

"Tie this around your eyes," Sotaro said, handing Toyo a long black sash.

Toyo tied the blindfold around his head. With the sash covering his eyes, the light from the dojo's oil lamps was completely blocked. The sound of the rain beating down on the roof filled his ears.

Sotaro took the bokkoto away from Toyo and guided him to the pedestal.

"Climb up," Sotaro said.

Toyo was a little nervous that he couldn't see, but he did as he was told. There was enough room on the top of the pedestal for Toyo to fit both feet, and it wobbled as he found his balance.

"Stand," Sotaro commanded.

Toyo slowly raised himself up. The total darkness was disorienting. For a moment, he feared Sotaro meant to attack him. He put his hands out warily, and his father pushed the wooden sword into his hands. *How am I supposed to defend myself blindfolded and balancing on a pedestal?*

"Now," Sotaro said. "Five hundred practice swings."

"There's no room to move my feet."

"Then do not move them," Sotaro said.

Toyo set his teeth. *Fine. I can do this.*

With a deep breath, Toyo focused on the perfect swing. In one quick motion, he raised the bokkoto and sliced the air in front of him.

The pedestal rocked wickedly beneath his feet. Toyo windmilled his arms, and the base responded by tipping back sickeningly. Fighting for balance and crouching low, Toyo brought the pedestal back under control and then shakily stood back up.

"One," Sotaro counted.

Toyo's blood boiled.

"Balance. Grace. Awareness," Sotaro said from somewhere behind him. "All these things a warrior must have to be a true samurai."

What does Sotaro know about being a real samurai? Toyo thought bitterly. *All he does is write complaining, bitter editorials. Koji was the true warrior, not Sotaro. Why wasn't Koji my father?*

Toyo swung harder. The pedestal tilted underneath him, and once again he fought to bring it under control.

"Two," Sotaro said.

Toyo's hands tightened around his wooden sword. *This is just another of Sotaro's stupid tortures meant to hurt me and humiliate me.* Toyo raised the bokkoto high over his head, swinging it harder and faster than he had before.

The pedestal pitched forward, and Toyo dropped his sword as he fell, reaching out blindly with his hands. The ground met him with terrifying speed, and his right hand twisted underneath him as he slammed to the wooden floor of the dojo.

Wincing in pain and disgust, he yanked off the blindfold to look at his wrist. He glared up at his father, seeking some sign of sympathy. Sotaro watched without expression.

"My wrist hurts," Toyo spat.

"A samurai never admits pain," Sotaro told him. "You may say only that it itches."

Toyo massaged his injury. "Then it itches," he told his father. "A lot."

Sotaro picked up Toyo's bokkoto and offered it to him. "The heart may burn, but the body must be made to obey," he said.

Toyo snatched the bokkoto away and stood up. He quickly retied his blindfold and climbed back on the pedestal. Taking a deep breath, he conjured the image of the wind in the sakura again, blocking out his throbbing wrist and his pounding heart.

And with a controlled, measured movement, Toyo swung the bokkoto. This time, he rocked with the pedestal, keeping his feet planted and his weight centered until it finally came to a rest.

"One," Sotaro counted.

• • •

After Toyo completed one hundred blindfolded swings without falling, Sotaro told him they were finished. Toyo stripped off his blindfold and hopped to the ground. The pedestal tipped backward, and he let it fall. Outside, the rain continued to pour down in sheets, which meant there would be no baseball practice before tomorrow's game against Third Higher. Right now, all Toyo wanted to do was curl up on his futon anyway. He handed his bokkoto back to Sotaro.

"Keep it," his father told him. "Take it with you tonight."

"Take it where?"

"To the Shinto shrine."

Toyo frowned. "What?"

"Leave Ichiko after the dinner hour," Sotaro told him. "Make your way to the Shinto shrine in the clearing. There you will spend the night, practicing your meditation and your swordsmanship."

"Why can't I practice my sword and meditation here in the school dojo?"

"Because," Sotaro said, righting the pedestal, "you are not afraid of the dojo."

"I'm not afraid of some little shrine in the woods either!" Toyo insisted.

"Good," Sotaro said as walked away. "Then this will be an easy task."

Toyo closed his eyes and listened to a warm night's sleep wash away in the torrent of rain on the roof.

Chapter Twenty

"BUT YOU'RE always trying to convince me *not* to go sneaking out," Futoshi protested.

"Can you help me or not?" Toyo asked.

Futoshi pulled out paper and a brush and drew a simple map of the Ichiko campus.

"The best place to climb over the Wall of the Soul is here," he said, marking a place near the entrance. "But that is also the easiest place to get caught. I recommend you take this route, skirting the classroom building, then around by the dining hall."

"Maybe I can swap a cafeteria shift with someone," Toyo thought aloud. "If I'm on clean-up duty, I can be the last to leave and go straight from there."

Futoshi tapped his chin with his brush and nodded. "That's good. I never thought of that."

"We're not trying to work out better ways for you to sneak out," Toyo whispered. "We're trying to get me over the wall and back for one night only."

"All right. All right," Futoshi said. "Follow the yamabuki

shrubs along the wall to this point. The ground rises there, and the view is hidden by the bushes. I could come with you—to show you the way."

Toyo shook his head. "I have to prove that I'm not afraid to do this alone. Besides, it's much more dangerous now with the Mainstream Society watching everyone." He checked Futoshi's map once more and leaned back. "Okay, once I climb the wall, I can find my own way to the Shinto shrine."

"But shrines are full of kami, especially at night!"

"This one more than most," Toyo said. "It's where my uncle died."

"That little shrine in the woods!? No, no, no," he said. "You're not going there. That wood is definitely haunted. Not even the kami of your great uncle Koji will be able to protect you. And besides, there are wild creatures there. Wolves. Panthers. *Tengu.*"

"Tengu? Come on, Futoshi. Are we still in grade school?" Tengu were monsters parents told stories about to keep their children safe in their beds each night.

"Besides," he continued, "if any imaginary creatures attack me, I'll have this." Toyo pulled his bokkoto out of his bedroll on the shelf.

Futoshi marveled at the wooden sword, then stood and took a couple of practice swings into the bedding of his futon. He shook his head.

"Not good enough." Futoshi picked up Toyo's baseball bat and weighed it in his hands. He slammed it into his bedroll with a satisfying thud and handed it to Toyo.

"Take this instead."

"The great samurai Miyamoto Musashi didn't need anything but his wooden sword to defeat the best swordsmen in all of Japan," Toyo said.

"Are you the great Miyamoto Musashi?" Futoshi asked.

"No," said Toyo, trading the bokkoto in favor of the bat.

"Here," said Futoshi. "Let me show you how to stuff your futon so it looks like you're asleep in it. And save some fish from dinner. Headmaster Kinoshita always puts his cat out when he is ready to sleep, and if you don't give Benki something, he will meow and give you away."

"Exactly how many times have you done this?" Toyo asked.

Futoshi just grinned.

• • •

A senior named Sakai was happy enough to trade his clean-up shift for a cooking shift, and Toyo switched off the light in the dining hall when the mopping was finished. Dark clouds from the afternoon rainstorm still hovered overhead, but a few lamps in nearby windows gave enough light to find his way around to the back of the kitchen. His bat was waiting for him against the back wall, and he tucked it into his sash like a sword.

Toyo selected an empty vegetable crate to help him climb the wall, then heard footsteps. Ducking among the scattered crates and kitchen rubbish, he held his breath as someone the size of a senior walked by. A Mainstream Committee patrol?

The boy passed, and Toyo lingered a few more heartbeats.

Exhaling slowly, he tried to step carefully out from the crates, but his bat knocked one and it clattered to the ground. Dashing down the path, he slipped into the yamabuki shrubs and waited a few more moments to see if anyone had heard him. Cautiously making his way along the wall, he searched for the rise in the ground.

Something moved in the bushes ahead of him, and Toyo froze. He slid his bat out of his sash.

"Who's there?" Toyo whispered.

"Meow," purred a cat.

Of course. Benki, the headmaster's cat. Toyo fed him a bit of fish from his pocket, once again marveling at Futoshi's thoroughness.

The yellow roselike flowers of the hedge were beginning to bloom, and the scent of the yamabuki was strong as Toyo worked his way farther down the Wall of the Soul. He kept one hand on the wall to help him find his way in the darkness, and as he touched it he felt a chill pierce him. Toyo stopped and felt the wall with both hands. Was it pulsing with energy, or was that just his own heartbeat?

This wall surrounds our school, preserving Ichiko like . . . like an island of tradition in a sea of progress, Toyo thought, beginning to understand why men like Kinoshita revered it so much. *We might be learning Western philosophy and science in the classroom, but within this Wall of the Soul, we are distinctly Japanese. On this sacred ground is the pure soul of Japan.*

Toyo found the rise in the ground where Futoshi had predicted it would be, and he propped his crate against Ichiko's wall. The crate wobbled under his feet, but like the pedestal in the dojo, Toyo brought it back under control. When he had mounted the wall, Toyo thought about sitting for a moment and looking out over the complicated city beyond, but with Mainstream members about, there was too much chance of being seen. Toyo slid quickly over the wall and started the long walk to the shrine.

• • •

Toyo held his bat out in front of him like a sword as he walked the winding path through the woods. He strained his ears in the darkness. Did wolves really live this close to Tokyo?

Something snapped in the trees to Toyo's right, and he froze. He waited tensely, trying to make out vague shapes in the dark, trying to pick up any other sounds. A bird fluttered somewhere in the trees above him. Something small rustled in the undergrowth to his left. An insect chirped, and was joined by a small symphony.

Toyo inched his way down the path. Only the gray clouds against the black sky told him he had found the clearing. The wind was stronger here, and something rattled in the center of the clearing. Something metal.

Childhood stories of tengu and their rusty old swords came flooding back to him.

"Who's there?" Toyo asked. The sound of his own voice scared him, and he raised his bat.

Something tinkled in response.

Stupid. Futoshi's talk of kami and tengu was making his heart race. Everyone said Shinto shrines were magical places where kami and people met. But what if *this* kami wasn't

Koji? How many others haunted the clearing?

Toyo slapped his own face. *I'm just being superstitious. Uncle Koji is dead and gone.*

Isn't he?

Taking a nervous step forward, Toyo was suddenly overcome with images. Koji's head rolling to a stop in the grass at his feet, his father picking it up by the top knot to throw onto the funeral pyre. The empty stare on Koji's face that seemed to look deep into Toyo's soul . . .

His foot kicked something big and round. He screamed, and though he couldn't see one foot in front of him, he fled headlong into the darkness. Something caught him by the ankle, and he went sprawling. His bat thunked to the earth, and Toyo scratched himself badly reaching out to stop his fall. Crawling back to his feet, he felt the sting of fresh wounds on his palms and knees, and his injured wrist throbbed in pain. He stumbled a few more paces down the trail, but something touched his face and he recoiled, spinning away.

The sound of his own panting filled his ears, and he had to struggle to calm himself. Turning this way and that, trying to remember which direction was which, he knew he was completely and totally lost.

There was nothing to do but wait until his heart stopped thumping. Then Toyo remembered his training. Slowly he brought to mind the image of sakura in the wind, all the sights, the sounds, the smells. He pictured himself in the sun underneath the cherry trees back at Ichiko, but quickly the image was replaced by another.

In his mind, Toyo saw himself walking this path once

before, this time with clear skies overhead and the moon to guide his way. He followed his father up the path to the shrine, where they set about preparing for Uncle Koji's ceremony. In his memory, Toyo stripped a climbing vine from one of the temple's posts. He swept the dirt floor. He polished the little mirror that hung inside.

A breeze blew over his closed eyes, and something metal tinkled off to his left. Toyo crouched low to feel his way with his hands and kicked something that clattered away. Groping around, he found his bat and squeezed it tightly in his hands, feeling the power and confidence it gave him. If he could control his fear, his bat could take care of the rest.

Working slowly down the path took an eternity, but the metal tinkling sound continued to beckon him. Moving more calmly now, he discovered the thing that tripped him was a tangle of large roots, and the mysterious object his foot had found turned out to be a stump. Toyo cursed himself, and cursed Sotaro for being right. *Always so right. And never afraid. Not like me.*

Finally Toyo reached the center of the clearing. There, a small mirror *tink-tinked* as the wind brushed it back and forth against its post. It was the same one Toyo had polished to a shine for his uncle.

"If you really are a kami, Uncle, thank you for helping me find my way," Toyo whispered. His voice still seemed loud in the dark silence. He knelt and said a silent prayer for Koji.

A light rain began to fall as Toyo finished his prayer. He stood up and practiced his baseball swing, focusing on economy of movement.

"One," he counted. He set himself carefully and swung again. "Two." And again. "Three."

Toyo practiced five hundred swings, then stopped to meditate as Sotaro had commanded. In Koji's honor, Toyo meditated on the mystery of his uncle's death poem.

> In the darkness after the earthquake,
> The Flowers of Edo burn bright and fast—
> Only to be replaced in the morning
> By the light of a new day.

He understood the poem no more than the first day he had heard it here in this clearing, but that didn't stop him from trying. After meditating, Toyo rose again to take another five hundred practice swings. He meditated, practiced his swing, meditated, and practiced his swing, all through the night.

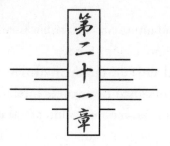

Chapter Twenty-one

THE OLD guard yawned as he unlocked the Ichiko gate early the next morning.

"Good morning, Nishimoto-san!" Toyo said cheerily as he passed through the gate. His baseball bat was tucked into his sash, and he carried a copy of that day's *Asahi Shimbun*. "Just went out to get the paper."

Nishimoto gaped and rubbed his eyes. "Toyo?" he said. "But, how did you . . . ?" The old guard glanced outside the gate, making sure there weren't any more Ichiko students he had missed. Toyo walked on past, toward Independence Hall.

The gatekeeper shook his head. "I need my morning cha," he mumbled.

• • •

Futoshi and the other boys were still asleep when Toyo slipped inside the room.

"Good morning, Futoshi," Toyo whispered.

"Mmmph," Futoshi said. He turned on his side and pulled his quilt-top tighter, then his eyes popped open as his brain realized Toyo had returned. "You're back. Nothing happened to you!"

Toyo pushed aside the clothes stuffed inside his futon and flopped on it. He closed his eyes. Something *had* happened to him. Toyo knew it, but he couldn't explain it to Futoshi.

"Wake me up when it's time for class," Toyo said.

The clock tower in the courtyard clanged the hour.

"It's time for class," said Futoshi.

• • •

Toyo sat up straight in his classes, but every now and then he caught himself swaying back and forth, ready to slip into sleep at any moment. By the end of the day, his Western philosophy lesson worked like a lullaby. He lost the lecture during a discussion of Plato and didn't snap to attention until the clock tower in the courtyard rang.

As always, Sotaro waited for him on a mat in the dojo. Toyo slipped his shoes off at the door and walked quickly and quietly to his place. He bowed deeply to his father.

"You look tired," Sotaro said.

"Hai, sensei," Toyo told him. Even so, he felt energized, and he wanted to share his breakthrough. "I did it. I meditated and practiced my swings all night long in the shrine."

Sotaro nodded. "Take your bokkoto and stand," he said. "Defend yourself."

His father attacked, but Toyo parried the blow. Toyo countered, knocking Sotaro back. His father's eyes widened, then grew sharp.

Twip! Thwak! Clack! Toyo and Sotaro traded advances, deflecting each other's moves. The bokkoto was much lighter than the baseball bat Toyo had practiced with all night, and though he was tired, his swings were swift and strong. Toyo had never felt so alive, not even when he was playing baseball. The thrill was electric.

Sotaro handed him a blindfold, and Toyo immediately tied it around his head. No longer was the darkness something he feared. He could hear Sotaro moving quietly around him, stalking him. Toyo pictured himself back in the Shinto shrine, the black of night surrounding him. His other senses came alive, and he closed his eyes under the blindfold.

Sotaro's lunge came from the right, and Toyo countered. Then his father seemed to disappear, but Toyo turned quickly, parrying a new attack from behind. From the left, from the right, Toyo's bokkoto was always there to defend him.

The floor of the dojo creaked, and Toyo thrust quickly. His wooden sword met flesh, and Sotaro grunted. "Ha!" Toyo laughed, pressing the attack. A quick hit to Sotaro's knees—*Thwack!* Up to the head—*Smack!* A broad swing at his stomach—

Swish. Toyo's bokkoto met air.

Sotaro smashed his sword into the back of his son's head, and Toyo went sprawling to the floor. Groggily, Toyo slid a hand under the blindfold and felt a warm, sticky place on the back of his head. Blood. He pulled the blindfold off and turned to look up at his father.

A tiny bit of blood trickled from Sotaro's lip, and he dabbed at it with a finger.

"It is unwise to attack from a position of weakness," Sotaro said calmly.

Toyo stood and squeezed his bokkoto in both hands. His voice came low and dangerous. "Thank you for the lesson, sensei."

Without warning he plunged toward his father and their wooden swords locked. Toyo pushed his father away and Sotaro stumbled, then regained control. He lunged for Toyo, but his son deflected the attack and countered. Toyo's bokkoto caught Sotaro in the ribs. He ducked another swipe from his father's sword, then rammed the pointed end into his father's sandal. Sotaro went down.

"Again," Toyo ordered.

Sotaro's eyes grew hard and he drew himself up. He let Toyo come this time. *Smack! Thwak! Tonk!* His father parried every blow—but Toyo was gaining ground. Back and back they went, until Sotaro's foot met the wall.

Toyo grinned like a wolf and pressed his attack. High, low, low again. Sotaro's returns weren't nearly quick enough. His father staggered back, but the wall kept him on his feet. Toyo hit a single to Sotaro's gut, smacked a double to his shoulder. He belted a triple that took his father to the ground and sent his bokkoto across the floor. Then Toyo drew his sword back for the home run swing and—

"Koji! Stop!" Sotaro cried, his eyes wide with fear.

Toyo froze. *Koji?*

"Toyo," Sotaro said, immediately realizing his mistake. "I mean—stop, Toyo."

Toyo's arm lowered as he saw the broken old man at his feet.

"Father, I—"

"*Sensei*," Sotaro reminded him. "I am still your teacher," he said, his breath rasping, "and this lesson is over."

• • •

Futoshi was bent over a little desk on the floor writing something with a brush when Toyo came back to the room.

"You're back already? Did I miss the bell?" Futoshi asked.

"The lesson ended early," Toyo said quietly. His futon was still unrolled from the morning, and he curled up on it.

"You going to sleep with that thing?" Futoshi asked.

Toyo looked down to find he still carried his bokkoto.

"Samurai sleep with their swords," he murmured.

"Well, don't forget you've got a besuboru game tonight, samurai-san," Futoshi told him.

Toyo closed his eyes and fell into a fitful sleep.

Chapter Twenty-two

TOYO FINISHED another round of meditation. Moonlight glinted off the mirror in the shrine, and he caught his reflection in it as he stood to practice his swings. Something wasn't right. He kneeled down for a closer look.

Uncle Koji's face stared back at him in the mirror.

Toyo shook violently.

"Toyo, wake up!" Futoshi said, rocking Toyo back and forth.

His eyes fluttered open.

"It's almost time for your game," his roommate said. "Here. I stole some rice balls for you from the dining hall."

"Thanks," Toyo said. He took a bite as Futoshi dragged him out of bed. "I had the weirdest dream."

"I hope it was about winning the game," Futoshi said as he handed Toyo his bat and glove. "You've got to hurry. I'll see you there, okay?"

Toyo stumbled to his feet. "I'll make it," he said. "Why are you in such a rush?"

"I have to get ready for the game, too," Futoshi said. He grinned as he left.

Toyo staggered toward the door, then paused. The dream still lingered, and he dug out a little mirror Futoshi kept under his bedroll.

When he looked in it, all he saw was himself.

• • •

Toyo could hear the screaming before he even got to the baseball field. It sounded like a hundred students crying out in pain. Futoshi stood before an enormous group of students all screeching at the top of their lungs. Futoshi waved as Toyo walked up.

"What's going on?" Toyo hollered over the screaming.

"Yelling practice!" Futoshi yelled.

"What for?" Toyo asked. Some of the boys were screaming so hard, they were spitting little drops of saliva.

"It's what's been missing," Futoshi yelled. "They're what you need to beat Sanko! Meet the new Ichiko oendan!"

Toyo wasn't sure more fans were what Ichiko needed, but they certainly seemed enthusiastic. Futoshi signaled for the screaming to stop, and the players on the field looked relieved.

"You'd better go," Futoshi told Toyo. "We have more practice to do before the game."

Toyo left Futoshi leading the oendan in warm-up stretches.

"Your idea?" Moriyama asked Toyo.

Toyo shook his head. "All Futoshi."

Futoshi's oendan sang a school song as the game began. Toyo settled in at shortstop, and wondered how many of their "fans" were actually watching the game. But the oendan clearly had the other team rattled. Futoshi urged the cheering section louder as Moriyama threw his pitches, and the first batter struck out on three straight.

"*Yu-sho! Yu-sho!*" the oendan chanted. Victory! Victory!

Moriyama and the oendan kept Sanko—Third Higher School of Kyoto—from reaching base in the first inning, and the Ichiko nine ran in to bat. Lead-off hitter Michiyo tried to bunt his way on base, but the Sanko catcher made a good play to throw him out at first.

The oendan erupted in celebration.

Toyo drew Futoshi aside as the third baseman, Kennichi, made his way to the plate. "Um, Futoshi? You might need to explain the rules to them."

Kennichi grounded out to the shortstop, and the oendan cheered again.

"Oh, right," Futoshi said. "Okay oendan, just do what I do from now on, all right?"

Junzo was up next, and he launched a fly ball to deep right center field. The center fielder ran the ball down and caught it for the third out of the inning.

The oendan aped Futoshi and booed the Sanko team loudly.

"This is going to be a long game," Toyo told Fuji as they jogged out onto the field.

Toyo's prediction came true in more ways than one. It was clear from the beginning Sanko was not as good as Ichiko. They made errors on routine plays in the field, they weren't aggressive on the base paths, and they swung at bad pitches. But Ichiko played just as poorly. Toyo was tired and still thinking about his battle with Sotaro, Fuji hadn't gotten his bearings as a batter, and something was seriously bothering Junzo. Two hours and five innings later, the score was 0–0.

Junzo tossed his bat away after striking out to end the bottom of the fifth.

"This is ridiculous!" he said. "This team is terrible, and we can't do anything against them."

Two more innings crept by with no score. With their oendan chanting loudly behind them, the Ichiko nine ran out onto the field and took their positions for the top of the eighth inning.

The first Sanko batter laid down a bunt. Moriyama pounced on it. He turned, fired to first, and overthrew Junzo's glove by two feet. The batter took second on the error.

Moriyama screamed and kicked the mound in disgust. Then he walked the next batter on four pitches, which only made him more riled.

Ichiko's bats had been silent all night, and Toyo worried a big inning would bury them.

"Play deeper," Toyo called to the outfielders. "Better to let a ball drop in front of you for a single than to let it go over your head for a double."

The outfielders stepped back a few paces.

"Katsuya, let's play deeper and look for a dabu pure," Toyo told the second baseman. "Kennichi, Junzo," Toyo said to the corner infielders, "guard the foul lines. Don't let them hit any doubles."

Kennichi moved closer to the bag at third, but Junzo waved Toyo's advice away.

"You worry about your own position," Junzo said.

Moriyama was still steaming, and he reared back and threw as hard as he could. The batter swung late—*Thwack!* The ball tore down the first-base line. Junzo dove, but the ball was too far away. It kicked into the right field corner, and before Sachio could get the ball back in, the hitter was at second with a stand-up double. Both base runners scored.

"You should have listened to Toyo and guarded the line!" Kennichi yelled at Junzo.

"You should play your own position!" Junzo yelled back.

Whack! The oendan watched mutely as Moriyama gave up another hit. Runners stood at the corners with no outs. Moriyama finally threw a curveball, and the next batter tapped it right to Toyo. He flipped the ball to Katsuya, who swept the bag and fired to first for the double play. Amazingly, the runner on third base stayed put instead of going in for the easy score.

Toyo called time out for a meeting on the mound.

"So stupid!" said Moriyama, smacking the ball into his glove. "I've fielded bunts like that dozens of times."

"Maybe you've got something else on your mind today," said Junzo.

"What's that supposed to mean?" Moriyama asked.

"You should have stopped that ball at first," Katsuya told Junzo. "We could have had a dabu pure."

"Look, you be quiet about that," Junzo said. "I'll get both those runs back with my bat, and one more to beat them. You'll see."

"We have to get one more *out* first. We're lucky the runner on third didn't try to score."

"He should have," said Kennichi. "These guys are terrible."

"Which is why we have to get this last out and come back and tie it up," said Toyo. "The next batter has two hits, right, Moriyama? Moriyama?"

Moriyama was eying Junzo. "What? Um, yeah," the pitcher said. "He's got uh, two hits and a walk. I should have thrown him a slider instead of a fastball last time. I can't believe I did that."

"What about the next batter?"

"Hmm? What? Oh, um . . ." Moriyama tried to think.

"Two strikeouts and a groundout to second," Fuji offered.

"Good. Okay," said Toyo. "Why don't we walk this guy to get to the next one?"

"You want to put another runner on base on purpose?" Fuji asked.

Toyo nodded. "That way we have a play at first or second if he manages to get the bat on the ball. What do you think, Moriyama?"

The pitcher thought it over. "Hai," he agreed.

"Same places as before," Toyo said as they broke up. He took up his position, noting that Junzo still refused to play the line. Toyo shook his head. It was hard to find harmony when one wouldn't join the others.

Moriyama threw four pitches way outside, and the batter trotted down to first.

"Okay, Moriyama, you're better than this guy. Go get this batter," Toyo called.

The pitcher nodded. Pitch one zipped inside. "Strike one!" Pitch two broke outside, and Fuji framed it perfectly. "Strike two!" cried the umpire. Moriyama bent low and Fuji laid down the next sign. The ball came twirling in, daring the light hitter to take a hack.

The Sanko batter flinched, but didn't swing.

"Ball one!" the umpire cried.

Moriyama twitched.

"Put him away, Moriyama!" Kennichi called.

"Don't play with your food!" one of the outfielders called.

Moriyama laughed. Fuji gave him the sign, and he reached back and hurled his best fastball over the heart of the plate. All the batter could manage was a *doink* down to second, where Katsuya scooped the ball and tossed it to Toyo at second base for the out.

"All right," Toyo said as he ran in with the infielders. "Now let's see if we can tie it up."

The bottom of the order was up, and they went down flailing. A pop up, a strike-out, and a weak grounder to third.

In the top of the ninth, Moriyama took the mound with renewed determination. He equaled the Third Higher pitcher, setting the Sanko lineup down one-two-three.

As dusk fell on the field, Ichiko found themselves down to their final three outs. The score was Third Higher 2, Ichiko 0.

"Little Locomotive!" the oendan chanted as Michiyo led off the inning with a bunt hit. Kennichi moved the speedy center fielder over to second on an error that should have been a double play, and with one out Junzo stepped to the plate.

Without wasting any time, Junzo slammed the first pitch he saw over the sacred Wall of the Soul for a two-run home run. The oendan went berserk, hopping up and down and embracing each other with unabashed tears of joy.

Third Higher threw their baseball into play, and Futoshi was dispatched to track down the Ichiko ball. The score was 2–2 in the bottom of the ninth, but the sun had almost set.

"Hurry! Hurry!" Toyo cried.

Moriyama worked a time-consuming walk off the pitcher, but they had a man on. For their part, the Sanko team was honorable, working quickly and not stalling for a tie as darkness fell.

Katsuya bunted Moriyama into scoring position, sacrificing their second out, and Toyo stepped into the batter's box. For some reason, all he could see were Sotaro's horrified eyes staring up at him. He was tired too—so tired, he could barely lift his bat. He called time out and rubbed his eyes.

"Get in there, Shimada!" Junzo called from the sidelines. "You can still see!"

Toyo stepped back in and tried to focus on the sakura, now shadowy forms on the edges of the field. He listened for the sound of the wind in the trees, and as he took the first pitch for a ball, he began to hear his memory of the sakura.

A base hit right now would win the game. The pitcher

went into his motion, and time slowed for Toyo. The ball came spinning in slowly, and he saw the seams on it as clearly as if he were holding it. His bat rose to meet the ball, and for a moment time froze as leather met wood.

Thwack!

Time exploded back to full speed. The bat kicked, the ball flew toward left field—

—and right into the glove of the shortstop.

Toyo didn't even finish running to first base. The inning was over, the score still tied at two.

Fuji brought Toyo's glove out to where he stood.

"That was a great shot. I thought you had a hit for sure."

"You're weak, Shimada," Junzo called. "You should hit lower in the lineup."

The sky was almost completely dark now. Toyo was sure they could squeeze in one more inning if they were quick about it, but for some reason the Third Higher players began wasting time, making unnecessary lineup changes and calling batters back for strategy sessions.

"What are they doing?" Junzo cried. "Why are they wasting time *now*? If they score, they could win."

Fuji stood from his position at catcher and went to the Third Higher bench. Toyo glanced at Kennichi to see if he understood what was going on, but the senior shrugged. Fuji and the Sanko bench exchanged bows, and the umpire was called over. After a brief consultation, he waved his hands in the air and called the game.

"What!?" Junzo yelled. "He can't call off the game! It's not completely dark yet!"

The oendan celebrated as though Ichiko had won. The teams hastily lined up to bow to each other, and the Ichiko team stayed behind after their cheering fans left for Independence Hall.

"Will somebody tell me what happened?" Junzo demanded.

"We agreed to end in a tie," Fuji said.

"'We' who?" Junzo barked. "Who made you our negotiator!?"

"The Third Higher players had no intention of hitting again," Fuji explained. "I heard them. They knew we were the better team and should have beaten them, but they were afraid they might go ahead this inning and win. With darkness coming, they allowed us to escape with a tie. It was an honorable gesture."

"What do *you* know about honor?" Junzo said.

Fuji bowed his head and said no more.

"Well, you can be sure American Meiji won't be so kind," Junzo told them. "I suggest we *all* focus our thoughts on playing better in tomorrow's game against Tokyo School of Commerce. At least *that* one we should win."

Toyo followed Junzo as the team broke up for the night.

"What right do you have to speak to Fuji that way?" demanded Toyo.

"What *right*?" said Junzo. "I think being on the executive council has made you forget your place, first-year. I'm an Ichiko senior. I can talk to anybody I want to any *way* I want to."

"You don't treat Fuji like dirt because he's a first-year. You do it because he's not samurai."

"Well?" said Junzo. "What does a peasant know about honor? Respect? I let him on this team because we need a catcher, but as soon as I find someone to take his place, he's gone."

"You criticized my father for longing for the old ways, and now you refuse to accept that we're all commoners. Which is it, Junzo? You can't have it both ways."

"Don't get too comfortable in your bed tonight, Shimada," Junzo said, walking away.

"What? I thought the storms were over," Toyo said.

Junzo turned. "The storms are never over, Shimada. But that's not what's happening. Tonight there is to be a clenched-fist punishment, and you, first-year, are going to take center stage."

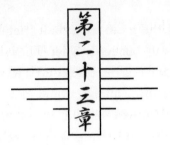

Chapter Twenty-three

WORD GOT around the dorm quickly that night, though no one seemed to know who was being punished or why. Toyo and his roommates remained in their Ichiko uniforms, legs pulled tightly up under their chins or quilts pulled tight around their shoulders, heads bent low. They relived each mistake, examined every error, and weighed all possible offenses they might have committed.

Toyo picked his own life apart piece by piece. Greedily hoarding his precious whalebone brush set? Momentarily entertaining his attraction to the girls in Tokyo? Assigning the seniors to cafeteria duty? Talking back to Junzo? But while any of those might justify a quiet word from the Mainstream Society, none warranted the clenched-fist punishment. Did they? Not like Toyo's biggest offense—climbing over Ichiko's sacred Wall of the Soul to sneak out last night.

The door slid open with a bang and all the heads in the room jerked up.

"It's time," Junzo announced.

Futoshi glanced at Toyo, and without a word they stood

and filed out of the room with their friends. The hallway was filled with boys, but eerily quiet. They shuffled together down the steps and out into the courtyard with the hushed air of a crowd awaiting an execution. Here was the perfect world for the Mainstream Society, Toyo realized—the Ichiko boys moving and acting as one, each hoping he was enough like the others to be anonymous.

"It's me," Toyo said, so softly that Futoshi almost didn't hear him. "I'm sure of it."

Six hundred boys marched solemnly out of Independence Hall to the baseball field, passing the faculty building on the way. Toyo noticed that every light was out, and not a teacher was to be seen. Kinoshita was true to his word—the students would be allowed to run their own affairs.

No matter how far we go? Toyo wondered.

A large paper lantern hung from a pole on the pitcher's mound, casting a fragile, flickering light on the faces of the boys as they formed a circle as broad as the infield. Without being told, they lined up along the base paths, creating a human wall around the infield.

Toyo stood near his position at shortstop. Across the diamond, the faces that looked back at him were dark and expressionless.

A hole in the students opened, and Junzo stepped through into the light. He walked to the hill near the middle of the diamond and studied the crowd, casting eyes of blame on them all.

"Tonight we gather to do the greatest and most terrible duty we have as members of the Ichiko family," Junzo told them. "Tonight, we must administer that most sacred of ceremonies—the clenched fist."

The wind picked up, slapping the paper lantern against its pole. A sound like a raging river filled the air, and with a shiver Toyo recognized it for what it was: the wind tearing through the sakura lining the field.

"Let no man here believe we perform this ceremony for a common criminal," Junzo warned them. "This is not some base animal or eta we condemn tonight. He is one of us. Our brother. He is Ichiko. This is less a punishment than a cleansing, and you here will be witnesses to a rebirth. Tonight we extract the evil that inhabits a friend, and set him on the path to manly virtue."

The wind became a roar in Toyo's ears now, almost deafening, and he stood transfixed.

"I now call on the executive council to step forward and take your place as student leaders," Junzo said, his voice rising above the wind.

The council emerged from the wall of students to form an inner ring around the pitcher's mound. As if his brain were disconnected from the rest of his body, Toyo felt his legs lurch forward to join them. Toyo stood with his back to the pitcher's mound, clutching his arms to his chest to hide his own quivering.

"I call too the members of the Mainstream Society," Junzo said, "as guardians of Ichiko's past, present, and future."

More boys stepped from the crowd. They formed a smaller circle halfway between the ring of executive council members and the pitcher's mound. When the two groups had taken their places, the crowd grew still.

"One among us left his family in Independence Hall by night and scaled Ichiko's sacred Wall of the Soul," Junzo announced.

Toyo's knees lost their strength, and he wobbled. He caught himself, vowing he would stand for his punishment like a man. He forced his legs to hold him upright and bit his tongue to regain his senses. The sharp, salty taste of blood filled his mouth.

"Worse than the climb over the Wall of the Soul was his reason," Junzo told them. "He abandoned his brothers at Ichiko to seek the pleasures of a *woman*."

Not me, Toyo realized with relief and panic. *Futoshi*.

"For proof," Junzo said, "I offer these letters of affection, written to a girl in his own hand, under the very roof of Independence Hall. And here the register of an inn, where they have spent the night in each other's arms!"

Toyo looked to his friend in dismay, but Futoshi was shaking his head with desperate innocence.

"The register and letters are signed," Junzo cried, "with the name of Moriyama Tsunetaro!"

Toyo couldn't believe it. *Moriyama?* The best pitcher in Tokyo? *Junzo's best friend?* But then he realized how, like Futoshi, Moriyama had missed the tea assembly the other night, as he said, to "study." Was *he* the shadowy figure Toyo had hidden from behind the kitchen?

All Ichiko shared Toyo's shock in silence as the paper lantern knocked restlessly against its wooden pole. Moriyama stepped out of the crowd and into the lamp's inconsistent light, and the hole that opened to admit him closed quickly behind him. The Ichiko fireballer walked to the center of the circle, the pitcher's mound, without being told what to do. He staggered, his legs betraying him, and Toyo watched Junzo start to move toward his friend, then hold himself back.

On the mound, a place he had owned and commanded for almost three full seasons, Moriyama pulled himself up to his full height. The light from the lantern framed the look of anguish on his face.

"It is the verdict of the Mainstream Society," Junzo said, his voice breaking on the word *verdict,* "that our brother Moriyama Tsunetaro has violated the Ichiko code of honor both on campus and off, and therefore that he be given the clenched-fist punishment."

Moriyama bowed his head in shame.

"It is never easy to punish your brother," Junzo said sincerely, "especially when he is your friend." Junzo met Moriyama's gaze. "As always, we will carry out our sacred duty with tears in our eyes and resolve in our hearts. And when we are done, he will rejoin his mother school."

Moriyama nodded, and Junzo made his way to where the pitcher stood. As he passed, Toyo could see Junzo was really crying.

Junzo stood before his friend. A moment passed, punctuated only by a sob. Toyo couldn't tell if it was Moriyama or Junzo.

Then, without warning—*Whump!*—Junzo slammed his fist into Moriyama's stomach.

The pitcher doubled over on the mound, spitting up part of his dinner. He coughed violently. Junzo waited for Moriyama to collect himself, then—*Whump!*—hit him again. Moriyama vomited a second time.

Toyo didn't want to watch, but he couldn't stop himself. All around him the students along the infield lines watched too, unable—unwilling—to look away.

Whump! Junzo struck Moriyama a third time. As the first baseman stepped away, light from the lantern glittered in the tears that ran down his cheek. Junzo didn't bother to wipe them away.

A boy from the Mainstream Society took Junzo's place. Toyo flinched as the second-year boy hit Moriyama another three times—in much quicker succession. Moriyama fell to his knees, but was able to pull himself up on the pole before the next member of the society stepped forward. Moriyama was struck three more times—this time in the face—as yet another of the Mainstreamers took his turn.

Blood streamed from Moriyama's nose and mouth, and one of his eyes was already swollen shut. Toyo felt nauseous as he watched Moriyama receive the clenched-fist punishment from all seven members of the Mainstream Society.

The bouncing light from the lantern danced in six hundred pairs of eyes as their dark faces bore mute witness to the violent rebirth of Moriyama Tsunetaro. No student made a sound.

"Next," said Junzo, "I call the members of the executive committee."

One by one, the elected officials pummeled Moriyama.

When he could no longer stand, he curled up into a ball on the pitcher's mound and the council members kicked him.

Dully, Toyo realized he was on the executive committee, and that he was next in line.

Once again, his legs carried him with only partial consent from his brain. Toyo cried openly at the sight of Moriyama, remembering the senior's kindnesses on and off the field. In the salty tears and the harsh sting of blood in his mouth, Toyo could taste some part of his Ichiko brother's pain.

In the emptiness that accompanied him to the inner circle, Toyo once again heard the wind in the sakura. He climbed to the top of the pitcher's mound, where Moriyama lay whimpering. Then, with tears in his eyes and resolve in his heart, Toyo Shimada kicked Moriyama Tsunetaro hard in the ribs.

And again.

And again.

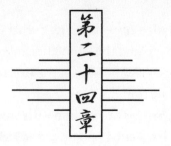

Chapter Twenty-four

TOYO STOOD outside the dojo and wondered how he would face his father. What had passed between them last time could not be taken back, no matter how many layers of apology Toyo might use to mend it.

He was startled to see Sotaro sitting in his usual place, his face marked and bruised, one of his hands wrapped tight with a bandage. Toyo felt his face flush with shame. He closed his eyes and sat across from his father without a word.

Toyo had a hard time meditating, and wondered if Sotaro was having any success. Trying to picture the wind in the sakura, the only image that came to mind was of a howling beast, roaring in the darkness around six hundred still and silent boys.

"Clearly," Sotaro said, startling Toyo, "you have mastered the bokkoto."

Toyo opened his eyes. He expected Sotaro to be angry, but his father just looked tired. Toyo looked to the ground.

"It is time you wielded your family's sword," Sotaro said.

The metal blade sang as it was removed from its scabbard,

and the light from the oil lamps on the wall glinted down its long, curved edge. It was horrible, yet strangely intoxicating. Like the boys in the darkness, Toyo could not take his eyes off it.

"This blade was made by the great swordmaker Tadayoshi, more than two hundred years ago," Sotaro told him. "The Shimada family crest is even older."

Intricate carvings worked their way up the metal, and there was an elaborate golden design on the hand guard. The Shimada crest, a simple outline of a cherry blossom, was set into the blade near the handle.

"Why a cherry blossom, sensei?" Toyo asked, his lips dry with his first words.

Sotaro nodded. "The sakura was chosen to remind us we may die in the prime of life, just as the cherry blossom may be blown from the tree while in full bloom. They are beautiful, and yet may be short-lived. Like samurai."

Sotaro held the katana out to Toyo, who bowed and took the sword from his father's steady hand.

"Stand," Toyo's father told him.

Toyo immediately tensed, then understood that his father did not mean to test him. Standing, he let the magnificence of the sword wash over him. It felt right in his hand, as though it belonged there, an extension of himself, its weight perfectly balanced for his body. The katana was much heavier than his bokkoto, yet Toyo felt quicker with it. He practiced one of the moves his father taught him, and the sword cut the air with a *whhht*.

The guard at the top of the handle that protected

Toyo's hands was made of gold. Deep cuts in the soft metal spoke to a well-used past, and Toyo ran his fingers over the craggy surface. Despite its battle scars, he could still make out a little scene delicately carved in the guard—a samurai handing his sword to another warrior on a bridge as arrows flew past.

"Have I told you the story of Yoshitsune and the broken sword?" Sotaro asked.

"No, sensei," Toyo said.

Sotaro stood away from his son and tucked his hands inside his kimono. He spoke quietly. "Yoshitsune lived hundreds of years ago. He was unequaled with the sword, unparalleled at poetry, and unbeatable in battle. But once, while battling his way across the Goto Bridge in Kyoto, Yoshitsune's katana snapped in battle."

Toyo stared at the sword in his hands. *How could this ever break?*

"He thought he was finished," Sotaro continued. "His enemies would soon be upon him, and he readied himself for death. But at the last moment, his faithful retainer Benki offered his own sword to his master. It was an inferior blade, but in the hands of Yoshitsune it became a glorious weapon."

Toyo smiled despite himself—Benki was the name of Kinoshita's cat.

"After the battle, Yoshitsune bought the finest blade in all of Japan for Benki. For himself, Yoshitsune kept the inferior blade—in honor of his retainer's faithfulness. The story of Yoshitsune and Benki on the Goto Bridge is a reminder to all Shimada samurai that friendship and loyalty are more important than any sword," Sotaro explained.

Sotaro stepped forward to take the sword, and Toyo passed it back.

"There are techniques that are difficult to teach only with the bokkoto," Toyo's father said. Holding the sword out in front of him with one hand crossed over the other, Sotaro found his balance and closed his eyes. With a carefully controlled motion he brought the sword over his head so it was parallel to the ceiling. When Sotaro's eyes opened, Toyo saw a fire there that made him take a step back.

"*Heeeeeeeeeeeiaaaaaaaaaaaa!*" Sotaro cried, carving a downward path through the air so powerful, his body shook with barely controlled energy.

Sotaro held the pose for a moment, then relaxed.

"Now you," Sotaro said, handing the blade to Toyo. His father helped him position his feet, his legs, his arms, his hands, and step by step he walked Toyo through each position in the move. When Toyo understood, his father stepped back and nodded for him to begin.

Toyo held the sword out and raised it over his head. He tried to clear his mind, to focus his body and soul on the swing, but with his eyes closed he saw only Moriyama curled up into a ball at his feet. His forehead wrinkled as he tried to push the image from his mind, but Moriyama became his father, cowering beneath Toyo's bokkoto. With great strain, Toyo forced the vision out, replacing it with the wind in the sakura. But not the gentle summer afternoon—the swirling black chaos of the harsh night winds, shearing the sakura of their beauty.

Harnessing that violent energy, Toyo opened his eyes wide with fury and frustration. "*Yaaaaaaaaaaaaaaaaaaaaaa!*" he cried, swinging the sword with more power than he had ever felt in his life. He stopped the sword short as he was supposed to, and as the force of his attack left him, so too did his anger. Clarity came then, a break in the storm that had raged inside him since last night.

Toyo breathed deeply, savoring this experience. With proper control and follow-through, he realized, such a swing could be a devastating weapon in a baseball game.

Sotaro nodded. "We have much to work on, but . . . it is a good start."

"Perhaps you can delay writing your death poem for another day then," Toyo said, bowing low to acknowledge the rare compliment.

Sotaro looked surprised. "I have already written my death poem. I wrote my first death poem when I was your age, and I have written many since. I wrote one on the occasion of your mother's death, and another the day of Koji's death."

Toyo felt the sword slipping from his hand, and recovered in time to keep it from falling to the floor.

"Shall we practice the killing stroke again?" Sotaro asked.

"The what?"

"The killing stroke is the name of the sword maneuver you just learned."

"No, sensei," Toyo said, handing the katana back to his father. "If it's all the same, I would rather train with the bokkoto."

Chapter Twenty-five

THE SUN was shining, boys were laughing and running about, and teachers walked the school grounds. But for Toyo, stepping out onto the field before the Tokyo School of Commerce game felt like returning to the shrine where Koji died and finding the happy festival.

Amazingly, he saw that Moriyama could still stand. His face was black and blue, lips cracked and broken, and one eye was still swollen shut. Moriyama carried his right arm in a sling, his glove dangling almost uselessly from his wrist.

"This is crazy," Toyo told Kennichi.

"He insisted," the third baseman said with a shrug.

The School of Commerce team was whispering among themselves, watching as Moriyama grunted in pain with each pitch.

"What happened to your pitcher?" one of them asked.

"Nothing," Junzo said, stepping forward to answer for the team.

The oendan crowded the sidelines, and Futoshi whipped them into a frenzy. It looked as if every boy at Ichiko had come to see the game. As he took his place at shortstop, Toyo had an eerie sense of déjà vu. Six hundred boys were looking on again, and standing on the same mound was Moriyama Tsunetaro.

The oendan slowly began to chant his name. *Mo-ri-ya-ma, Mo-ri-ya-ma, Mo-ri-ya-ma.*

"Pu-re boru!" yelled the umpire. The game began, and Toyo watched in awe as Moriyama pitched like a hero. He guided the ball in and out over the plate as though he had it on a string. The ball danced on the outside corner—*strike one!* It curved and slipped and dropped—*strike two!* It came in heavy, thudding dully as the hitter beat the ball into the ground toward first. *You'rrrrre out!* Three up, three down. The oendan went wild.

Toyo came to bat in the third inning with one out and the bases empty. He practiced his bokkoto shadow swing. Not only was he better rested than last game, his bushido workouts were having noticeable effects on his muscles.

"Slam it out, Shimada!" the oendan screamed, but as Toyo settled in to his batting stance, he focused only on the sound of the sakura. This time, he was able to recall the gentle afternoon when he had first experienced the power of meditation, and he felt himself unwind.

Before the pitcher delivered the first pitch, Toyo closed his eyes. Today, he would let the sound of the wind guide him. Today, he would hit the ball without seeing it, the way he had fought his father blindfolded in the dojo.

With his eyes closed, he could smell the ball, a wonderful mix of leather, dirt, and tea leaves. He heard it hum toward him. In his mind's eye, he *could* see it.

Thwack! Toyo made contact. A thrill ran through him—

—followed by searing pain as he fouled the ball off his own foot. Toyo hopped away into the grass near home plate, where Fuji joined him.

"I forgot," Toyo told his friend. "Never attack from a position of weakness."

"Are you all right?" Fuji asked.

"Hai," Toyo said. He limped a little as Fuji helped him up. "It just . . . itches."

His teammates laughed. Toyo pulled on his sandal and stepped back into the batter's box.

"Strike one!" the umpire called.

Toyo kept his eyes open this time and watched two pitches go by for balls. He called time out and stepped away from the batter's box to focus on the next pitch. His shadow swings had prepared him to make proper contact, but he knew he needed something more. Something to get the ball out of the infield.

He needed the killing stroke.

Toyo stepped back into the batter's box and lifted his bat high above his head, just as Sotaro had held the sword over Koji's head. His anger and sadness welled up inside him, and Toyo channeled that energy into his arms, into his hands, into his legs.

The ball came whistling straight over the plate. Toyo raised his bat and brought it down in one swift motion. *"Hii-iiiiiiiiiiiyaaaaaaaaaaaaaaaa!"* he cried. Wood met leather in an explosion of dust and powder. The baseball leaped off Toyo's bat. The shortstop timed his jump—

—but the ball sailed over his head.

The oendan wailed for joy, chanting, *"To-yo! To-yo! To-yo!"* as he jogged to first with a clean single.

Fuji was up next, and the outfielders came in close. Someone had told them the Ichiko catcher couldn't hit.

"Remember how we practiced it," Toyo called to his friend from first base. "Use your whole body, and don't open yourself up."

Fuji nodded. The first pitch zoomed over the heart of the plate, and Fuji did everything he was supposed to. He planted his feet. He kept his eye on the ball. He brought the bat clean and level through the strike zone—but he swung long before the ball even got to him.

"Strike one!" the ump called.

"Relax," Toyo called. "Now you're trying too hard. What did you do to get ready for sumo?"

Fuji stepped out of the batter's box for a moment to gather his thoughts. When he stepped back in, he planted both his feet methodically, slapped his knees, and tossed a bit of dirt over his shoulder. The School of Commerce boys laughed.

"This one thinks he's sumo wrestling!" the catcher joked.

"He's big enough," the pitcher said.

"Hrah!" Fuji bellowed, snarling as though he might charge the mound any minute and heave the pitcher from the field.

The pitcher got serious and reared back to pitch. Fuji attacked the ball as it crossed the plate, his form perfect. The ball rocketed off his bat into deep left field, well over the head of the drawn-in outfielder. Toyo scored as the ball bounced all the way to the Wall of the Soul and Fuji lumbered into second base with a double. The big catcher acknowledged the screaming oendan with a nod, then bowed to Toyo.

"Mt. Fuji got lucky," said Junzo as Toyo returned to the bench

"Not lucky," said Toyo, smiling. "Better."

Toyo got a double his next at bat, and another single in his third at bat. He finished the day three for four, but there had never been anybody on base ahead of him and he had only been batted in the one time. Suguru, Michiyo, and Kennichi each had two hits, but the real story of the day was the masterful pitching of Moriyama. On the strength of the pitcher's arm, Ichiko won 5–3. The oendan carried Moriyama on their shoulders down the hill to Independence Hall.

Toyo and Fuji lagged behind the celebration.

"Moriyama was incredible," said Fuji.

"He pitched like he was a new man," said Toyo.

"Wasn't that the purpose of last night?" Fuji asked.

"Hai," Toyo said. "I suppose."

They walked along in silence until Fuji spoke again.

"You also look like a new man."

"Me?"

Fuji nodded. "You're getting hits, you're swallowing everything that comes your way at short, you even helped me get my first hit." He smiled. "You're a whole new player."

"It's the bushido," Toyo confessed. He hated to say it, but knew it was true.

Neither of them said anything for a time.

"I could teach you, if you want."

Fuji stopped. *"Bushido?"*

"Sure," Toyo said. "Why not?"

Fuji grunted. "I am not samurai."

"Neither am I," Toyo told him. "Neither is my father. Neither is Junzo. There *are* no samurai anymore, remember? Only commoners like you and me."

Fuji shook his head.

"I know you don't believe it, but let me try and prove it to you. Meet me here on the field tomorrow morning, an hour before the first bell."

Fuji considered the offer.

"You will teach me to hit like you?" he asked.

"Better," Toyo promised.

• • •

That night in the dorm, Toyo and his roommates were already on their futons when their door banged open and Moriyama burst inside. Toyo jumped. Had he come for revenge?

"Moriyama, I didn't—I'm s—"

The pitcher dragged Toyo out of bed with his good arm.

"Grab your bat, Toyo. Let's go, Mt. Fuji," Moriyama said, kicking Fuji's futon.

Toyo stood blinking in nothing but his underwear. "What's going on?"

"A storm," Moriyama told them.

"You're—you're storming?"

"We're storming," Moriyama told him. "A *victory* storm."

Fuji climbed out of bed, his fat belly rolling over the top

of his little loincloth. Someone in the hall screamed happily, and Toyo saw Kennichi run by, smacking at the walls with his bat. More players followed him—Suguru, Katsuya, Michiyo. They were shrieking and dancing and whacking anything in sight with their bats. As though nothing had happened the night before, Moriyama let out a whooping yell and joined his friends in the frenzy. Fuji shrugged his massive shoulders, and he and Toyo grabbed their bats and ran out into the hallway to join the storm.

• • •

Hours later, after the victory storm had blown through Independence Hall once, twice, three times, the baseball team danced as one around a bonfire on the pitcher's mound, celebrating more than Ichiko's first win of the year.

They knew they had become a team.

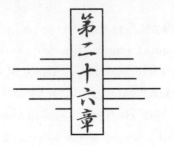

Chapter Twenty-six

The remains of the bonfire still smoldered on the pitcher's mound the next morning as Toyo and Fuji finished their first five hundred swings. Fuji dropped his bat and sat down.

"It gets easier," Toyo told him. "It hurts now, but it'll make you stronger. And you won't have to think as much about your swing when you're in a game."

"Is this how you were able to get three hits in the School of Commerce game?"

"Partly," Toyo said. "I also learned a new sword move from Sotaro. Let me show you."

Toyo held the bat high, bringing it down with controlled fury. *"Hiiiiiiiiiiiiyaaaaaaaaaaaaaa!"* he screamed. He turned to Fuji. "See? The bat starts much higher, which allows you to generate lots of power and not swing under so many pitches."

Fuji hauled himself to his feet and tried to imitate Toyo.

"Don't forget to give a battle cry," Toyo told him. "It makes you breathe out."

"But what do I say?" Fuji asked.

"I don't know. Anything."

"What do you say again?"

"It's kind of like a 'Hi-ya!' You know, like in judo."

Fuji tried it out. "HI-YA!"

"No, longer now. More like—*hiiiiiiiiiiiiiiiyaaaaaaaaaaaa!*"

Fuji tried to do the yell while he practiced the swing. It came out more like *"Hnnnnnnnnnnnnh!"*

Toyo bent over laughing.

"What?" Fuji asked, looking slightly offended.

"Nothing. Nothing," Toyo said, still laughing. "It's very . . . sumo."

"Thank you," Fuji said, grinning and bowing.

"The killing stroke will make a samurai out of you yet," Toyo said.

Fuji paused in the middle of a swing. "The what?" he asked.

"The killing stroke," Toyo said. "That's what the move is called."

Fuji dropped his bat.

"What's wrong?" Toyo asked.

The big first-year wouldn't meet Toyo's eyes. "That stroke was used to kill my grandfather," Fuji said quietly.

"What are you talking about?"

Fuji looked up. "Before they lost their swords, my grandfather was killed by a samurai."

Toyo didn't understand. "What did he do?"

"Nothing," Fuji said.

"No, I mean, what did he do to make the samurai kill him?" Toyo asked.

191

"He did nothing," Fuji repeated. "He was killed for looking up when he should have been looking down."

Toyo shook his head. Fuji wasn't making any sense. "What? Looking up when—"

"My family are peasants. My grandfather was walking through our village, and he looked a passing samurai in the eye instead of looking to the ground. The samurai punished him by chopping off his head."

Toyo rested his bat on the ground. "There had to be some other reason."

"The samurai had too much sake," Fuji told him. "But drunk or not, samurai always punished peasants any way they wanted for such supposed disrespect."

"I don't believe it," Toyo said.

"That's because you don't know what it was like," Fuji told him. "What it is *still* like."

"Surely you can't mean the samurai still wear their swords in Akita," Toyo said.

"No," said Fuji. "But they still wear the same samurai attitude. Here in Tokyo, the samurai already had no use for their swords when they were taken away. They were bureaucrats. Politicians. In Akita they are still overseers, foremen on farms and work crews. Their swords have been taken away, but they still carry the same swagger."

Toyo frowned. "Bushido would never allow that."

"Maybe your father isn't teaching you everything there is to know about bushido."

Toyo bowed. "I am sorry for the loss of your grandfather."

Fuji returned the bow. "It is nothing," he said. A polite lie.

"Maybe we should go back to the five hundred practice swings," Toyo told his friend.

"Hai," Fuji said. "I would like that."

• • •

In his classes that day, Toyo could not get his conversation with Fuji out of his mind. Could a samurai who lived by bushido—the warrior's code—actually be so dishonorable as to take someone's life for such a petty reason? And why should there be no recourse for such behavior? He knew Fuji wouldn't lie about such a thing, but could he be mistaken? Fuji's family might have kept the real reason from their son, to hide their shame. Still, to lose your head in a village street. . . .

The day crept by as Toyo watched the clock. When his school day finally ended, Toyo went straight to the dojo. Sotaro had yet to arrive, and Toyo sat on the building's front steps. Slowly he became aware of a thumping coming from somewhere nearby—*Thump, thump, thump.* At first Toyo thought somebody might be building something, but the sound came too regularly and too steadily. *Thump. Thump. Thump.*

Toyo followed the sound around the corner. Peeking around the back wall, he was surprised to see Moriyama hurling a baseball at the dojo wall. His right arm was still in a sling, but he went through his pitching windup the best he could and punished the brick wall with his fastball. The ball skipped back toward him, and he picked it up to throw again. *Thump. Thump. Thump.* The look of determination on his face was ferocious.

Toyo thought it best not to interrupt. There were plenty of brick walls around campus, and Moriyama had obviously chosen this one because he didn't want to be disturbed. He walked back to the entrance of the dojo, and found Sotaro was now inside. Toyo bowed, slipped off his shoes, and entered the room. When he took his place on the mat across from his father he bowed again, but when he sat up he did not begin to meditate.

Sotaro opened his eyes when he sensed Toyo was not participating.

"You do not meditate," Sotaro said.

Suddenly Toyo was back in middle school, sitting across a table from his father, trying to find the words to speak with him.

"Hai, sensei. I—I need to—I have questions."

Sotaro waited.

"About . . . bushido."

Sotaro said nothing, and Toyo stumbled on.

"I—my friend Fuji—Fujimura—told me today his grandfather had his head taken off by a samurai. For no reason."

"This Fujimura, he is a student here?"

"Hai."

"Is he samurai?"

"No," Toyo said. "I mean, his parents weren't samurai."

"Then he is mistaken," Sotaro said.

Toyo frowned. How could Sotaro know that?

"He says his grandfather was killed for looking at the samurai the wrong way."

"Ah," Sotaro said. "Then there was a reason."

"That's no reason!" Toyo cried.

Sotaro's face was hard and cold. His eyes narrowed.

"You're saying because Fuji's grandfather wasn't samurai, he deserved to have his head cut off? How can there be a place for such senselessness within bushido?"

Sotaro waited a long time before he spoke.

"Your bokkoto looks damaged," he said.

Toyo blinked. "W-what? My bokkoto?"

Sotaro picked up Toyo's wooden sword and examined it.

"Hai. Your bokkoto is weakened from our sparring, as is mine."

"I'm not talking about bokkotos," Toyo protested. "I'm talking about cruelty. I'm talking about blatant abuse of power—"

"This is easily remedied," Sotaro said.

Toyo stilled his tongue and waited for Sotaro's answer.

"An animal bone should do the trick."

Toyo shook. His father was still talking about the stupid bokkoto!

"You're changing the subject!" Toyo complained. "Have you finally run out of answers? Well?"

Sotaro set the wooden sword aside.

"Today instead of our usual lesson you will go to the eta village at the edge of the city," he continued. "There you will find a butcher who will give you an animal bone. Return to me here in the dojo when you acquire one."

Sotaro closed his eyes and began to meditate.

"That's your answer then?" Toyo demanded.

Sotaro ignored him.

Toyo pushed himself up to leave. So his father would rather send him away than discuss the crimes of the samurai. Or he was buying time to think up a believable excuse. Toyo stood over his father for a moment, giving him one last chance. When it was clear Sotaro was not going to answer him, Toyo stormed away.

Chapter Twenty-seven

TOYO HAD never been to the eta village, but the smell
alone was strong enough to lead him there. The eta handled
the burial of people and the butchering of animals. They
lived and worked in blood and filth, and most people in
polite society avoided them and their village. Toyo and
his father had done eta work to clean up after Uncle Koji's
seppuku, and Toyo's skin still crawled at the memory of the
nasty business.

But they weren't really eta anymore, Toyo told himself
as he worked his way through the streets. As he'd been
reminding Fuji, the emperor had made all Japanese equal.
Everyone was heimin now—commoners. In this new Japan,
wouldn't the son of an eta have as much opportunity in life
as the son of a samurai?

As Toyo entered the eta village, the stench of burnt
flesh, rotting meat, and animal feces made him clutch a post
as his lunch came up. Some workers rebuilding a shop nearby
watched him for a moment, then went back to work without
a word. A man in tattered clothes ran up to Toyo with a

bucket of water and offered him a drink from a ladle. The water was warm, but it helped rinse the vomit from his mouth.

"I'm so very sorry," the man muttered.

"I'll be all right," Toyo told him. "Thank you for the water." He began to ask where he could find a butcher, but the man was already backing away, bowing to Toyo again and again.

"Wait," Toyo said, but he was too dizzy to follow and had to wait until he was a little more used to the smell of the village to continue. As he regained control, he noticed how much construction was going on here. There must have been a bad fire recently, for burned-out houses and shops were being rebuilt up and down the lane. Men were working with amazing speed, clearing out the charred boards and replacing them with fresh lumber.

Toyo searched for someone he could talk to, but though the villagers watched him, no one would come near him.

"Hello," Toyo called out, "could someone help me, please?"

In response, the villagers disappeared into their houses and huts. Only the man who brought him water was brave enough to approach, bowing with each step he took.

"Hai, my apologies, my apologies," the man groveled.

"Why do you apologize?" Toyo asked.

"Such a poor reception, and clearly you are here on urgent business, samurai-san."

Toyo balked. Not only had the man used -san, the suffix Toyo used to show respect for his elders, the man had called him a samurai.

"Why do you—" Toyo began, wondering if he had worn something with the Shimada crest on it. But all he wore was the Ichiko uniform, and that didn't mean he was samurai. "My name is Toyo. Shimada. Toyo Shimada."

The man bowed again. "It is an honor to serve you, Shimada-san."

"No, just Toyo."

"Toyo-san. Hai," the man said, bowing again.

Toyo sighed. "I'm looking for a butcher," he said.

The man's eyes went wide. "Oh, no, Toyo-san. There could be nothing you need at a butcher's. If so, a servant should go in your place. Let me go. I will get whatever you need."

"No, really, it's okay," said Toyo. He touched the man's shoulder to stop him, and the man dropped into the muck to bow. "Wait, no, get up, please," Toyo said. "What's your name?"

"Tanner, honorable Toyo-san," the man said. He tanned animal hides to make leather.

"No, not your job," Toyo told him. "Your name."

"Tanner, Toyo-san."

"All right," Toyo relented. If the man wanted to think less of himself, there was nothing Toyo could do about it.

Ahh. This is the reason Sotaro sent me to the eta village, Toyo realized. *Not to get an animal bone, but to see this tanner and others like him, cowering men and women and their filthy, loathsome lives.* Sotaro's answer had become clear: Toyo was better than these people, no matter what the emperor chose to call them. And the eta knew it too.

As much to spite his father as to honor his guide, Toyo bowed respectfully to the tanner.

"My father has commanded me to see a butcher," he told the man. "If you would tell me where I could find one, Tanner-san, I would be most grateful."

The man fell all over himself bowing at the use of *-san* with his name.

"Hai. Hai, Toyo-san. I will take you there. Hai," the tanner promised.

Toyo bowed his thanks and fell into step beside his guide. As they walked through the village, Toyo noticed again the massive rebuilding effort under way.

"Why is there so much construction?" Toyo asked.

"The Flowers of Edo," the tanner sighed.

Toyo stopped. "The what?" he asked.

"The Flowers of Edo, Toyo-san. When the earthquakes come, lanterns overturn, paper walls catch fire, houses and shops burn. The flames are called the Flowers of Edo, for they blossom suddenly and are gone."

Koji's death poem, Toyo thought. *In the darkness after the earthquake, the Flowers of Edo burn bright and fast—*

"And this happens often?" Toyo asked.

"Hai, Toyo-san. The latest earthquake was yesterday."

"These homes burned down only yesterday?" Toyo said. He looked around at all the new and mostly finished houses. "You've rebuilt them so quickly."

The tanner shrugged. "What else can we do? The Flowers of Edo come and go, and we rebuild in their ashes. But always better than before, Toyo-san. Always better."

• • •

Sotaro was still meditating in the dojo when his son

returned with a thick piece of horse bone. Toyo sat across from his father and laid the bone between them.

Sotaro opened his eyes and watched his son.

"Do you understand now?"

"I understand why you sent me to the eta village," Toyo told his father. "They treated me differently there. A man called me Toyo-san and wouldn't tell me his name. He would say only to call him Tanner."

"Eta have no name other than what they do," Sotaro explained.

"Surely his mother did not call him Tanner," Toyo countered.

Sotaro narrowed his eyes. "You are not his mother."

"He is heimin now, sensei. A commoner like us. He should never have to bow in the mud and call me Toyo-san."

"And yet he did," Sotaro said. "The Emperor Meiji may say they are elevated, but the eta know their place."

"But where is the honor in subjugation?" Toyo wanted to know. "Where is the harmony in oppression?"

Sotaro sighed. "Clearly you have misunderstood."

"Clearly," said Toyo.

Sotaro regarded his son coldly. "Honor and harmony are not the birthright of the eta, nor of any other peasant. They belong to the samurai and the samurai alone. How can creatures such as the eta ever hope to understand the concepts of honor? Harmony? Loyalty? Courage?"

"They can understand it if they are taught honor," Toyo said. "If they are taught courage."

"Such efforts would be wasted on them."

Toyo shook his head. What his father was saying went against everything he felt bushido stood for.

"A smooth animal bone will not mar the surface of your bokkoto like a rock or a stone," Toyo's father said, resuming a conversation they were not having. Sotaro ran the bone down the length of his wooden practice sword, mashing the pulpy white ash back down. "Proper application will harden your bokkoto like the day it was cut from the tree."

Sotaro held the bone out to Toyo. "Now you."

• • •

At practice, Toyo stared dully, coming alive only when his senses told him the ball was coming his way. He dove at ground balls. He went back on pop-ups. He barehanded slow rollers. On a hard bunt down the third-base line, he cut Kennichi off to make his own play.

"Um, I can handle those, Toyo," the third baseman said. "I've got the better angle."

"Right. Sorry," Toyo said, returning to his X in the dirt.

"Is everything all right?" Kennichi asked.

Toyo just stared at the batter, waiting for the next hit.

When it was his turn to bat, he found he didn't have the energy for the killing stroke. A Moriyama curveball bent away from him, and instead Toyo reached out to slap at it with his bat. *Twink!* He looped the ball easily over Junzo's head at first base.

Moriyama frowned. The pitcher got set again and threw another curveball. Toyo did the same thing—dump it into right field for a hit.

"All right," Moriyama said. "What are you doing?"

Toyo shook himself awake. "Wha—? I was just . . . hitting."

"Come on, Moriyama, pitch already," Junzo called from first.

"No. Nobody gets hits off that pitch," Moriyama complained. "If I throw it right, everybody strikes out or grounds out."

"Maybe you didn't throw it right," Junzo told him.

"Come on, Toyo. Tell me what you're doing so I can stop you."

Toyo looked at his bat and shrugged. "The ball wanted to go to right field, and I didn't feel like fighting it."

"That's stupid," Junzo said. "A ball doesn't 'want' anything. It goes where you hit it."

"It wants to go where it's pitched," Toyo said.

Moriyama threw a curveball that broke over the outside corner of the plate. Toyo reached his bat out again, smacking the ball in the hole between first and second.

"I guess I keep hitting the ball where it doesn't want to go," Michiyo joked as he threw it in.

Fuji batted after Toyo. *Whap! Crack! Smack!* Fuji drove the ball to all corners of the outfield. He used everything Toyo taught him—everything except the killing stroke.

Moriyama got the ball back and sniffed it. "Maybe this thing got harder when the old man boiled it in his cha. Okay, Fuji. See if you can hit the fastball."

Fuji performed his sumo ritual and grunted his challenge to the pitcher. Moriyama answered, hurling the ball across the plate. *Whack!* Fuji drove the ball to deep center field, where it bounced off the Wall of the Soul.

After practice, Toyo complimented Fuji on his batting. Kennichi and Michiyo stood nearby.

"I owe my success to you." Fuji bowed. "Same time tomorrow? Before the first bell?"

Toyo was tired of bushido, uncertain about the true values of the samurai. But abandoning Fuji's lessons would only be giving in to Sotaro.

"Hai," Toyo said. "Bushido at dawn."

• • •

In his room after dinner, Toyo sat on his futon and rubbed his bokkoto with the animal bone. He wondered why he bothered. Maybe the samurai *shouldn't* belong in the new Japan. But as mad as he was at Sotaro, he hated to think what that would mean.

Toyo set his bokkoto aside and pulled his baseball bat to him. The wood was soft from too much batting practice, and he smoothed the barrel slowly and carefully with the horse bone as his father had shown him.

When he was finished, Toyo curled up with his bat and glove and fell into a deep sleep.

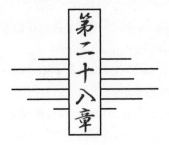

Chapter Twenty-eight

THE AIR was crisp and cool, and Toyo could still see his breath as he and Fuji met on the baseball field at dawn.

"Ready for five hundred swings?" Toyo asked.

"Wait," Fuji said. "Look."

Kennichi and Michiyo were coming up the path, baseball bats and gloves in hand. Moriyama, Katsuya, and Junzo were with them.

Toyo and Fuji waited for everyone to gather around.

Kennichi cleared his throat. "We, ah, we want to be besuboru samurai like Fuji."

"Besuboru samurai?" Fuji said.

"We play American Meiji in two days," Katsuya said. "You know we're not ready."

Toyo crossed his arms. He couldn't deny bushido had made him a better baseball player, maybe a better person. But he refused to be called a samurai, even for Koji's sake.

Though maybe they *could* take the warrior code and leave the worst elements of the samurai behind. He knew Sotaro would never approve. But wasn't that what Japan herself was doing—taking the best of what the rest of the world had to offer and making it her own?

"I cannot and will not teach you to be samurai," Toyo told his friends. "But I *can* teach you bushido—the way of the warrior—and *that* will make you better besuboru players."

"I don't care what you call it," Michiyo said. "I just want to learn to hit a ball where it wants to go."

Toyo nodded. "Then we must have some rules. First, you must join me here each morning, and be on time. Second, you must call me sensei, for I will be your bushido teacher."

"*Sensei?*" Junzo scoffed. "It's bad enough I let Moriyama drag me out here to pretend you know more about hitting than I do. I am *not* calling you sensei. Forget it. I'm going back to bed."

Junzo stalked away, and Toyo waited to see if anyone else would follow him.

"When do we start, sensei?" Moriyama asked.

Toyo bowed. "We begin this moment."

"Can we work on defense first?" Katsuya asked.

"We usually begin with five hundred swings," Fuji told them.

"*Five hundred swings?*" worried Kennichi.

Toyo waved them all quiet. "Everyone put down your bats and gloves and follow me."

Leaving their equipment behind, Toyo led his students to the line of cherry trees that bordered the baseball field. He sat down underneath one, and his teammates settled in a half circle around him. The ground was cold, but they waited without complaint.

"Sit very still and watch the sakura," Toyo told them. There were some skeptical looks, but Fuji and Moriyama did as Toyo asked and the rest followed suit.

A strong breeze came, and one of the cherry blossoms shook free from its branch and drifted to the ground between them.

"Besuboru is like the sakura in the wind," Toyo told them. "There are long moments when you wait—at the plate, in the field, on base—and nothing happens. Then, as suddenly as this cherry blossom was torn from its branch, there is action: a pitch, a ground ball, a stolen base. . . . And now, the sakura is still, until the wind comes and pulls another blossom from its branches."

"How will this teach us to field better?" Kennichi whispered.

"Shh!" Moriyama hissed. "We're learning bushido."

"Kennichi, when you understand the wa of the game," Toyo explained, "when you are a part of it and can feel its harmony, *then* you will become a better third baseman."

"Hai, sensei."

The wind blew through the sakura, and Toyo closed his eyes. It was a sound he could conjure up for himself any time now, and it calmed him.

"Listen," said Toyo. "Listen to the wind in the cherry trees, so you can remember it when it's gone."

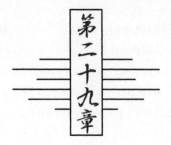

Chapter Twenty-nine

TOYO WAS early for his lesson with Sotaro. Despite his differences with his father, he had resolved to teach his friends bushido, and he owed it to them to learn as much as he could. What he silently disagreed with he would *not* pass along.

A familiar thumping sound came from the back of the dojo, and Toyo snuck around the side to watch Moriyama practicing his pitching. The pitcher's hair was wilder, more unkempt than before, and for a boy who had always prided himself on his clean good looks, Moriyama hadn't shaved in days. On his face, he wore the same grim resolve to perfect his pitching Toyo had seen before, but there was something more. Anger? Frustration? Shame?

Moriyama caught sight of Toyo and started. When he realized who it was, the pitcher relaxed, bowing silently to his sensei. Toyo bowed back and left Moriyama to his penance.

Sotaro was arriving as Toyo turned the corner, and they stopped awkwardly at each other's approach. For lack of a better greeting, Toyo bowed. Sotaro returned the politeness with a nod.

"I thought you might not return," Sotaro said.

Toyo acknowledged his father's concern with silence. Then, before Sotaro could interpret his quiet as a challenge, Toyo said, "I still wish to understand more about bushido."

Sotaro nodded. "Then let us begin."

Toyo followed his father inside the dojo, and together they laid out the tatami mats for meditation. As Toyo settled in, he could still hear the soft thumping of Moriyama's fastballs on the wall outside. *Thump . . . . Thump . . . . Thump.* He found it soothing.

Sotaro stirred and frowned. "What is that sound?"

"It is a besuboru, sensei."

"Besu-boru?"

"The Western sport I played in middle school."

"You played a sport in middle school?"

"Hai," said Toyo. "And I play on the First Higher team as well. I am the shortstop."

"I do not understand what that means."

"All the infielders have a base except the shortstop," Toyo explained. "He floats in between second and third."

"Second and third what?"

"Bases," Toyo said, happy to finally be explaining baseball to his father. "There are four bases in all, only the home base is called a plate. When you reach home plate you score a—"

"Is this a game you and your friends invented?" Sotaro interrupted.

"No, sensei. It's a gaijin game. The American businessmen play besuboru down by—"

"And must this game be played against the wall of the dojo?" Sotaro demanded.

"We have a field, beyond the dormitories. Moriyama is putting in extra practice. We have a big game soon against American Meiji."

"I am surprised the headmaster allows such a waste of time," Sotaro said. He closed his eyes again and tried to focus on his meditation.

"Actually, I think you would like besuboru," Toyo pressed. "There is much in it that reflects traditional samurai ways."

Sotaro opened his eyes and peered at his son. "I doubt that very seriously."

"No, it's true," Toyo said, "I've discovered it myself. In the last few weeks, I have been able to incorporate almost all of my bushido lessons into the game. The—the flower arrangement, for example, it helped me understand how to, how to arrange everyone. So that we were one, not nine fielders all acting independently. And the killing stroke! When I learned that, I was able to finally hit the ball out of the infield. Oh! And the wind in the sakura—that's the most important of all. It helps me focus on the game, on that moment—"

Sotaro scowled. Toyo shook his head. He wasn't saying it the way he wanted to.

"I just need to tell you how the game is played. Then you'll understand—"

"I have not been teaching you bushido so you may become better at a gaijin game," Sotaro spat. "Have you missed the point of our lessons *entirely*?"

"No. I didn't—I mean—just give me a chance to—"

"I have taught you bushido so you might understand Koji and myself better. So you might one day be samurai."

"I don't *want* to be a samurai," Toyo countered, suddenly angry. "Not if people cower in the muck when I approach. Not if someone else has to be eta. Why can't everyone be a commoner as the emperor commanded, and then aspire to be something better? Aspire to be like the best of the samurai?"

"Samurai are *born*, not made," Sotaro told his son

"Then you will find it impossible to make me a samurai," Toyo replied, "for I was born a commoner."

Sotaro stood. "Then I see no reason to continue our lessons."

Toyo bowed his head, and his father left without another word.

Toyo put the mats away and left the dojo, noticing on the way out that the thumping had stopped. He went around back and put his hand against the wall where Moriyama had concentrated his frustration, much as he had once put his hand to the Wall of the Soul, to see if he could feel its energy.

Weakened from the onslaught, the bricks shifted under his touch.

• • •

The ball kicked past the pitcher's glove as he tried to field Fuji's little tapper back to the mound. Moriyama ripped his glove off in disgust and flung it away as far as he could.

"No!" cried Toyo. Storm clouds threatened to put an early end to their practice, but he still stopped everything to get the pitcher's glove for him. "You have fighting spirit, Moriyama, and that's good. But a samurai's most important possessions are his swords. They are his heart and soul. Yours are your bat and glove. You should never disrespect them."

"I thought you said we wouldn't be samurai," Moriyama said.

"We won't," Toyo promised. "But there is much we can learn from them."

"Hai, sensei. Sorry, sensei," Moriyama said with a bow.

Junzo snorted at first. *"Hai, sensei. Sorry, sensei,"* he sang in a high-pitched voice.

Toyo ignored him. "Think of yourselves not as samurai but shishi, Men of High Purpose," he told the team. "Men of High Purpose show their courage and strength in their actions. If you make an error, you must not get angry. If you get a hit, you must not celebrate. If you strike out, you must smile as if it doesn't matter."

"Smile when you strike out?" Junzo said. "Where's the fighting spirit in that?"

"Fighting spirit must be tempered with control," Toyo said, looking at Moriyama now. "The heart may burn, but the body must be made to obey."

"Burning besuboru," Fuji said. "That should be our motto."

Toyo nodded. It reminded him of the line from Koji's death poem. *The Flowers of Edo burn fast and bright.* "I like it," he said.

"Good. Can we practice now?" Junzo complained. "This is our last chance to practice before the Meiji game, and soon it's going to rain!" As if on cue, it began to sprinkle.

"Let's get some hitting practice in," Toyo called. "Hurry!"

The team gathered around Toyo as he demonstrated the hitting techniques he had learned from his bushido lessons, adding some of his own observations.

"Contact is the most important thing," he told them. "If the pitcher throws the ball on the outside of the plate, make contact there and try to send the ball where it wants to go. When we try to send the ball where it doesn't want to go, we make outs."

"I don't care what the *ball* wants," Junzo said. "*I* want it to go over the Wall of the Soul."

Toyo ignored the big first baseman as the rain got stronger. "Keep your swing sharp," he said over the noise of the wind. "Keep your legs shoulder-width apart, feet straight, with the bat held high over your head."

"Who says there is only one way to hit?" Junzo demanded. "I don't stand like that."

"There is a right and wrong way to arrange flowers, a right and wrong way to write with a brush, and a right and wrong way to hit a besuboru," Toyo explained. "There is a perfect way to do everything we do if we take the time to look for it."

The heavens truly opened up then, and the rain came like a monsoon.

"Guess you'll have to look for it another time," Junzo yelled. "Practice is over."

"Wait," Toyo called. "Why don't we keep practicing?"

"What?" Moriyama cried. "In this? My fastball would be blown off course in this typhoon."

"And it's freezing!" Michiyo complained.

A small lake was already forming in the infield.

"Burning besuboru, remember?" Toyo said. "Burning besuboru will keep us warm!"

"A burning fire back in Independence Hall is what will keep me warm," Junzo said.

"You said it yourself," Toyo told Junzo. "This is our last chance to practice! This is about *effort*. Fighting spirit. My uncle Koji used to stand under waterfalls in the dead of winter to test his spirit. He called it a guts drill."

"He sure showed his guts with his seppuku, didn't he?" Junzo sneered.

The wind howled through the sakura on the edge of the field, and all eyes fell on Toyo. Water streamed down his face like tears.

"Hai," Toyo said finally. "He did."

"I will show my fighting spirit, sensei," Fuji said, and the other players nodded in agreement.

"Stay here and show whatever you want, then," Junzo told them. "*I'm* going back to the dorm and show myself a hot bath."

The team watched Junzo as he walked away.

"All right," Toyo called over the storm. "Get your bats and line up for the five hundred swings drill!"

• • •

Late that night, the storm raged on as eight boys sat in a circle around a flickering candle in Independence Hall. The door to the dark room slid open, and Junzo Ueda stepped inside.

"I got your message," Junzo told the group. "I didn't know

the Mainstream Society was investigating someone else so soon."

"We are always watching for those who do not choose to fit in," a boy said.

"This person has just come to our attention," said another.

"Toyo?" Junzo said, recognizing the first-year in the darkness. "What are you doing here? Who is the offender?"

"*You* are."

Junzo was stunned speechless, but the moment quickly passed.

"*I* am the offender!?" he cried, shifting quickly to a whisper. "I argued for the Mainstream Society. This group owes its very existence to me!"

The head of the Mainstream Society took charge. "Is it true you walked away from your teammates on the besuboru field tonight?"

Junzo laughed nervously. "Is *that* what this is all about? What does it matter what I do on the besuboru field?" he asked. "That's just an athletic club."

"The athlete is to the school what the warrior is to the country," the head boy told him. "Was Moriyama's behavior any less excusable because it took place away from the hallowed grounds of First Higher? An Ichiko man is an Ichiko man wherever he goes."

"This is crazy," Junzo said, looking more uncomfortable.

"Did you walk away from your Ichiko brothers this evening?" the head boy pressed.

"It was *raining*. Listen to it out there. It's a typhoon."

"When the rest of your team changes position, do you change with them?" another asked.

"You must be kidding," Junzo laughed. "I'm not taking orders from a first-year."

"Nor were your teammates," the head boy told Junzo. "They were playing together, with one mind. There is no room for individuality at Ichiko, whether in Independence Hall or on the besuboru field."

Hearing the echoes of his own words in the head boy's reprimand, Junzo looked to the floor.

"There is great evidence here," the boy continued. "Swinging for homu rans and personal glory where a new approach might benefit the team. Blaming others for team losses. Refusing to accept your new catcher as part of the team—"

Junzo glared at Toyo. "Fuji was not born samurai," he protested.

"Have you forgotten our bodies and souls were born in the womb of Ichiko?" the head boy answered. "None of us existed before. We were nothing until Ichiko made us men. Made us *brothers*."

Junzo stammered to find a defense for himself. Nothing came of it.

"The Mainstream Society has found you guilty of crass individuality. In your words and deeds, you have violated the unwritten spirit of Ichiko unity. Your sentence has been passed."

"You—you don't mean—the clenched fist?" Junzo whispered.

"No," the head of the Mainstream Society said. "Consider

this a 'quiet word.' But from this moment forward, you must swear to change your behavior for the better."

Junzo bowed low to the members of the Mainstream Society. "I so swear," Junzo said.

"Think always of Ichiko first, Junzo Ueda," the head boy said. "We will be watching."

● ● ●

The few boys in Toyo's room were reading or talking quietly, and he pulled his futon down and sat by himself in the corner. His bat and glove lay next to a candle where he had left them to dry. He toweled off the bat and held it the way Sotaro had taught him to wield a katana. An idea struck him, and he took out the brush set his father had given him for his birthday. Using the finer of the two brushes, Toyo carefully drew a cherry blossom, the Shimada family crest, on the barrel of his bat.

Futoshi slid into the room, as dripping wet as Toyo had been after practicing in the storm for two hours. Toyo immediately worried his friend had been out to visit his girlfriend.

"*Futoshi*," Toyo hissed.

"I wasn't out to see her, I swear," Futoshi promised.

"Where *were* you, then? You're drenched."

"Just a little errand," said Futoshi. His friend grinned, and Toyo knew he was in trouble.

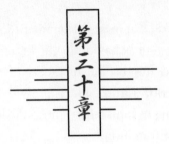

Chapter Thirty

THE DAY of the Meiji game, the path to the baseball field was packed with hundreds of students—some from Ichiko, and some, amazingly, wearing Meiji uniforms. As Toyo wove his way through the crowd, Ichiko students slapped him on the back and shouted, "Get a hit!"

On one side of the field, Futoshi had arranged hundreds of Ichiko students and fans. On the other side, Futoshi's Meiji friend Shigeo was organizing hundreds more supporters for *his* school. Fuji and Moriyama stood in the middle of the diamond, shooing fans off the field.

"What's going on?" Toyo asked.

"Futoshi's brought more oendan," Fuji explained. "I think this is going to be the biggest besuboru game in the history of Japan."

Great, Toyo thought. *As if playing Meiji weren't big enough.*

Futoshi was getting his troops warmed up for their shouting exercises when Toyo walked up.

"Futoshi, what have you done?"

"Hm? Oh, this?" Futoshi said. "This is where I went last night. I challenged Shigeo and the Meiji judo club to see who could cheer the loudest."

"You invited the Meiji *judo club* here?" Toyo asked. He had a sick feeling in his stomach. "Didn't both clubs get into a fight the last time you had a judo match?"

"Hai," said Futoshi. He smiled at the memory. "Maybe we will again today."

"Just wait until *after* the game, all right?" Toyo asked.

"Okay, oendan!" Futoshi cried. "Let's stretch those tonsils! One, two, three—scream!"

More people came up the path, and fans began to spill over onto the field. The Ichiko nine gathered on the pitcher's mound, eyeing the human foul line down both sides of the field.

"If we hit a foul ball we might kill someone," Fuji pointed out.

"Just try to hit all your fouls down the third-base line into the Meiji fans," Junzo said.

Kennichi scanned the crowd. "I think every student and teacher from Ichiko is here. Even Nishimoto is here!"

True enough, the old gatekeeper was working his way into the crowd.

"Nishimoto-san, who's watching the gate?" Toyo called.

"No one. It's closed," said Nishimoto. "Enough people here already! If Junzo hits one over the Wall of the Soul, I'll have to go unlock it for you. Good luck!"

The home plate umpire pulled his mask over his face and cried, "Pu-re boru!"

"You heard the man," said Junzo.

"Burning besuboru," Toyo told the team.

"Burning besuboru!" everyone but Junzo yelled back.

The team ran out to their positions, and Fuji put down the sign for Moriyama's first pitch. The ball zipped in. "Strike one!" the umpire called.

Futoshi whipped the oendan into a frenzy. Three pitches later, the batter grounded out to Katsuya at second, and the Ichiko fans never let up. After a fly ball for the second out, Meiji's third hitter singled. Moriyama stayed cool. Toyo saw how he was pitching to the cleanup hitter, and moved into better position. The big Meiji hitter grounded a ball right to Toyo, and he flipped the ball to Katsuya at second for the third out of the inning.

Futoshi's oendan erupted as if Ichiko had won the game.

The Meiji pitcher was almost as good as Moriyama, though, and while his pitches weren't as fast, he had a wicked one he threw much slower than the rest. Michiyo struck out swinging at it for the first out of the inning.

"I don't know what that was," Michiyo told them when he got back to the sidelines, "but when I thought I had his timing down, he threw that pitch and it mixed me up."

"Maybe it's something the American taught them," Katsuya said.

Kennichi grabbed his bat to head to the plate, but Junzo stopped him. "I think Toyo should hit higher in the lineup," he said, surprising everyone.

Kennichi nodded, and Toyo took up his bat.

"Do your best, Toyo," Junzo said. He tapped Toyo's bat with his own for emphasis.

Toyo stepped up to the plate and focused on the wa of the game. He was aware of the fielders' positions, the chanting of the oendan, the pitcher's motion—even the sakura, hidden behind the swelling crowd.

The first pitch missed off the corner, and he let it go. "Ball one!" the umpire cried. The next pitch came in slow, like Michiyo said, but Toyo waited back on it and shortened his swing. *Smack!* He sent the ball where it wanted to go— right over the head of the third baseman and down onto the left-field corner.

The Meiji fans on the third-base line scattered, throwing jeers at Toyo as he rounded first and then pulled in safely at second base. On the other side of the field, the Ichiko oendan waved banners and sang, "Behold, the flaming red of our school flag—dyed o'er the fumes of our seething blood!"

Junzo came to bat, and the outfielders moved deeper, playing almost all the way back to the Wall of the Soul. The pitcher stayed away from him with two straight balls, and Junzo dove at the third pitch, yanking it high and deep to left field. It was caught five steps from the wall.

Toyo tagged up at second and sprinted for third base, sliding in safely under the throw. The Meiji judo club swarming the third base foul line cursed him.

Kennichi got his turn to bat, and the oendan applauded as he worked a walk on six pitches. Fuji stepped in next, and after being ridiculed by the Meiji fans for his sumo warm-ups at home plate he lined a solid hit. Toyo scored to the screams of the oendan as Ichiko took a 1–0 lead. "Victory!

Victory over the evil invaders!" he heard Futoshi cry. The next batter, Moriyama, grounded out to end the inning.

Toyo ran Fuji's catcher's mitt out to him.

"We can beat these guys!" said Fuji.

"I know!" said Toyo. "Burning besuboru!"

"Burning besuboru!" everyone cried—everyone but Junzo.

Ichiko and Meiji held each other scoreless for the next two innings, but in the bottom of the fourth, First Higher got another rally going. Michiyo bunted his way on and stole second, and Toyo drew a walk to put men on first and second for Junzo with only one out.

The first baseman's previous at bat had been identical to his first—a long fly ball out to left. The Meiji pitcher knew to keep the ball as far away from Junzo as he could, but on his third pitch he made a mistake. He left a fastball out over the plate, and Junzo jumped on it, blasting the pitch to deep left center. No one could get to it, and it bounced to the wall. As he scored right behind Michiyo, Toyo watched Junzo pull in to second with a stand-up double.

In the next inning, Meiji struck back. A walk, a hit, a double, and the score was 3–2 with only one out. The Ichiko oendan had been taunting the visiting fans all game long, and now Meiji returned the favor. The two judo clubs surged onto the field, but teachers on both sides managed to keep the groups under control so the game could continue.

Moriyama got a strikeout for the second out of the inning, but his next pitch was ripped for a single. Michiyo got to the ball quickly and hit Toyo as cutoff man, and the shortstop turned and fired the ball at Fuji's huge target.

The ball popped into Fuji's mitt. The runner slid. Fuji swept the tag—

"Safe!" the umpire called.

"Second base!" cried Junzo. The hitter was trying to advance on the throw home. Fuji gunned to second, and the ball and the runner arrived at the same time. Katsuya put down his glove. The Meiji player slid in hard, and they tumbled off the bag in a tangle of arms and legs.

"Out!" called the umpire.

Katsuya struggled to free himself of the Meiji player, and Toyo and Junzo rushed to his aid.

"Get off him, you baka!" Junzo cried. He planted a foot on the Meiji player and pushed him aside. At once, players spilled out from the Meiji bench, and the Ichiko nine rushed to second base to protect Junzo. An umpire held the players apart, while the teachers on the sidelines struggled to keep the oendan from joining the fray.

"He's all right," Toyo told his teammates. "Katsuya's all right. There's no harm done."

The teams backed down, and order was restored. The inning was over, but the damage was done. The score was tied 3–3.

"They hit good pitches," Moriyama said on the sidelines. He set his glove down respectfully and got his bat to hit. But he and the next two Ichiko batters were retired in order, and the fifth inning ended with the score still tied.

In the top of the sixth, Meiji went to work again. The first hitter fouled off pitch after pitch, finally lining a single. The next batter bunted the runner to second, and a triple, a walk, and a double later, Meiji was leading Ichiko 6–3.

"Time out," Toyo called. He ran to the mound to help settle Moriyama down, and the rest of the infielders joined him.

"I'm sorry," Moriyama told them. "I'm doing my best."

"I can't believe that guy actually caught up to your fastball," said Kennichi.

"I think he had his eyes closed," Junzo grumbled.

"And that walk was a strikeout all the way," Fuji said.

"Forget about all that and get these next two guys out," Toyo told the pitcher. "We can score more runs for you."

"I'm going to hit a homu ran next inning," Junzo said. "No matter *where* the ball wants to go."

Moriyama slapped the ball back in his glove, and the infielders returned to their positions. The next batter fouled the first pitch back, and Fuji made a diving catch at the screen to steal an out. After that the Meiji third baseman grounded out to Toyo to end the half-inning.

"All right," Moriyama told his teammates. "Let's score some runs!"

Michiyo got a walk ahead of Toyo, who slapped a base hit to left. Junzo stepped to the plate with two runners on base again, and the Ichiko oendan chanted his name. *"Jun-zo! Jun-zo! Jun-zo!"*

"Here it comes, ladies," Junzo announced to the Meiji team. "Homu ran."

The catcher flashed the signal to his pitcher as Junzo settled in. From his position on first base, Toyo saw the ball come out of the pitcher's hand high and hard. Junzo tried to turn away, but—*thwack!*—the ball nailed him in the shoulder.

"Arrgh!" cried Junzo, falling to one knee.

The Ichiko oendan surged onto the field. "Kill the pitcher!" Futoshi screamed.

Junzo slammed his bat into the ground and started toward the pitcher's mound, but the Meiji catcher got in his way.

"You should have knocked me out," Junzo yelled at the pitcher. "Because I'm going to send the next stinking pitch I see over that wall!"

The pitcher grinned and gave an insincere bow of apology.

Junzo took his free base, and Toyo moved down to second.

"Are you okay?" Toyo called.

Junzo worked his right arm in circles and winced. "It itches," he growled.

Toyo smiled. Junzo would be okay, and while the Meiji pitcher had taken the bat out of the big hitter's hands, Ichiko had the bases loaded with nobody out.

The oendan tossed threats at each other across the baseball diamond, but quickly an eerie quiet settled over the field. Toyo, Junzo, and the entire Meiji team seemed to notice the silence at the same time. Both oendan were focused on something in the outfield, and Toyo turned to see what they were all staring at.

There, climbing his way over the Wall of the Soul— Ichiko's last defense against the modern world—Toyo saw an

American gaijin. That same red-hair he had seen coaching the Meiji team.

With a smile and a wave, the foreigner hopped to the ground inside Ichiko.

"That gaijin climbed *over* the Wall of the Soul!" Futoshi screamed. *"Kill him!"*

Toyo shrank as the Ichiko judo club streamed past him into the outfield. The Meiji judo club poured onto the field to meet them, and the startled American was engulfed by the mob.

Toyo ducked a fist, then a leg, as he bizarrely found himself still holding his place on second base. Weren't they in the middle of a game? Through the spin-kicks and roundhouse punches, Toyo spied Junzo, who seemed to still be anchored to his base too. Otherwise, all semblance of a baseball game was gone—it had become an all-out brawl. Toyo watched as Junzo shrugged and jumped on the back of the Meiji first baseman, riding him to the ground in a halo of blows.

Toyo gave up. "Burning besuboru!" he screamed, and turned to join the fight.

Chapter Thirty-one

"A DISGRACE. A disgrace!" the headmaster said. Toyo and Futoshi sat in Kinoshita's office for the second time in a month, their heads bowed while he paced the room. Futoshi's left arm was in a sling again, and his ear was bloody. Toyo had escaped with nothing worse than a black eye.

"Look at you," Kinoshita said. "Leaders of your clubs. Yet there you were, in the middle of the conflict."

"I was trying to stop them, but—" Futoshi began.

"Silence!" the headmaster barked. "I happen to know you led the charge. Whatever could have possessed you to attack a distinguished guest of this school?"

Toyo and Futoshi stole glances at each other.

"You mean, you weren't there, Headmaster-san?" Toyo asked.

"Of course I wasn't there," Kinoshita said. "I do not have time to attend sporting functions."

"Then you didn't see the gaijin climb over the Wall of the Soul?" Futoshi asked.

The headmaster stopped pacing. "He did *what?*"

"We thought you knew," Toyo said. "We were in the middle of a besuboru game, and an American gaijin came over the sacred wall."

"He—he climbed *over?*" Kinoshita said. "*Into* Ichiko? From the *outside?*"

"Hai, Headmaster-san," said Toyo.

"Seeing somebody climb over—and a gaijin, no less!—it drove us mad," Futoshi finished.

"Of course, of course," said the headmaster. "I had no idea. The very thought . . . I think I might have attacked him myself. You boys are to be commended."

Toyo and Futoshi exhaled in relief.

But suddenly the door to Kinoshita's office slid open and Sotaro stepped inside. Toyo and Futoshi stood quickly and bowed. Once the headmaster and Toyo's father exchanged greetings, the boys were told to sit back down.

"Thank you for coming, Shimada-san," Kinoshita said, "but this matter has been resolved."

"On the contrary," Sotaro said. "I fear it is far from resolved."

Toyo closed his eyes. He *knew* getting out of this had been much too easy.

"*Far* from resolved?" the headmaster said. "But I have already spoken with the headmaster of Meiji. He assures me—"

"This incident has gone well beyond school rivalry," Sotaro said. "All Edo is abuzz with the news of the attack on the gaijin."

"The, the American?" Kinoshita said. "Is he all right?"

"Minor wounds," Sotaro reported with a wave of his hand. "The real damage has been done to the relations between our two countries. You are aware Japan is in the middle of tense negotiations to rework the Unequal Treaties the United States forced us to sign?"

"Hai," said the headmaster. "Of course."

"Due to this incident, the Americans have withdrawn their representative."

Toyo felt his stomach tighten. He didn't understand the politics, but could negotiations over foreign policy really break down because of a fight at a high school baseball game?

Brrrrrring!—Brrrrrring! Toyo jumped at the sound. A black box on the wall made a terrible racket, and Toyo watched Kinoshita pull a small horn from the side of it and bring it to his ear. He spoke into the thing's nose.

"Hai? Hai?" he said. "Hello?"

Futoshi gasped, and Toyo guessed at once what it was. A *telephone*. He had never seen one in operation. The horn squawked in Kinoshita's ear, and his face told them it was delivering more bad news.

"Hai. Hai," the headmaster said. The horn kept squawking. "Hai, Minister. Hai. But the gaijin climbed *over* the—" Kinoshita began. The person on the other end of the phone cut him off. "I understand," said the headmaster. He bowed, though the person he was speaking with wasn't in the room, and returned the earpiece to its hook.

"That was the minister of education," Kinoshita said. "The incident is indeed as bad as you say, Shimada-san.

229

The emperor himself has ordered me to send a delegation to apologize to the gaijin at the American consulate."

"To think this could sabotage all we have worked for," Sotaro said. He looked straight at his son. "And all because of a worthless game!"

Toyo bowed deeply. "I will go to the consulate and apologize, Headmaster-san. Perhaps then the Americans will forgive us and everything will be as it was."

Toyo nudged his friend. "Me too," said Futoshi.

"Hai," Kinoshita said. "I will escort you to the American consulate tomorrow morning, where you will formally apologize. You may now return to your dormitory."

Toyo and Futoshi bowed to Sotaro and the headmaster and got ready to leave.

"Headmaster-san, a word or two with you about this besu-boru before I go," Sotaro said.

Toyo tried to put his outside shoes on slowly, but he heard no more before they had to leave.

• • •

The next morning before the first bell, the students of Ichiko gathered in the ethics lecture hall to hear an address by the headmaster. Toyo and Futoshi stood together in a row near the back. The Emperor Meiji looked down on them from his picture high above the chalkboard.

"Many, if not all of you, were involved in the incident on the besu-boru court yesterday," Kinoshita began. "And while your defense of the sacred Wall of the Soul was honorable, your actions were not. Later this morning, two of your student leaders will join me at the American consulate, where they will apologize for this disgrace. In the meantime, there will be no more besu-boru played at Ichiko."

Toyo's teammates found one another in the crowd, exchanging pained and angry looks.

"They can't do that!" Toyo whispered to Futoshi.

"It had nothing to do with the game," Futoshi agreed.

"The relationship of Japan with the rest of the world only highlights your purpose at Ichiko," the headmaster told them, returning to his favorite refrain. "You will lead this country into the next era, where Japan will finally stand on equal footing with the other great nations of the world."

It was the beginning of a speech Toyo had heard all too often at Ichiko, and he quickly tuned it out. What would the baseball team do if they couldn't practice? Was it just the season that was over, or did Kinoshita mean they could never play baseball ever again?

A better question was *why* Kinoshita had banned baseball, and Toyo knew the answer all too well: Sotaro.

Chapter Thirty-two

TOYO STOPPED and bought an *Asahi Shimbun* on the way to the American consulate.

"Come along, come along," said Kinoshita. "The consul is expecting us at precisely nine o'clock." The headmaster was already a few yards ahead of him, but Toyo didn't bother to hurry. He and Futoshi dropped back a few paces, and Toyo grunted as he perused the paper.

"What?" Futoshi asked.

"My father's article. 'The Evils of Besuboru.' He says the game has no honor. 'Besuboru is a pickpocket's sport, where players are encouraged to steal bases from their opponents.'"

"Has he ever even *seen* a besuboru game?" Futoshi said.

"No, and he never will," Toyo told him. "He refuses to understand, yet here he writes: 'Besuboru is too Western. It teaches bad lessons and doesn't have the tradition or harmony of Japanese sports such as judo or sumo.' He says, 'Judo stresses the development of character through martial training and an emphasis on the Zen way of the warrior.'"

"Really? I just like it because we get to hit people," Futoshi said.

Kinoshita turned and urged the boys to hurry.

Toyo wadded the newspaper up and threw it in the gutter. Futoshi let him walk along in silence until they reached the American compound. There, two bearded gaijin soldiers with long rifles consulted Kinoshita through a translator before they were allowed through the gate.

A soldier escorted them to a large building near the center of the compound, and Toyo and Futoshi followed the head-master inside. They started to leave their shoes at the door, but there wasn't a cabinet.

"You may keep your outside shoes on here," the headmaster told them. "Americans do not take their shoes off inside."

"The consul is expecting you," a Japanese man told them. He opened another hinged door and showed them inside.

The gaijin consul was a tall thin man with a thick gray suit and a bushy moustache and beard. He sat behind a large wooden desk, and he got up when he saw them enter the room.

"Come in," the consul said in Japanese. It took Toyo only a moment to realize he had seen the man before. Futoshi must have realized it as well, for his eyes were wide as rice balls. It was the gaijin Futoshi had knocked into the pond at Asakusa Park.

"You remember Mr. Smith?" asked the consul, nodding to the other man in the room.

Toyo did—it was the man who was coaching the Meiji

team, the same gaijin who had climbed over Ichiko's Wall of the Soul. The American baseball player blushed and bowed too deeply.

Toyo and Futoshi bowed respectfully, trying to stay clear of the consul, who shook hands very formally with the headmaster. Japanese did not shake hands when they greeted each other, but Kinoshita was clearly trying his best to be diplomatic.

The consul waved at three chairs and asked them to sit down.

"Have we met before?" the consul asked Futoshi.

"No, Consul-san," Futoshi said quickly. "I'm sure I would remember."

The consul studied Futoshi a moment longer, but apparently couldn't place him. Toyo hoped they could apologize quickly and escape.

"Please accept our humble apologies for the incident yesterday," he said.

Futoshi bowed his head. "Hai. We are very sorry. Good-bye." He started to stand up, but Kinoshita put a hand on his shoulder and returned him to his seat.

The consul smiled and translated for the American. Smith shook his head, and Toyo's heart sank. If he refused their apology, all was lost. The Meiji teacher said something in English, and the consul translated.

"Mr. Smith says you are not to blame. He says he has come to understand the wall held special significance to you, and he begs you to accept his own apology."

Toyo and Futoshi were stunned.

"We accept his apology, of course," Kinoshita said quickly, "if he will accept ours for not being gracious hosts." Toyo and Futoshi woke from their surprise and agreed, bowing respectfully. The gaijin did his best to duplicate their bows, and spoke again in English.

"Mr. Smith wishes to explain there are no such walls in America," the consul translated, "and he had no idea he was breaking a rule. He merely wished to see your besuboru game, and the front gate was locked."

"A terrible misunderstanding," the headmaster agreed. "Terrible."

"Mr. Smith wants to know if you are hurt badly," the consul interpreted, pointing to Futoshi's sling.

"Oh, this?" Futoshi said. "Just a sprain. You should see Shigeo."

"And who is Shigeo?" the consul asked before translating for the red-hair.

"The one who did this," Futoshi said.

The consul translated this for the other gaijin, and the baseball player laughed heartily.

"Are you sure we haven't met?" the consul asked the boys again. "You look very familiar."

"No, Consul-san," said Toyo.

"Absolutely not, Consul-san," said Futoshi.

Kinoshita eyed them suspiciously. "It is time the boys returned to school," he said. Everyone stood and bowed to one another again. Smith-san stuck out his hand and Toyo shook it, imitating the headmaster. Suddenly Toyo had an inspiration.

"Perhaps you would honor us with a besuboru game," he told the gaijin. "Your Shimbashi team against the Ichiko nine."

The consul looked startled as he translated what Toyo said. The American was equally surprised, and he replied with a kind smile. The consul translated.

"Mr. Smith thinks your offer kind, but worries you might be, how do you say, overmatched?"

"Of course," Toyo conceded, "but it would be an honor to share the same field with them."

The consul translated this as well, but the gaijin baseball player was still reluctant.

"Hai, why don't they play?" Kinoshita said, stepping in. "It would be a gesture of goodwill on both sides. To let everyone know there are no bad feelings."

The consul seemed to see some wisdom in this, and he spoke with Smith-san at length. Finally he nodded—the Ichiko nine were back in business! They set a date for the game and did another round of hand-shaking and bowing.

Outside the consul's office, the headmaster complimented Toyo on his quick thinking.

"This game will go a long way toward repairing the damage done between our two countries," Kinoshita told them.

"So we can play besuboru again?" Toyo asked eagerly. "We can practice?"

"Do whatever you like," the headmaster told him. "Just as long as you lose."

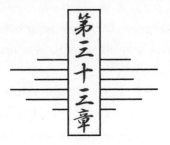

Chapter Thirty-three

THE ICHIKO nine gathered around Toyo excitedly as he stepped onto the baseball field.

"Is it true?" Katsuya asked. "Did you really challenge the gaijin to a besuboru game?"

"What should we start with?" Moriyama asked. "Five hundred swings? A hundred ground balls? We can beat them. I know we can beat them!"

"No," Toyo said. "We can't." His teammates' faces fell.

"Well, they're better than we are," Michiyo said. "Bigger too. But that doesn't mean—"

"Yeah," Junzo cut in, "what happened to 'burning besuboru'?"

"You don't understand," Toyo told them. "The headmaster has ordered us to lose."

No one spoke for a moment, and Toyo watched as his friends began to understand what he was saying.

"But . . . why?" asked Fuji.

"To make the Americans happy and repair the damage done in the Meiji game."

Toyo searched the boys' faces for answers. He could see they were as angry and upset as he was, but none of them could see a way out either.

"Will it?" Moriyama asked. "Make them happy, I mean? Fix things?"

Toyo shrugged. "Kinoshita seems to think so."

"So what do we do, deliberately strike out? Make errors?" Junzo demanded.

"If that's what it takes to honor Ichiko and defend Japan," Toyo answered.

Fuji shifted uncomfortably. "So, we're just giving up?"

"What choice do we have?" Toyo asked.

He waited for someone to argue with him, for someone to find an answer. When no one did, he kicked at the dirt and stalked back to the dorm.

● ● ●

"Toyo Shimada," a first-year called. "Message for you."

The delivery boy caught Toyo at the door to his room in Independence Hall. The piece of paper bore the Shimada family crest. A note from Sotaro. Toyo unrolled it.

"Toyo, please join me at dawn in the Shinto shrine in the clearing," Sotaro wrote in neat, beautiful characters. "There you will assist me with my seppuku."

Toyo's arms fell to his side and the message dangled between his fingers. Everyone else was at athletic club, and Toyo passed into his empty room like a sleepwalker. He had never felt so distant from his father, so out of touch, and yet he could not imagine a world without him. As much as his father angered him, he still couldn't bear to see Sotaro die—much less help him.

He lifted the note to read it again, but the characters swam before his eyes. Breathing deeply, he willed himself to conjure the image of the wind in the sakura, but nothing came.

Toyo sat on his bedroll and stared at the wall. Without thinking, he slipped on his baseball glove and smacked his fist into it, over and over again. First Koji, now his father. For all he had learned about the way of the warrior, he still didn't really understand why *Koji* had killed himself. Yes, the emperor had commanded it, but *bushido* was what supposedly demanded it—

Did that mean Koji had two masters—Emperor Meiji and the way of the warrior? Toyo's uncle had chosen to turn his sword against the emperor in a civil war. But bushido demanded absolute loyalty to one's master, and what was the emperor if not the greatest master in the land? Toyo began to understand—in challenging Meiji, Koji had violated the very laws of bushido he was fighting to preserve!

And while the consequences of Toyo's decision were not life and death, he realized that he too was faced with choosing between two masters. If he and his team threw the baseball game against the Americans, they would bring dishonor upon themselves, their school, and their nation. Yet to win might mean expulsion from school or, worse, another international incident.

What had Koji done in this situation? He had chosen what he felt was right—no matter the cost. And though he had challenged the emperor, Meiji had still honored him by allowing him to commit seppuku. That meant the emperor understood bushido—perhaps even respected Koji for his challenge.

In that moment, Toyo finally understood the emperor's command, and his uncle's acceptance.

And why it had taken Sotaro so long to decide to die.

Chapter Thirty-four

BEFORE DAWN, Toyo laid out clean tatami mats on the dirt floor of the Shinto shrine. He swept and cleaned everything, pausing to make sure it was his own reflection he saw in the mirror. After giving it an extra shine, he cleared the newly grown kudzu.

Everything had to be perfect for his father's seppuku.

Toyo wore his best Ichiko uniform and hat, with its twin symbols of oak and olive leaves polished to a glow. Sitting on a mat at the foot of the shrine, he waited for first light. Beside him lay his baseball glove and his bat, decorated with the Shimada family crest.

His father arrived a few minutes later, wearing a brilliant white kimono, the Shimada family swords hanging at his side. Sotaro sat down on the mat Toyo had prepared for him, and they waited quietly for nearly half an hour until the sun broke through the trees to the east.

Sotaro offered him the katana, and Toyo accepted it with a bow. Without being told, he rose and stood beside his father. The long sword sang as he drew it from its sheath.

Removing the wakizashi, Sotaro touched the flat part of the blade to his forehead, then placed the short sword before him on the mat. Next he undid his sash and pulled his kimono open, baring his shoulders and chest.

Toyo's father closed his eyes and recited the poem he had written for the occasion of his death.

> "Blow if you will,
> Fall wind,
> And steal the last
> Blossom of spring."

When he was finished, Sotaro picked up the wakizashi and pointed it toward his stomach. Gripping it tight like a baseball bat, Toyo raised the katana high, clenching his teeth in a desperate attempt to hide how much he was shaking.

"Toyo, please wait until I have finished my task."

"No."

The wakizashi flinched in Sotaro's hands, almost imperceptibly. He did not look up.

"You dishonor me. If you cannot fulfill your part, I will still commit seppuku."

"I can do it," Toyo told him. "And I will. After I hear your reasons. Uncle Koji gave his reasons for killing himself. He fought in a civil war, and the emperor ordered him to die. But Meiji did not give *you* permission."

Sotaro held the short blade perfectly still, mere inches from his skin.

"I do not need his permission."

"If that's true, you betray both your masters—the emperor

242

and bushido. Koji fought and failed. That's why he had to commit seppuku. Can you say the same?"

"I am not a fighter," Sotaro said tiredly. "Your abuse of me in the dojo is proof enough of that." His father suddenly looked smaller to Toyo. Older. Weaker.

Toyo stabbed the katana into the hard-packed dirt in front of his father. "But you *are* a fighter! Your soul is not in this piece of metal, but in your brush! You fight with every word you write, with every article you publish. It is the emperor's duty to move Japan forward into a new era, but it is *your* duty to remind us where we come from. And your work is far from over. You have no reason to die."

"I have a hundred reasons."

"No! You may be tired, angry, unhappy—but those are not proper reasons for seppuku. Koji had a good reason. Like the forty-seven ronin, he disobeyed his ruler and fought for what he felt was right, knowing that he must die for his actions. Emperor Meiji honored his choice—and his failure—by allowing him to commit seppuku. But Meiji *rejected* your request. He *wants* you to keep fighting. Where Koji failed, you succeed!"

Toyo breathed hard, unable to take his eyes off the wakizashi his father still held before him.

Sotaro's whole being seemed to sigh, and he lowered the blade.

Toyo closed his eyes and dropped his head, relieved. "That's why you waited so long, isn't it? You knew it was wrong."

"That may be. I have fought long and hard with myself

243

over this." Sotaro stared into the distance, then pulled on his kimono. "You understand bushido better than I could ever have hoped. Maybe that is proof enough that my fight has value."

Toyo sat next to his father.

"I was thinking again last night . . ."

"Hai?"

"The Flowers of Edo are the fires after the earthquakes. The houses destroyed are replaced quickly, and always better. But Koji wasn't talking about buildings, was he?"

"No," said Sotaro. "The new light that shines is you."

"And you. I think he meant us both."

Father and son sat together in the light of the new day, watching the wind play in the treetops.

"What made you finally understand? Koji's poem, his death . . ." Sotaro asked.

"Besuboru."

Sotaro grunted unhappily.

"Your soul is contained in a brush," Toyo challenged him. "Why can't mine be in a besuboru bat?"

Toyo's father viewed him from the corners of his eyes.

"And what about this besu-boru has anything to do with Koji?"

"Headmaster Kinoshita has ordered us to lose to the Americans. They are bigger and better. They would have beaten us anyway. But now we're not even supposed to try. Like Koji, I have to choose between two masters, Kinoshita and honor. And either way I lose."

Sotaro was quiet for a long time, and Toyo worried he had undone everything by bringing up baseball.

"You mentioned the forty-seven ronin," Sotaro said finally. "When they could not decide whom to obey, they went on a *yamagomori*."

"A yama—?"

"A trip to the mountains. An ancient tradition where one gains insight through meditation. You should do the same."

"Hai, sensei," Toyo said, somewhat surprised. "Thank you for the advice."

Sotaro stood, offering his hand to his son to pull him up.

"No—not sensei. Your bushido lessons are over. You have mastered them."

Chapter Thirty-five

JUNZO FROWNED at the entrance to Asakusa Park. "I don't understand why we're here. I thought we were going on a trip to the mountains."

"There is our mountain," Toyo said as he led them into the park. Before them stood the miniature replica of Mt. Fuji. They each paid for a climb up the mountain and then hiked around its winding trail to the tiny observation platform at the top.

"Now what?" Moriyama asked.

Toyo shrugged. "We meditate, I guess."

"On what?" Kennichi asked.

"What do we always meditate on? The sound of the sakura trees, you baka," Katsuya whispered, his eyes already closed.

"I thought we were trying to decide whether or not to throw the game," Junzo said.

"*Shh,*" Moriyama hushed them. "We're doing bushido."

The team became quiet and still. A young couple wandered up the path, but turned around abruptly when they saw the mass of Ichiko robes camped on top of the mound.

Toyo's mind wandered to the events of the morning, but he quickly focused on what his father had told him about the samurai tradition of yamagomori. According to Sotaro, the forty-seven ronin had gone on a trip to the mountains to solve their problem, but no answer was presenting itself. Maybe it didn't work with fake mountains.

Toyo opened his eyes and saw his teammates practically sitting on top of one another, their eyes screwed tight in thought. If this wasn't a real mountain, they weren't exactly the forty-seven ronin, either.

It was then Toyo realized Sotaro had already given him the answer. *You should do as they did,* Sotaro had said, but he meant more than the yamagomori. The forty-seven ronin had decided to do what was *right*.

Sometimes a man must do what is in his heart, Sotaro had told him at the Shinto festival, *not what the law tells him.*

"I don't want to lose," said Fuji, suddenly breaking the silence.

"Neither do I," said Moriyama.

"Me either!" said Katsuya.

"Now we're talking like real men," Junzo agreed.

Toyo nodded. "All along, I have been thinking that to honor Ichiko and Japan we must honor the wishes of Headmaster Kinoshita," he told his teammates. "But where is the honor in losing? What does it say about Ichiko—about Japan—if we would willingly lose rather than challenge those who are stronger than we are?"

"Who are we?" Junzo asked.

"We are sons of Ichiko!" they cried as one.

"What is our name?"

"Our name is Ichiko!"

"Where do we come from?"

"Our bodies and souls were formed in the womb of Ichiko!"

"Why are we here?"

"To honor Ichiko and defend Japan!" they yelled as one.

"To win!" Toyo cried.

• • •

The team sang school songs all the way back through town on the streetcar, scaring the salarymen on the way home from work. "I'm going to hit three homu rans off the gaijin!" Junzo boasted to a stranger. "No, four!"

Toyo smiled. There had been a time when he hated the very idea that the harmony of a game might be interrupted by a ball leaving the field of play. But home runs were part of the game, he now realized. Every so often you had to shake things up and belt one over the wall.

• • •

Though the sun had begun its descent by the time they returned, the Ichiko nine went straight to the field to practice. When it got too dark to see, they did guts drills without the ball far into the night. They returned to Independence Hall bruised, battered, and about to collapse. And as they leaned out their windows for one great dormitory rain, their urine ran red with the blood of their effort.

Chapter Thirty-six

AT THE sight of the Ichiko nine, the Japanese crowd at Shimbashi field screamed and cheered. Kinoshita had bought them all baseball uniforms—white jerseys with black trim, and black and white hats the boys had decorated with the brass badges from their Ichiko caps.

It felt to Toyo like they were conquering heroes, home from some victorious campaign. The game hadn't even been played yet, and already the crowd was celebrating. *"Ich-i-ko! Ich-i-ko!"* they chanted, singing and dancing in the newly built bleachers. For a moment, Toyo thought he understood how Fuji must have felt, met by well-wishers at every train station on the way out of Akita. It was both daunting and exhilarating.

Toyo's team walked over to the section of the bleachers filled with Ichiko students and were greeted with a school song and the pounding of huge drums. Futoshi was down front, readying his oendan for battle. He wore a headband that said *hissho* on it—"desperate victory!"

"The whole school is here, and all of Meiji too!" he yelled.

Sure enough, the bleachers nearby were filled with Meiji students. Futoshi's friend Shigeo was challenging his troops to cheer louder than the Ichiko oendan. They sang a song they had written especially for the occasion.

"These Meiji students are rooting *for* us?" Junzo asked.

The Meiji shortstop climbed out of the oendan and bowed to Toyo and the rest of the team.

"The Meiji team hopes you win today," he said.

"Really?" Fuji asked.

"Of course," said the shortstop. "We may be American Meiji School, but we are still Japanese. Do your best!"

Toyo bowed respectfully to the shortstop, and the Ichiko team broke up until the American players were done taking infield practice. Some headed off into the bleachers to say hello to friends, while others like Toyo went over to the free concession area to see what the Americans were offering.

In the line at the concession stand, Toyo noticed a tall man who wore a kimono and still had his hair in a topknot. At first he almost thought he was dreaming.

"Father?" Toyo asked.

Sotaro turned around. "Toyo."

They bowed to each other and Toyo joined his father in line. "Are you covering the game for the *Asahi Shimbun?*"

"Not . . . officially," Sotaro said. He hesitated. "I am of course interested in the outcome of the game, in that it may affect trade agreements between our two nations."

Toyo looked around at the huge crowd. "I wonder how all these people heard about the game," Toyo said.

"I may have said something about it in the *Asahi*

Shimbun," Sotaro said cryptically. He nodded at the front of the line. "Apparently, we are waiting for a drink made from lemon fruit, and some kind of frozen cream treat flavored with beans. They are supposed to be Western delicacies. Watch."

At the table ahead of them, a gaijin man squeezed juice from a yellow fruit into a pitcher of water, while a gaijin woman added two white cubes that dissolved.

"Sugar," Sotaro explained.

Toyo took a cup of the drink, and his father took a ball of iced cream on a little cone. After bowing their thanks, they moved away to taste their treats. Toyo screwed up his face at the sour taste of the lemonade, and Sotaro put a hand to his temple as the cold ice cream gave him a sudden headache. They looked at each other, then swapped treats. Sotaro tasted the lemonade carefully, and appeared surprised and not wholly unpleased. Toyo devoured his ice cream.

"Father, was your influence the reason I was accepted into First Higher?" Toyo asked.

Sotaro seemed shocked by the question. "Where did you get such an idea? You earned your place at Ichiko, on your own merits."

Sotaro withdrew one of the ice cubes from his cup to examine it.

"Then it was not because our family was once samurai?" Toyo asked.

"Of course not. None of that matters anymore," said Sotaro.

"Well, to most people it doesn't," Toyo added.

Sotaro conceded the point with a nod. "It is, after all, a new day," he said, raising his cup of sugared lemon water.

When he discovered it was edible, Toyo ate the cone as Sotaro drank the last of his lemonade. Behind them, the American players jogged off the field, done with their pregame exercises.

"Time for me to go," said Toyo.

Sotaro stopped him. "May I ask what you and your team ultimately decided?"

Toyo smiled. "We have sided with the forty-seven ronin."

His father nodded. "Do your best, Toyo."

Toyo bowed low and ran onto the field to start the game.

Chapter Thirty-seven

THE ICHIKO team bowed to the Americans as they took the field. Some of the Americans laughed, and others tried to bow back. Since Ichiko was representing Japan, they were given home field advantage, and would bat last in the inning. Toyo wondered if this, like the lemonade and ice cream, wasn't also a gift from the Americans. From the way they were talking and goofing around, it didn't seem as if they thought Ichiko would be much competition.

Everyone gathered on the mound before running out to their positions. Moriyama had a sack with him, and he opened it to reveal a wooden chest protector woven together with leather.

"What is that?" Kennichi asked.

"Samurai armor," Moriyama said. There were also shin guards and arm protectors in the sack, as well as an elaborate and beautiful helmet with a faceplate. "These belonged to my grandfather."

Moriyama held the chest protector out to Fuji. "For our honorable catcher. To protect him against all of my curveballs that bounce five feet in front of the plate."

When Fuji made no move to take the chest protector, Moriyama slipped it over his head.

"It's a little small for you," Moriyama said. "But it should protect you well enough from foul balls."

"I don't—I don't know what to say," Fuji told him.

"Say you will wear them with honor and respect," said Moriyama with a deep bow.

"But I am not samurai," Fuji protested.

"None of us are," Moriyama said. "But we are still Men of High Purpose. Right, Toyo?"

"Hai." Toyo nodded.

Fuji donned the rest of the samurai gear and bowed low to Moriyama. "Men of High Purpose," he repeated.

Suddenly Katsuya cried, "Burning besuboru!"

"Burning besuboru!" the team answered. They ran to their positions, and the umpire called, "Pu-re boru!"

The first American batter chuckled at the samurai armor Fuji was wearing, pointing it out to the rest of his team. The big catcher signaled for the first pitch while the hitter was still laughing, and Moriyama zipped a fastball across the plate.

"Strike one!" the umpire cried.

The strike prompted even more laughs from the Americans on the sidelines. The gaijin tipped his cap to Moriyama, then settled in for the next pitch. Moriyama threw a terrific curveball that dipped as it crossed the plate.

The gaijin smacked it into right field for a hit.

Moriyama got the ball back and slammed it into his glove.

"It's okay, Moriyama," Toyo called to him. "You'll get the next batter."

He saw Moriyama take a deep breath and stare in at the hitter. This gaijin was as big as the first. Fuji laid down the sign for a fastball, and Moriyama threw hard down the heart of the plate.

Crack!

The American hit the ball so high and so far, Toyo thought it might never come down. He watched as Michiyo turned and sprinted, but the center fielder was still far from catching it when it hit the ground. Without a wall at Shimbashi field, the ball kept bouncing, and by the time the outfielders had gotten it back in, both runners had scored.

Moriyama crouched on the mound. Toyo rushed in to comfort his pitcher, and the rest of the infielders joined him.

"Moriyama, you can't let them get to you," Toyo told him.

"You're just nervous," Kennichi told him.

Moriyama's eyes said he was elsewhere. Junzo took the ball from his glove.

"We must take a moment to focus," Toyo said. "Remember our bushido training. Think of the sakura . . ."

Moriyama came back to them a little then, but he shook his head. "I practiced those over and over," Moriyama muttered. "They were perfect pitches." Moriyama turned toward the outfield. "Michiyo is already playing so far away, I can't see his face. If they're going to stand up there all day and hit homu rans like that, I—"

"Who are you!?" Junzo screamed, making them all jump.

Moriyama blinked. "What?"

"*Who are you?*" Junzo repeated.

"I'm Moriyama—"

"No," said Junzo. He slapped Moriyama hard across the face, startling everyone again. "*Who—are—you?*" Junzo said, repeating the words with heavy emphasis.

"I am a son of Ichiko," Moriyama said automatically.

Junzo nodded. "What is your name?"

"My name is Ichiko," Moriyama said a little more strongly.

"Where do you come from?"

"My body and soul were formed in the womb of Ichiko!"

"Why are you here?"

Moriyama threw back his head and yelled to the sky: "To honor Ichiko and defend Japan!"

"Again!" Junzo commanded.

Moriyama screamed so loud, the oendan could hear him. "*To honor Ichiko and defend Japan!*"

"Good!" Junzo said, slamming the ball back in Moriyama's glove. "You're the best pitcher in all of Japan. So get them out already. I want to hit!"

Moriyama nodded sharply, and Toyo saw the focus return to his eyes. As he got ready to pitch again, the infielders took their positions.

Then Moriyama went to work like one of the forty-seven ronin avenging his daimyo, attacking batters up and in, feinting away with breaking balls, challenging them down the middle of the plate. By the time he was finished he had struck out three batters in a row.

As the Ichiko team ran off the field, Toyo saw some of the Americans kidding their teammates about striking out.

"Show them what we're made of," Toyo called to Michiyo, who led off their attack. From the start, it looked like an uphill battle; when the American catcher crouched low, Michiyo was barely a head taller than him.

The pitcher sniffed at the baseball and laughed, saying something to his teammates, who laughed with him.

"Burning besuboru!" Michiyo screamed, startling the gaijin. But they simply grinned at his challenge, and the pitcher tipped his cap and went to work.

Doink! The speedy Ichiko center fielder laid down a terrific bunt down the third-base line. The third baseman charged, picked the ball up barehanded, and threw it across the diamond. Michiyo slid headfirst into the bag, raising a cloud of dust.

"Out!" the umpire called.

The oendan booed loudly at the call, but Michiyo popped to his feet and ran back to the Ichiko sidelines without a word. His teammates nodded bows to him for his effort.

As Toyo finished his practice swings in the on-deck circle, he caught sight of the Shimada family crest painted on his bat and a strange feeling came over him. Suddenly, he thought of Uncle Koji, and how he had never run from a fight. It was as though Koji's kami were there, filling him with his own fighting spirit. The bat was a sword in his hands, and with it he would battle the gaijin.

Working the count in his favor, Toyo gave the pitcher a mischievous grin and settled in, knowing the next pitch would be one he could hit. The next pitch was a fastball, and Toyo drove it into right field for a single and slid into first base headfirst. The Americans laughed at him, and one of them pulled an umpire aside and spoke to him in English.

"The gaijin asks me to tell you that you are not required to slide into every base," the umpire translated. "Especially headfirst."

"Thank you," replied Toyo. "We know."

The Americans might not understand, but Toyo could see his teammates on the sidelines had gotten the message. This game was a guts drill, played by Men of High Purpose.

"Like Koji," Toyo whispered.

As Junzo strode to the plate, his eyes were cold and his jaw set. Toyo knew that look, and got ready to run. The American pitcher stared in, received his sign, threw his leg high in the air, and came toward the plate. The ball shot from his hand.

"*Rrrrraaaaaaaaaaaaaaa!*" Junzo roared as he swung.

He launched the ball deep to left field, where it soared over the outfielder's head.

Toyo pounded around the bases and slid into home. The left fielder got the ball back to the cutoff man as Junzo was passing third—but Junzo didn't slow down.

"Slide! Slide!" Toyo yelled.

"*Slide! Slide!*" mimicked the crowd.

The ball hit the catcher's glove just as Junzo slid in headfirst. Toyo saw the catcher's mitt coming down on his head, but Junzo's hand snaked through the big gaijin's legs.

"Safe!" the home plate umpire cried.

The Ichiko supporters went wild. The game was tied 2–2.

Toyo helped his teammate up, and they ran back to the

Ichiko sidelines without so much as a smile. But the oendan did the celebrating for them. "Jun-zo! Jun-zo!" the Ichiko side chanted. "To-yo! To-yo!" the Meiji side countered. They went back and forth, raising the volume each time.

The gaijin pitcher looked surprised, but just shrugged and said something to his catcher, who laughed. The third baseman taunted him, but the pitcher waved him off too.

"They're obviously not taking us seriously," Fuji said on the sidelines.

"That's why we have to hit them now," said Toyo, "while they're not expecting it."

Suguru earned a walk, running to first base and following Toyo's lead by sliding in headfirst. Fuji followed him with a single. The gaijin outfielder took his time throwing the ball back in, and Suguru stole third base with another headfirst slide. Katsuya was up next and drove the ball deep to right for an out, allowing Suguru to tag up and score on the sacrifice.

The gaijin third baseman tried to joke with his pitcher again, but Toyo noticed that this time the pitcher didn't laugh.

Moriyama stepped confidently to the plate and smacked a double, and with two outs, Fuji began to rumble around the base paths, sliding in safely at home when the throw from the outfield was off target.

"Victory! Victory at all costs! Desperate victory!" Futoshi screamed over the roar of the oendan. His face was bloodred, and Shigeo was shouting so hard, he was a deep shade of purple.

The pitcher yelled something at the catcher in frustration, who said something snide in return. The gaijin got Kennichi to ground out to third base for the last out, but Ichiko ran onto the field with a 4–2 lead over the Americans after one inning.

Toyo glanced at the scoreboard. Still eight innings to go.

Each inning will be a battle, he thought, *but Ichiko must win the war.*

Chapter Thirty-eight

MORIYAMA STORMED through the top of the second inning, striking out the first batter but giving up a weak single to the following gaijin. Toyo watched the way the next batter stood as he took his practice swings in the on-deck circle, and repositioned Katsuya at second. The second baseman made the adjustment, and Toyo nodded to Moriyama that they were ready.

Moriyama pitched away from the hitter, who slapped the ball to the right side—exactly where Katsuya was positioned. He scooped the ball and shoveled it to Toyo, who jumped over the sliding American and threw out the batter at first to end the inning.

Then the Ichiko batters picked up where they left off the previous inning. Their right fielder bunted for a single, and Michiyo caught the gaijin off guard by bunting again. The surprised catcher thought too long about trying to throw out the runner at second, and both players were safe. Toyo stepped to the plate with two men on and no outs and an opportunity to drive the runners home.

But now the Americans were beginning to think. Toyo watched the outfielders shift to where he had placed his first inning single. The infielders were also playing deeper, looking for a double play.

The first pitch was too low, and Toyo let it go. The second pitch looked good. Time slowed for Toyo as the ball broke over the plate, and he attacked it with the killing stroke.

"Hiiiiiiiiiiiiyaaaaaaaaaaa!" Toyo cried.

A sickening crack split the air as the ball bounced away into foul territory. With horror, Toyo realized he had shattered his bat.

"Time out!" the umpire called. "You'll have to find another bat," he told Toyo.

"But—but *this* is my bat."

His heart sank as he saw that the place where he had painted the Shimada family crest was split clear down the middle. He looked to the sidelines hopelessly, catching a glimpse of his father in the stands. Sotaro was watching the proceedings with intense interest.

As he stood and stared, Fuji jogged over and bowed to him, holding out a bat.

"What's this?" Toyo asked.

"My bat, sensei," Fuji said. "It is unworthy, but it would honor me if you used it."

"The honor is mine," Toyo said, taking Fuji's bat.

With some doubt, Toyo tested the bat. It was far heavier, and he liked the handle and control of his own bat better, but Toyo bowed his thanks.

In the batter's box once more, Toyo noted how deep the

infielders were playing. To everyone's surprise, he dropped another bunt—the third straight bunt of the inning. By the time the third baseman slid to the ball, everyone was safe and the bases were loaded for Junzo.

The pitcher turned and motioned his outfielders to move farther back. Toyo knew that if Junzo tried to swing for a grand slam without a wall to send the ball over, the best he would get would be a sacrifice fly. But did Junzo know that too? The pitcher got set on the mound, and Toyo moved off first base, ready for anything.

A sweeping curveball dipped away from Junzo. He swung hard, but came up empty.

"Strike one!" the umpire called.

The crowd buzzed, and Toyo could feel their anticipation. An abrupt hush fell over the oendan as the pitcher looked in for another sign.

It was a breaking ball again, and Junzo lunged for the pitch, trying to yank it to left.

Dink! It caromed off Junzo's bat and shot back over his head for a foul.

Toyo saw the pitcher smile as he walked back up the mound. Junzo was behind. No balls and two strikes. But the oendan still had faith, chanting Junzo's name.

He took a few practice swings while the pitcher and catcher decided what pitch to throw him. Everyone in the park knew Junzo desperately wanted to hit a grand slam, but Toyo knew he couldn't do it. Not here, not now. And Ichiko needed to score.

"Junzo!" called Toyo. When he had the senior's attention,

he held up his open hand, then clenched it slowly into a fist.

The message came across loud and clear. As soon as the pitcher was ready, Junzo called time out, first eyeing the distant left fielder, then scowling at Toyo. The senior hesitated, then beckoned Fuji over from the sidelines. They whispered together for a minute before the umpire called Junzo back to the plate.

The American pitcher moved his first and third basemen in at the corners, guessing the conference had been about a surprise bunt. Junzo laughed, making the fielders take a step back. Toyo saw him shift his hands a few inches higher on the handle of the bat. He smiled and got ready for what came next.

The pitcher reared back and threw a fastball, daring Junzo to catch up to it.

Whack! Contact! But instead of lifting the ball in the air to left, Junzo deflected the pitch on a low line drive to the huge gap between right and center field.

Sachio and Michiyo scored ahead of Toyo, who stomped happily on the third-base bag. Junzo slid headfirst into second.

The oendan hopped up and down in tears. Ichiko led the Americans 6–2.

Junzo shrugged and called to Toyo, "The ball didn't want to go for a homu ran."

Thereafter, the Ichiko nine kept sending the ball where it wanted to go, and the American team got madder and madder. Seven to two, eleven to two, fifteen to two—Ichiko poured it on.

Hitting, stealing bases, bunting runners over—the oendan was in such ecstasy, they sang nonstop. Toyo held back a moment to watch the waves of people dancing and screaming—all except Kinoshita, who looked furious. Behind the headmaster, Toyo thought his father looked almost . . . *amused.*

"Burning besuboru!" Toyo cried, and ran out to join his teammates on the field.

• • •

The Americans scored only two more runs all game—one in the fourth, and another in the sixth inning. Moriyama struck out fifteen batters, looking as sharp in the ninth as he had in the first. The Americans held First Higher scoreless for only one inning, and the inning after that Ichiko responded by scoring seven runs.

When the game ended, they had defeated the Americans 29–4.

When Toyo and his teammates rushed over to the American sidelines to bow to them after the game, many of the gaijin were so mad, they turned their backs. Others tried to bow politely, obviously humbled by their loss. The shortstop who had climbed over the Wall of the Soul tipped his cap in respect.

Next the Ichiko players ran to bow to their loud, faithful fans. Futoshi led the oendan as they streamed onto the field, swallowing the boys in enthusiastic embraces. Junzo and Moriyama were lifted up on the shoulders of their classmates and paraded around the field. Toyo worked his way through the mob to Fuji, and bowed as he returned the catcher's bat.

"We did it," Fuji said.

"That we did," Toyo agreed.

Sotaro appeared next to the boys, and Fuji bowed as Toyo introduced his father.

"You showed your true samurai nature today," Sotaro said. "Both of you."

"Forgive me, Shimada-san," Fuji said, his eyes on the ground, "but I am not samurai."

"You mean that this is—but your armor—"

"These belong to my teammate Moriyama. They were his grandfather's."

"This is my friend Fujimura," Toyo told his father. "The one I spoke to you about. A Man of Higher Purpose."

Sotaro looked Fuji over. "You fought like a samurai today," he told the catcher.

Toyo saw Fuji blush with pleasure as he bowed. They were joined by Headmaster Kinoshita and the American consul. More bows were exchanged, and Sotaro stepped back for the boys to address the two men.

"The outcome of your game was," the headmaster said, "*unexpected.*"

"Ichiko was lucky this day," Toyo responded.

The consul glared and crossed his arms. "I think the proceedings very *un*lucky."

"Luck had nothing to do with it," said Sotaro. He stepped forward. "The Ichiko team was clearly superior in every aspect of the game, from effort to execution."

Headmaster Kinoshita stared at Sotaro.

The gaijin shortstop worked his way over and spoke through the ambassador.

"Mr. Smith, ah, hmm," the consul said, clearly not wanting to translate what the shortstop said, "Mr. Smith wishes me to tell you that you were the better team today. He says it was an honor to play you, and he looks forward to a—to a rematch."

Toyo beamed and bowed politely to the gaijin, thanking him for the offer.

"Does this mean we may continue to play besuboru?" Toyo asked Kinoshita.

"Hai," the headmaster sighed. "If you can give me your word as a samurai that what happened during the Meiji game will never happen again."

"I thought there were no more samurai left in Japan," the American consul said.

"Ahh," said Sotaro. "Quite the contrary."

Epilogue

From the *ASAHI SHIMBUN, MAY 1891*

THE BENEFITS OF BESUBORU

by Sotaro Shimada

THERE IS an old Japanese proverb that says, "The frog in the well does not know the ocean," and for too many centuries, Japan has been that frog in the well. I and others have argued Japan should close her ports and reject the West, that we should remain in our well, content never to know the vast depths of the ocean. And our reasons for this way of thinking were not unfounded: Already we have lost many things that made us uniquely Japanese. As the influence of Europe and the Americas grows, we may lose more still.

But while the West may have replaced our samurai with businessmen and our swords with umbrellas, they cannot replace bushido in our hearts. Nowhere was this more evident than in yesterday's game between Ichiko and the gaijin Shimbashi besuboru club. Those who witnessed the Ichiko victory saw a display of bushido unmatched since the Men of High Purpose rebelled against the overthrow of the shogun.

Due to this success, the editors of the *Asahi Shimbun* have decided to sponsor a yearly summer besuboru tournament. Through this National High School Besuboru Summer Championship Tournament, it is hoped the sport will grow in popularity both here in Tokyo and throughout the land.

While I have, in the past, condemned besuboru as yet another Western plague, perhaps we should instead see it as an opportunity for the advancement of samurai values in our changing nation. Though an American import, besuboru appears to have many elements that make it a truly Japanese game. While not the sport of ancient gods, the one-on-one showdown between the "pitcher" and the "batter" is reminiscent of the shobu seen between sumo wrestlers in the ring, and while there is an emphasis on individual strength and effort, there is a powerful team aspect to the game as well. Together, nine must become one, and without seamless execution they fail as one.

Besuboru is a sport in which effort may overcome skill, and where intensity overcomes size. It teaches patience during its lulls, quick thinking during its action, and looks to be good physical exercise for the arms, legs, and the entire body. The weapons of the game, the bat and the glove, may be favorably compared to the sword and shield of the old samurai. Besuboru incorporates teamwork, strategy, intelligence, physical strength, grace, agility, speed, and accuracy—in short, all the qualities that samurai have valued and developed for centuries.

As those who remember the days of old, we have a duty to teach the next generation the ways of bushido and the traditions of Japan, to keep all the stories and principles alive. Now rather than be absorbed by Western culture, we can absorb that which is most useful to us and our way of life. On the outside we may wear top hats instead of topknots, or use besuboru bats rather than swords, but on the inside, bushido can still fill our souls and guide our lives.

Western science teaches us the light we see from distant stars may be the energy from celestial bodies long since dead. So too bushido is gone yet lives on. Though the samurai may have passed as roughly as a cherry blossom torn too soon from its branch, the *spirit* of the way of the warrior lives on in us. And in our sons.

In the words of my honored brother, the Flowers of Edo have burned away in the night, and been replaced by the light of a new day.

Author's Notes

I HAVE long been interested in Japan, but I wasn't inspired to write *Samurai Shortstop* until I stumbled across a curious photograph in a travel guide. In the picture, a Japanese man wearing a kimono and sandals throws out the ceremonial first pitch for the 1915 National High School Baseball Summer Championship Tournament. *1915!* I knew of Japan's love affair with baseball, but I had always assumed the sport was imported by American GIs during the Allied occupation at the end of World War II.

I started reading everything I could about the history of baseball in Japan. One thing led to another, and soon I was checking out books about samurai, bushido, and the radical transitional period now called the Meiji Restoration. A story began to form about baseball and bushido, but at its heart *Samurai Shortstop* is really the story of a nation's difficult, overnight transition from feudal society to industrial power, and of one boy's struggle to prove that his samurai father still has a place in the new Japan.

The clenched-fist ceremony and the storm scenes were

among the hardest for me to write. Toyo and his classmates engage in violent rituals that would be unacceptable in today's world, and it was a challenge to be true to history and at the same time still paint Toyo as someone we like and respect. It is important to understand that Toyo, like his classmates, was a product of his time and his culture. To him, the question of the clenched-fist ceremony was not "Is this wrong?" but, "Do I have the strength to do what must be done?"

Hazing and bullying may never go away in any culture, but violence on a school-wide scale was eventually outlawed at Ichiko. In the meantime, caught in a moment between Japan's brutal Middle Ages and its suddenly gentler modern era, Toyo makes some decisions that seem very wrong to us, and others—like standing up for his friend Fuji—that are exactly what we would do. I hope that Toyo's inconsistencies make him all the more human, and that his choices will inspire discussion and debate.

• • •

When American Commodore Matthew Perry sailed his steam-driven Black Fleet into Yokohama harbor in 1853, life in Japan was turned upside down. The ruling shogunate, which had managed to keep almost everyone from the West out of Japan for nearly three hundred years, was forced to open the country to Western ideas and culture. In the turmoil that followed, a group of powerful samurai overthrew the shogun and put Emperor Meiji in power.

Meiji realized three centuries of isolation had left Japan far behind its Western neighbors in scientific advancement, and he and his advisors hurried to catch the nation up to speed. Almost overnight, Japan went from the Middle Ages to the modern era. Streetcars and locomotives were a radical shock to a nation that still walked and rode horses. Inventions and advancements that were discovered slowly in the West appeared all at once in Japan—telephones, electric lightbulbs, skyscrapers, gas heating, plumbing, movie theaters, even baseball, were all imported at the same time.

Still a relatively new sport in America, baseball was introduced into Japan in the 1870s by a young American named Horace Wilson who taught history and English at a Tokyo school. The sport quickly caught on, and Ichiko, the First Higher School of Tokyo, soon became one of the new sport's powerhouses. While baseball programs like Ichiko's were later to have professional coaches, many were originally organized and run by the students themselves, like Toyo's team.

Throughout my story, I incorporated fictionalized versions of several incidents that happened at the real First Higher School of Tokyo during the 1890s. In 1891, in front of thousands of baseball-mad fans, an American did in fact climb over the sacred Wall of the Soul at Ichiko. He too was attacked by Ichiko students, and the incident really did damage Japanese-American relations at the time. No goodwill baseball game was actually played, but after several rounds of official apology, the matter was settled.

Though my gaijin Shimbashi athletic club is fictional, the Ichiko nine did play a team of American workers from Yokohama in 1896, and that First Higher team also won by the incredible score of 29–4. It was a huge moment for a nation struggling to prove they could play on equal terms with the other nations of the world, and the victory was written about in newspapers from one end of Japan to the other. The Ichiko team went on to defeat the Americans twice more, by the equally ridiculous scores of 35–9 and 22–6. Ichiko was only defeated when the Americans recruited a professional baseball player from a U.S. Navy ship stationed in Yokohama harbor. Even then, the final score was 14–12.

Besides Headmaster Kinoshita, the only character in *Samurai Shortstop* based on a real person is pitcher Moriyama Tsunetaro. As I've said, storms and clenched-fist ceremonies were a real part of the culture of the day, and though Moriyama was likely to have taken part in some form of both, his romantic offenses and punishment here are completely fictional. The story about the loose bricks where he practiced against the wall, however, is real. Next to the hole in the wall is written: "The traces of Moriyama's fierce training." Remembered as the greatest pitcher in the history of Ichiko, Moriyama once threw a shutout against the American team from Yokohama. He was so popular in his day, it was said: "To be hit by a Moriyama fastball is an honor exceeded only by being crushed under the wheels of the imperial carriage."

• • •

Today, baseball is by far Japan's favorite sport. The annual National High School Baseball Summer Tournament, begun in 1915 by the *Asahi Shimbun,* is one of the world's largest amateur sporting events. Dozens of teams from across Japan play a single-elimination tournament in front of almost one million fans, and many millions more stay home from work to watch the televised games. The competition is fierce, but boys who persevere and win are regarded as national heroes, and often go on to play baseball in Japan's major leagues.

Until recently, workouts for professional Japanese baseball players were sometimes as rigorous as the legendary Ichiko workouts where the boys were said to practice so hard, their urine ran red with blood. Nippon Professional Baseball players began practicing hours before games. Pitchers threw hundreds of warm-up pitches, and batters took hundreds of swings each day. On defense, the "Thousand Fungo Drill" saw fielders take one thousand ground balls without resting. Players were often black and blue and ready to collapse after Nippon Professional Baseball practices—just in time for that night's game. Workouts have mercifully begun to loosen up, but like Toyo, Japanese players and managers believe discipline and intensity make the best baseball players.

The oendan at Nippon Professional Baseball games are even more fanatical than Futoshi and his troop. Some create shrines to their teams, where they pray before and after each game for victory. They also wear matching uniforms and sing special songs to their teams from the first pitch to the last out. They beat drums so loudly and wave so many banners and pennants that anyone sitting near an oendan section has trouble actually seeing or hearing the game. Oendan can become violent too. One group attacked a crew of umpires for canceling a game due to rain.

In recent years, baseball in Japan has come full circle. Once an American import, Japanese baseball has now sent players like Hideki Matsui, Hideo Nomo, Kaz Matsui, and Ichiro Suzuki to play Major League Baseball, proving Japan *can* beat us at our own game after all.

• • •

A number of people helped make *Samurai Shortstop* a reality, including my insightful and inquisitive editors, Cecile Goyette and Rebecca Waugh, readers Anne Thomas Abbott, Paul Harrill, and my wife and sensei, Wendi. Many thanks to the family of Kimberly Colen and the Society of Children's Book Writers and Illustrators for the generous Kimberly Colen Memorial Grant that helped pay the bills through the writing of *Samurai,* and thanks too to Dr. Wayne Farris, Sen-Soshitsu XV Chair in Traditional Japanese Culture and History at the University of Hawaii, not only for reading the first draft and offering his expertise, but also for steering me toward the enormously useful *Schooldays in Imperial Japan.* Any errors that remain are my own.

A great deal of research went into making *Samurai Shortstop* as realistic as possible, but the works of author Robert Whiting deserve special mention. *The Chrysanthemum and the Bat, You Gotta Have Wa,* and *The Meaning of Ichiro* are extraordinarily accessible and entertaining studies of baseball in the land of the rising sun. Many thanks to Mr. Whiting and the other authors whose works I used in researching this novel:

Daikichi, Irokawa. *The Culture of the Meiji Period.* Translation edited by Marius B. Jansen. Princeton, New Jersey: Princeton University Press, 1985.

Figal, Gerald. *Civilization and Monsters: Spirits of Modernity in Meiji Japan.* Durham, North Carolina: Duke University Press, 1999.

Gordon, Andrew. *A Modern History of Japan: From Tokugawa Times to the Present.* New York: Oxford University Press, 2003.

Hillsborough, Romulus. *Samurai Sketches from the Bloody Final Years of the Shogun.* San Francisco: Ridgeback Press, 2001.

McClain, James L. *Japan: A Modern History.* New York: W. W. Norton & Co., 2002.

Nitobe, Inazo. *Bushido: The Soul of Japan.* New York: G. P. Putnam's Sons—The Knickerbocker Press, 1905.

Roden, Donald. *Schooldays in Imperial Japan: A Study in the Culture of a Student Elite.* Berkeley: University of California Press, 1980.

Seidensticker, Edward. *Low City, High City: Tokyo from Edo to the Earthquake.* New York: Alfred A. Knopf, 1983.

Sinclaire, Clive. *Samurai: The Weapons and Spirit of the Japanese Warrior.* Guilford, Connecticut: The Lyons Press, 2001.

Passin, Herbert. *Society and Education in Japan.* New York: Columbia University—Teachers College Press, 1965.

Whiting, Robert. *The Chrysanthemum and the Bat.* New York: Dodd, Mead & Co., 1977

——. *You Gotta Have Wa.* New York: Vintage Books, 1989.

——. *The Meaning of Ichiro: The New Wave from Japan and the Transformation of Our National Pastime.* New York: Warner Books, 2004.

Whitney, Clara A. N. *Clara's Diary: An American Girl in Meiji Japan.* Edited by M. William Steele and Tamiko Ichimata. Tokyo: Kodansha International, Ltd., 1979.

• • •

A note on the text:

When introduced, I have italicized Japanese words that have not found their way into English vocabulary, with the exception of proper names. I have also tried, when possible, to use Japanese baseball terms, most of which are based on the English words that mean the same thing (*Pu-re boru* = Play ball; *homu ran* = home run). Some baseball conventions that were not so easily translated however, including positions (first base, shortstop, etc.) and pitches (fastball, curveball, etc.), I left in English to avoid confusion.

In Japan, a person's family name, what Westerners would refer to as a "last name," actually comes first. Thus, Toyo's name should actually be written Shimada Toyo. Again, to avoid confusion, I have written all names in *Samurai Shortstop* in Western fashion.